Equinox

Ruth Aylett
Greg Michaelson

Stairwell Books

Published by Stairwell Books
161 Lowther Street
York, YO31 7LZ

www.stairwellbooks.co.uk
@stairwellbooks

Cover design: Alan Gillott
Cover art: Northern lights over Callanish stones - Luca Quadrio

ISBN: 978-1-913432-70-6
p5

Also by Ruth Aylett:

Handfast: Poetry Duets with Beth McDonough, Mothers Milk, 2016
Pretty In Pink, 4Word, 2021
Queen of Infinite Space, Maytree Press, 2021

Also by Greg Michaelson:

The Wave Singer, Argyll, 2008
Napier's Bones, McStoryteller, 2017

Chapter 1

Helen - Tuesday 9th September

The first I knew about the Alba na Cuan's unfortunate encounter was when our Engineering Officer, Bodger Jones, stuck his head through the door.

'Hey, Hulkie, Skipper wants you, main deck aft, pronto. Bring your med kit he says.'

Unwelcome news. I was checking out the dynamic position controller, our Kongsberg, because we had a trawl out and keeping on station was pretty important so close to the coast. And I was enjoying the quiet of the Hebridean lee after several weeks bouncing around the Minch in the usual gale. But when the Captain calls, you go, especially if some crew member has injured themselves.

'Aye, aye Sir' – the only possible response. I grabbed the First Aid Box and a box of latex gloves.

Before we go any further, you may wonder why, since my name is Helen McIver, Bodger was calling me 'Hulkie'. Or you may not, but I'm going to tell you anyway, just to get things clear.

I've been working in all-male – except for me – environments pretty much since I left school. Prenticing at Nissan was much the same as being at sea in that respect. Being a canny lassie, as my dad always told me, I learned quickly you had to choose which pieces of nonsense to push back on. Nicknames is not one of those. Everyone has a nickname. The trick is to get one you can live with.

Now I'm a big lass. No, not my bust, all of me. At just short of six foot, I can look down on plenty of men, including Bodger, who's a small Welshman. My Dad calls me Topsy because I just kept growing. I picked up Helen-the-Hulk at Nissan, and the reason I stuck with it was that otherwise, the minute I open my mouth outside Wearside, I'm going to get *Geordie*. Nobody from Sunderland will accept that for a minute – we are Mackems not Geordies, and woe betide anyone who gets it wrong.

In fact, the way I got to be Hulkie was stepping into a bust-up between my Nissan shop floor boss and some tool from Newcastle who reckoned Mackems were Georgies with the brains bashed out. Neither party could hit a lassie, especially a large one giving them both a good glare. So I became Helen-the-Hulk and then Hulkie.

When I got aft, there was a huddle round the trawl net, only just winched in and still streaming water. No obviously bleeding crew member. We'd had a trawl out because the sonar had picked up a subsurface object that might just possibly be a lost signal buoy we were supposed to be retrieving, unmoored by one of the Minch storms. This had looked the right sort of size and it was drifting, so not sealife.

But I could see from the crew's faces that whatever we'd fished out, it was definitely not the buoy. Young Jimmy, our deckie, had gone a sickly white, and the others seemed pretty upset too. Of course everyone calls Jimmy 'Riddle', and the way he looked, a trip to the heads would do him good.

'McIver, I've called you out here as our stand-in medic'.

Even the Captain sounded upset, though he was carefully pointing out he didn't want me for any dogsbody stuff. That is one of the things I would push back on. Having the Electro-Technical Officer/Medical Certificate combo was how I got this Maritime Scotland gig. Their permanent crew broke his leg – playing football on shore apparently.

So if nobody was injured, why did they need my med cert knowledge?

'It looks like we've trawled a body.'

Luckily it's not the first body I've seen fished out of the sea so I knew what to expect. And in fact when the crew finally got it out of the trawl net, which took a good half hour, it was less bad than I expected. Looked as if he – clearly a he – hadn't been in the water all that long, since there wasn't much swelling and no evidence of bits nibbled away. Definitely dead. So the med-cert bit was mainly documentation and protecting the evidence. Latex gloves all round, plastic bags over the body's hands, a set of photos, since by the time we got the body into a port for autopsy, all sorts of changes could have taken place.

He was wearing a dark zipped anorak a size too big for him with lumpy bulges at the sides.

'I think we'd better unzip the jacket.' I said. 'Look for ID and find out what those great big bulges are. Russian gold, let's hope.' Nobody laughed.

Tipping the pockets out gave us a pile of beach pebbles, up to the size of small rocks. So that was why the body had been subsurface. Weighted down. Not an accident then. I took a picture of them.

'Sir, is there any other traffic in the area?' I asked the Captain.

He gestured at young Riddle. 'Baillie, up to the Bridge and ask Murray if he's seen anything on the ARPA. And bring a body bag back from Stores as well.'

Noticing a suspicious boat seemed a forlorn hope. We were in among skerries at the entrance to Loch Liurboist, which was why I had been watching the Kongsberg. A tender-size boat would have plenty of radar cover. And what if the Mate had seen something? Would we head over to ask if they'd chucked a body overboard? It smelt of drugs or some other kind of smuggling; not what you wanted to casually encounter.

Still, someone might ask later, so better to check.

The inside breast pocket of the anorak had a credit card and a driving licence in the name of Gray McMalkin. The licence address was in Glasgow. So not a local. I bagged them. There was nothing in the pockets of the jeans, nor in the check shirt under the anorak. There was a black cord round the body's neck. This turned out to be a leather thong with one of those amulet-like pendants some men wear – a little chipped-stone arrowhead in this case. Probably turned out by the thousand in China. I left it there.

I took pictures of everything, and some close-ups of the face and head. He had been a thin and rather elegant-looking man, younger than his thick grey hair suggested. His dead eyes were a startling shade of green, a bit creepy somehow, as if they could still see you.

'You done, McIver?' the captain asked.

At my 'Yessir', he motioned to the crew to load it into the body bag young Riddle had brought back. The message from the Mate was that he'd sighted no other traffic. The body – he, it – was to be stashed in the cold store.

'I'll go and radio Stornoway,' the Captain told us. 'Up to them to deal with this. I'll get a new schedule plotted with Murray. Sailing in ooh, thirty minutes I should think.'

The rest of the crew looked glum. Once we'd dealt with the buoy, still not located, the last task in our three-week tour of duty was south-west towards the Uists, not north-east to Stornoway. This would add at least a day to our programme even though Stornoway was only an hour or so away. There'd be all the faff when we got there – police statements and such – and we'd have to moor there overnight.

I was left with the pile of pebbles on the deck, a couple of dozen or so. Well, evidence, I supposed. Maybe a rocks expert could tell which beach they'd come from. My cousin Malcolm, a bit of a geology freak, would certainly know what type of rock they were. Riddle was standing there looking disconsolate as the others heaved the body away.

'Cheer up laddie,' I told him. 'Worse things happen at sea. Can you see if Gammon has got a box or a bag in Stores I can put the rocks in? We'd better deliver those too.'

He gave me a weak smile and off he went again. Running around is what deckies do.

I started sorting the pebbles into rough size order, as all that training on stowing things kicked in. Larger objects first. Most of them were irregular shapes in dull colours, but then one caught my eye. It had that smooth egg shape that fits your palm. Felt really good in my hand and was light green in colour. Very smart. Oh, they won't miss one, I thought, and slipped it into my pocket.

True to the skipper's word – he was good like that – we were underway in half an hour. But it took nearer two hours than one into Stornoway with a brisk north-easterly and a moderate swell against us. Early September, and summer was long over in these latitudes.

I don't know the coast below Stornoway, but when we got close it was all familiar landmarks. Dad's a Lewis lad, though he left in his late teens. We used to visit the grandparents every summer when I was a kid.

But by the time me and my brother Donnie were teens, we went off it. Stornoway makes Sunderland look exciting. And then there's all the heavy religious stuff. Which unfortunately the grandparents were well into. That was one of the reasons Dad left, or so he let slip once.

We were last there five years back to bury Ganny McIver and though it was interesting meeting a load of cousins, there was a terrible row about whether women could attend the burial or not. And when it was finally agreed we visitors could, there was another row about what we wore. Dresses, hats, that sort of thing. I was working for a boutique cruise line at the time, so in the end I wore their rather smart uniform, which included the only proper hat I had. A series of elderly gents in baggy suits did double-takes when they realised I wasn't a man. If the resulting glares had been bullets, I'd have been bleeding to death on the ground in the first ten minutes. And me Mam wasn't very impressed either.

When we got close to the berth at the back of the ferry terminal we could see our reception committee. A candy car, with a paddy wagon for the body. Two bobbies came up the gangway with a stretcher as soon as we'd tied up. Followed by a balding guy in a tweed jacket who was presumably a detective.

It was nearly six, which is when we normally ate, but of course we had to wait while the detective took statements in the lounge that doubled as our mess area. I was in and out in about five minutes, and handed over the SD card with my pics.

'You're not from round here then,' he said in that soft Lewis accent when he heard my voice. I couldn't resist pointing out that in some sense I was. An error as it turned out.

Still, with eight of us plus the one scientist on this mission, we were an hour late by the time he was done, and Gammon Findlay, our cook, was in a right old strop.

'Don't give me "overcooked",' he snarled as he plonked our plates down. 'And where's the skipper?'

The Captain reappeared after another half an hour, sticking his head into the galley to apologise to Gammon. Then sat down at the head of the table with a sigh and started into the dried-up chicken leg.

Protocol dictated that the crew waited for the Captain to get up before they left the table. As most of them had finished eating, there was some awkward shuffling and very desultory chat. Eventually the Captain noticed.

'OK guys, off you go. Murray – shore leave rota please, but everyone back by 11pm. We need to make an early start. McIver, stay will you, I need a brief chat please.'

I sat down again. I wasn't on the shore leave rota anyway. As the newbie in this crew my slot came round last.

'McIver, I've just had a long conversation with the Inspector trying to resolve our conflicting requirements. He wants us to stick around tomorrow in case there are further questions, and it's true I need a copy of the police report for the log. That won't be available until they finish the autopsy, which will be later tomorrow. On the other hand, we need to finish the mission.' He sighed. Then said decisively: 'Well, I can square the circle if I leave a crew-member on shore, and come back day-after-tomorrow. I hear you know Stornoway, and no offence intended, but leaving you is the least disruptive choice. OK?'

'Aye, aye Sir,' I muttered. That was the required answer. Though he was taking a risk. Strictly speaking they did need me on board in case anything went wrong with kit or people. Still, I could see they ought to manage for the odd 24 hours though it would mean longer watches all round. While for me, a whole day hanging around in Stornoway to look forward to.

'Good. I'll put a favourable comment in the log for you.'

That was worth something. A good track record would help me if Maritime Scotland needed crew in the future.

'Get your shore kit ready for first thing then, McIver. The police will find you a billet for tomorrow night and we should be back for you mid-morning the day after.'

I had an evening shift in the engine room, and with some of the crew ashore everything was pretty quiet except for the ferry coming in around eight. I did the day's checks and then settled down with my Kindle. Half-an ear open for anything unusual and the rest of my attention on my latest swords and sorcery.

The shore leave contingent were back in good time. Stornoway pub culture was probably even less groovy than the last shore leave in Tobermory, more than a week back. Our other stops had involved mooring near out-of-the-way locations with little or no habitation. A bit different from boutique cruising, and it meant Bodger and I had played a lot of Scrabble. He was a fanatic, but with my vocabulary of obscure electronic terms, I occasionally beat him.

I turned in and sorted out enough kit for my one day lay-over. Lucky I'd been keeping up with the laundry and still had clean underwear. Getting my clothes off I felt something hard in a pocket and realised it was the pebble I'd abstracted. Maybe not one of my better ideas, thinking about it, but done was done. It sat neatly in my palm, even greener than I'd thought, and warm to my touch after all that time in my pocket. My hand liked it.

Yes, that last trip to Stornoway. The grandparents both came from large families and there were lots and lots of distant cousins I'd never met before. Mostly more fun than the one cousin I did know a bit. Malcolm was my only first cousin, via Dad's sister. It wasn't just that he was a good bit older than me, by at least ten years. More his inability to do family small talk but then to go off on one if you hit one of his topics. He was working as a warden on some Scottish moor. God help the tourists if they ask him any questions.

And off to sleep – their early start meant I had to be off the ship for 8. Oh joy.

Chapter 2

Malcolm – Tuesday 9th September

The owl woke me. It was barely light but I couldn't get back to sleep. Owls are unusual. So I got up and peered blearily out of my bedroom window.

The sky was grey and the rain fell steadily. The owl was perched in the rowan tree, silhouetted in the half light, staring straight at me, as if it wanted something from me.

'Sorry,' I said, 'but the cat gets all the mice.'

The owl winked and flew away.

I got up and fed the cat, who seemed pleased, if surprised, at such excellent service. Then I showered, dressed, made myself a cup of tea, and checked the schedule. A minibus full of Japanese eco-tourists was due mid-morning, escaping from a cruise ship docked at Fort William. They could have chosen a better day, not that they'd had much choice.

I made my packed lunch, left the cottage and fired up the Land Rover. I'd always wanted a Land Rover when I lived in the city. Now that I had one, I realised how impractical it was, especially the lack of heating and the flimsy windscreen wipers. If only I hadn't bought fifth hand. Still, the four wheel drive often came in handy.

I drove slowly down the track, dodging sheep, and accelerated onto the empty main road: the road climbs steeply and the truck needs every last ounce of momentum. As we wheezed round the long hair pin bend, up onto the Moor of Rannoch, I spotted a cyclist in front of me, sustaining an impressive pace along the incline.

I overtook the cyclist at the Loch Tulloch Viewpoint, and pressed on across the moor. The vast boggy plateau is framed by ancient mountains that form a pinch point at the Pass of Glencoe. They're not so high by international standards, but the climbing routes can be treacherous. A big tourist draw, the peaks look particularly impressive capped with snow.

I pulled off the road at the Nissen hut at Loch Ba that passes for our headquarters. The hut, a relic from World War Two, had been listed as of historic interest by some jobsworth. To my mind, the only aspect of historic interest was that the corrugated iron walls hadn't rusted away. At least it had been painted green, which made it marginally less visible.

I parked outside the hut, opened up the visitor area and turned the sign to *Welcome!* Then I went behind the counter and turned on the laptop. I don't have much time for the interweb, but the mobile network's a godsend when you work in the middle of nowhere.

While the laptop fired up, I dug out a bundle of maps and guide books, and arrayed them on the desk. There weren't any Japanese ones left, so I hoped English would do. Next, I checked the email. There was just one new message, from the back office: the minibus tour had been cancelled due to the weather.

As I tidied up the maps and guidebooks, the door opened, and into the hut came one of the oddest looking people I've ever seen. Short and stout, they wore a leather aviator hood and goggles, and were enveloped in a grey cloak of loden.

'Welcome to Rannoch Moor,' I said. 'How can I help you?'

As the visitor took off their dripping cape and hood, and shook out their long tawny hair, I realised I was talking to woman, of indeterminate age. Her clothes were ill matched, and ill fitting, as if they'd been selected from a charity shop by someone who'd never met her.

The woman reached into her satchel and took out two pieces of stone.

'I'm trying to find another of these,' she said, in an indeterminate accent, holding the pieces out to me.

I took the stones and examined them. They fitted together to form an arrowhead, that had been knapped from flint. The leaf shape suggested it was Neolithic.

'Goodness!' I said. 'Calc-silicate hornfels!'

The woman looked at me blankly.

'It's metamorphic rock,' I said. 'Very old.'

'I really don't care,' said the woman. 'I need to find another one.'

As she spoke again, I realised that her accent was Scottish, though not one I recognised.

'You've come to the right place,' I said. 'That's a local stone. I'll show you.'

There was a large scale topographic map under the glass top of the counter.

'It was probably made here,' I said, pointing to the west side of Ben Lawers. 'Creag na Cailleach. It was a Neolithic quarry.'

'Is it far?' said the woman.

'Thirty miles or so to Killin,' I said. 'Half an hour maybe. But it's a fair walk from the road end. You're in a car, I take it.'

'No,' said the woman. 'Bicycle.'

'Gosh,' I said. 'Gosh. That'll take you three or four hours.'

'I'd best be on my way then,' said the woman.

'Fair enough,' I said. 'Could you sign the visitor's book, please?'

I pushed the book across the counter. The woman wrote down her details.

'The talisman,' said the woman, holding out her hand.

'Here you go,' I said, passing back the stones, and picking up the book. 'You know, those arrowheads used to be called witch stones.'

But the woman had already gone. I inspected the visitor's book. The woman's handwriting was like a child's, with letters formed in halting block capitals. Her name was Patricia Harper. The columns for nationality and email address were blank.

I was about to start on the chores, when a car drew up and two older people entered the hut. Both were dressed in what looked like brand new, top of the range, outdoor clothing. They seemed like New Age types: both bore a faint whiff of cannabis.

'Welcome to Rannoch Moor,' I said, proffering them the visitor's book. 'How can I help you?'

This couple were most forthcoming. From Southern California, they were recently retired, and exploring their Scottish roots. They particularly wanted to find the Menzies Stone, that marked the old

Perthshire boundary, in the centre of the moor. They'd read that it was an ancient seat of power. They even pronounced Menzies correctly: 'mingiss'.

Feigning enthusiasm, I handed them a map, and told them to head north to the Altnafeadh Hotel, and take the track east towards Rannoch Station, past the Black Corries Lodge. I also told them to keep well away from dead grouse. There was endemic cryptosporidiosis on the moor, that'd put paid to the shooting. Not that I'd ever actually seen any dead grouse. Still, they should be safe from toffs in tweeds.

The rest of the day was quiet. Late in the afternoon, I was about to shut up shop, when I heard the older couple's car returning.

'You've got to help us!' cried the man, barely through the door. 'There's a body up by the Menzies Stone!'

'That's dreadful!' I said. 'Have you any idea what might have happened?'

'All we saw was the body,' said the man, 'We didn't want to touch anything.'

'What did they look like?' I said.

'It was a woman,' said his partner. 'She looked so weird. Wrapped in a thing like a poncho, with a flying hat, like Amelia Earhart.'

Wow! That sounded like Patricia Harper! But what on earth was she doing there?

'Are you sure there was a body?' I said.

'Of course there was a body!' said the man. 'Do you think we're dumb?'

'Of course I don't think you're stupid,' I said quickly. 'Do you have any pictures?'

'No honey,' said the woman. 'We'd taken so many that we'd flattened the battery.'

'Have you told the police?' I said.

The man and the woman guardedly looked at each other.

'We don't want to mess with your authorities,' said the woman. 'We can't afford any hassle.'

I didn't ask why. Maybe I should have done.

'Someone needs to tell the authorities,' said the man. 'You've got to go and look. Just don't mention us.'

Before I could remonstrate further with them, they'd fled the hut.

Did I call the police? I did not. I knew fine that my neighbour Dougie, in the Achallader police station, would be less than delighted to head off on a wild goose chase on a dark, wet evening. Instead, I shut up the visitor centre and set off in my trusty steed.

The track across the moor is little more than a hiker's trail. Rocky and muddy in equal measure, it's ideal terrain for a Land Rover. Half way to the stone, the Black Corries Lodge was still boarded up. I didn't think anyone would be back there anytime soon.

As I neared the stone, the track ran along the high chain link fence that bounded the Fundamental Forces facility. F^2 took their security seriously: the fence was electrified, with huge warning signs every five metres or so. A Glasgow based enterprise, they were hoping to exploit basic properties of matter for sustainable energy. They'd chosen Rannoch Moor as a remote yet accessible site to search for cosmic particles. The geology is fairly complex but well understood; the Highland ranges and lochs mark major fault lines, but they're stable so long as no one messes with them. F^2 were said to be redeploying a long worked out lead mine, with detector tanks at the bottom.

All F^2's equipment came up the West Highland Line into Rannoch Station, much further to the east. So we heard little of them on our side of the moor, which suited me just fine, as I wanted as little to do with F^2 as possible. Did I mention that my ex-wife Bernie worked for them, in their Glasgow HQ?

I pulled up next to the fence. The sun was setting, so I retrieved the torch from the tool box, switched it on, and circled the stone, scanning all around. There was no sign of a body, but on the far side of the stone, deep in the heather, was a battered, sit up and beg bicycle. From her dress sense, it looked like just the sort of bike Patricia Harper might favour. But the stone's in the opposite direction to the quarry. How could she possibly have got there so quickly?

I righted the bike, lugged it back to the Land Rover, and stowed it in the back. As the light began to fade, I heard an owl hoot. I looked up and there was the familiar silhouette, perched up on top of the chain link fence. As I walked towards the owl, it hoots grew more acute. When I reached the fence, the hooting abruptly stopped.

'What is it this time?' I asked, feeling foolish. 'Still no mice?'

The owl winked, and looked down and round. Tracing the owl's gaze with the torchlight, I caught a sudden glimpse of green. I bent over and picked up a smooth round stone. At first glance, in the torchlight, it looked like green marble. Well that's really white marble suffused with green serpentine. But, as far as I knew, that came from islands like Iona, way over to the west. I'd need to check.

I rolled the stone around my fingers. The stone felt warm, as if it knew me. On impulse, I held up the stone to the owl. The owl hooted twice and flew off into the gloom.

I returned to the hut, and stashed the bike in the store room. Perhaps its owner would return. Then I headed down the hill to my cottage.

The cottage had been a bit of a wreck when I bought it. Bernie took one look and refused to live there. I really shouldn't have made it a surprise. But I'd endured the accident, and it was my compensation money that paid for it.

The cottage was supposed to be for holidays, and our retirement. Bernie said we should have put the money towards an even bigger house in a more upmarket area than Bearsden. But what's the point of having lots of bedrooms when all the kids have left home?

The long and the short of it was that I couldn't cope with going back to teaching, and Bernie couldn't cope with sharing the house with me in what she called 'my state'. I did offer her a divorce, but she said it was against her religion, as indeed it was, not that she'd otherwise paid much attention to it. So we sorted out our finances, I moved to the cottage, and we've had less and less contact ever since. At least I got to keep the cat.

Behind the front door, there was a pile of letters on the mat. I couldn't face them right then, so I added them to the stack on the hall table. Then I fed the cat, banked up the stove with peat, made myself an omelette, and, as I ate, watched the news on TV. Nothing seemed to be happening. Well, nothing out of the ordinary.

Replete, I settled down on the sofa, with an old compendium of Scottish myths and legends balanced on the cat on my lap. As I read about the strange beliefs concerning prehistoric arrowheads, I kept catching myself rolling the green stone between my fingers. And, when I finally went to bed, I carefully placed the stone on the bedside table next to my watch.

Chapter 3

Helen – Wednesday 10th September

I woke on time, before my seven o'clock alarm. The night's dreams flowed out of my mind the way dreams do when you try to grasp at them. Something vivid – my cousin, bodies, that pebble expanding and glowing, one of those dream chase sequences? Well, that's what you get if you read swords and sorcery after an eventful day. Though cousin Malcolm would make an exceptionally unlikely swords and sorcery character.

I golloped my scran and was on the quay for seven forty-five as the crew prepared to sail, and then cast off. I was looking out for a candy car but a rather smart black BMW pulled up instead. A bit of a waste on an island with single-track roads, where you'd be lucky to get past 40mph. And given the size of Stornoway, we could probably walk the town end to end in ten minutes.

There's something about plain clothes bobbies that makes it easy to tell them from normal folk. This driver was no exception. But he was also a bright-eyed and bushy-tailed youth, with added puppy enthusiasm. As I settled into the comfortable front seat he was already telling me his name – which was Steven McIver.

Oh.

'Nice to meet you Steven. Aren't you one of the cousins I met at my grandmother McIver's burial about five years back?'

Bingo. Off he went about it all; to my embarrassment told me I'd been a talking point in Stornoway for months afterwards. We were second cousins he explained, and seemed about to give me a whole family tree. Luckily, as we pulled out of the car park he had to stop the chat to avoid a van that whipped round the corner without looking. Not a white one either, lurid purple with some logo in red on the side.

'Tolla-thon,' Steven said loudly. Which for you non-Gaelic speakers means 'arsehole'. Not that I am a speaker, it's just that Dad, who grew up with the language, taught me a few choice terms.

'And if he wanted the ferry he needs to get out of bed quicker,' Steven added scornfully. I'd seen the ferry to Ullapool leaving earlier, at seven.

It was only about five minutes to the police station – along the front, back along it but a block in, a right turn, and in a couple more blocks we were there. We could have walked almost as quickly. It was a routine-looking 1970s building next to a big Georgian pile. I asked Steven what that was and he said 'The Masons,' rather shortly. I decided not to comment given all the stories about the police and funny handshakes, which were probably not just a Wearside thing.

Inside it had that quiet early-morning feeling. It was only just gone eight.

'I'm afraid it's too early to send you to your digs just yet,' Steven said. 'And the boss wanted a word but he'll be here after nine. I thought maybe the canteen?'

'I'll be fine,' I said, sounding as cheery as I could manage. 'No harm in another coffee and I'm in the middle of a book. I expect you have stuff to do, so just lead me there.'

More swords and sorcery. The coffee was at least as bad as I expected. Eventually I was summoned to meet Mr Tweed Jacket – or DI Sinclair to his friends.

'We appreciate your help Ms McIver,' he said, once I got settled, having refused the offer of yet another cup of coffee. This was my least favourite form of address, but I could hardly ask him to call me Helen and still less Hulkie. I gave him my cruise staff Customer Service smile.

'Delighted to be of assistance. Is there anything specific you need me to do?'

'The autopsy should be in process now, and we have passed on your photographs. We just need someone able to answer any questions the pathologist or ourselves may have.'

Damn, sounded like a whole morning in the canteen on the off-chance.

'I know that involves a lot of hanging around. I asked Steven if he could take you out for some lunch since we should be through by then. He can drop you off at the hotel down the street we've booked you into.'

As if by magic there was a knock at the door and before Sinclair could say 'come in' it opened and Steven appeared.

'Sorry to butt in boss, but something I thought you'd want to hear about our body.'

I stood up to go.

'Give me a shout then, if or when you do need me,' I said, trying not to sound grumpy.

I could see Steven was dying to tell Sinclair his news, and I should have been quicker closing the door behind me. But maybe carrying a kit bag slowed me down a little.

'He's a fake,' I heard Steven say as I finally shut the door. 'He doesn't exist.'

Of course it wasn't my business.

The canteen was busier now but police officers are not the most interesting people to people watch. On the other hand they are just as much into gossip over coffee as any other bunch of people. I sat there with my ears flapping, sure a lot of the them would be talking about the body. After all, a nice change from traffic offences. Frustratingly, they did keep their voices down and I only caught snippets.

Some of it could have been speculation about drug-running on the island. But I gathered someone had been asked to trace a Glasgow address, and from his face, it looked like he had failed. That was consistent with what Steven had said. There was also something about a car hire.

Pretty certain that Mr Tweed Jacket would be appalled at my hearing this, I decided I wouldn't mention it to him. Anyway, it wasn't my business.

It was getting on for midday when I was fetched back, this time to both Sinclair and Steven. I'd more than exhausted the potential of the canteen by then.

'Ms McIver,' Sinclair began. 'The autopsy is complete. You and your captain will be relieved to hear that we do not think this is a suspicious death. The Procurator Fiscal has authorised the death certificate and we have a copy here for you.' He handed it to me and I stared at it.

The certificate said 'death by drowning'. So that meant he wasn't killed first and then dumped. True, I hadn't noticed any obvious wounds or rope marks.

'So you think he made away with himself?' I asked, which I could see from their reaction wasn't a very diplomatic question. But it was the only other way to explain the pockets full of rocks.

'That is our current thinking,' Sinclair said. 'We have further investigations to carry out into the identity of the deceased and the circumstances of the drowning, but we have ruled out foul play.'

But who comes all the way to Lewis to drown themselves? Assuming he really was from Glasgow, he could have thrown himself into the Clyde.

'Thanks for the certificate,' I said, inserting it carefully into my kit bag. 'So I assume I can take in the sights of the town this afternoon?'

'Such as they are, Ms McIver, you can,' he said drily.

'Well, after lunch anyway,' Steven chipped in.

This time we left on foot and walked back down the street towards the harbour. The small hotel they had booked for me was about halfway down and I nipped in to register and drop my kitbag off.

The restaurant was another block or so in an arts centre with a fetching glass tower on the end. I was sure there hadn't anything so flashy when I used to visit the grandparents. Though that was a surprisingly long time ago now. We were upstairs with a nice harbour view, and they had some very decent seafood on the menu. We ordered, and I decided to tackle Steven about the body.

'Well, Steven, I've been hearing McMalkin was not all he seemed. So how are you guys going to investigate further?'

'Canteen chat, I guess?' I nodded. Steven might be a bit puppy-dog, but he wasn't stupid.

He leaned forward and lowered his voice.

'I suppose it does no harm to tell you, but don't go spreading it around. He didn't arrive on the ferry or by plane. Or not under that name. Indeed, we can't find anyone of his name and age in the UK or Ireland. Lucky he wasn't called McDonald or that search might have taken a week. His Glasgow address doesn't exist, there's no record of the driving licence at DVLC and the credit card was a clone from a completely different McMalkin – Gavin not Gray.'

He paused, then went on: 'Still, he managed to hire a car on Monday, and we're interviewing the car hire desk in case he let slip any useful information. The car might have been abandoned somewhere around Loch Liurboist, and there's only a couple of villages. I'll pop over to Leurbost and Crosbost this afternoon and see if anyone noticed him. And we'll be putting out a picture: STV will give us a short slot on tonight's news.'

They knew their stuff. 'Sounds impressive,' I said.

I could see a sudden idea strike him.

'Hey – do you want to be in the slot? STV love the human interest angle, I'm sure they'd want to interview you.'

I hesitated. What would the Captain think? Or Marine Scotland come to that? Oh, it was too tempting. Dad would be really tickled to hear I'd been on Scottish tellie.

'OK. Happy to help.'

It was fun being interviewed, and I got in some good points about the Marine Scotland mission. Then when I watched the segment on the evening news, that bit was edited out. My thirty seconds of TV stardom. Steven told me they got an artist to sketch McMalkin from my photo because dead faces are a no-no on TV. I thought it was a pretty good likeness. There was a separate photo of his pendant – they must have removed it from the body.

But that was all later.

Once the interview was over, I decided to walk off some of the seafood by going up to the Castle. Steven had offered to take me with him to the villages along Loch Liurboist, much against the rules I assume. He seemed to think that being family, as it were, he was responsible for amusing me. At least, I hoped that was the reason. I thought it wiser to decline. After all, McMalkin really was not my business.

The Castle is Stornoway's sole tourist attraction, but there is nothing medieval about it. It was some Victorian bigwig's pile. I used to go up there with my big brother Donnie on those summer visits to the grandparents so we could get out from under the eyes of the grownups for a bit. The Castle wasn't the attraction so much as the grounds. The only woods on Lewis we were told, pretty much every time the Castle came up. A great place for making dens or playing wars.

It was only a twenty-minute walk, but as I got to the Bayhead road, running along the inlet separating town and castle, I strode out for the first time in at least a week. The sun was shining, there was hardly any wind, and it was about 10 degrees warmer than the previous day. Climate change might be handy for Lewis. I enjoyed feeling my muscles stretch after the morning sitting down. Then stopped. Something was banging against me. It was the green pebble, which I must have put back into my pocket before I left Alba na Cuan.

I fished it out. The easy thing would be to dump it. I could throw it into the inlet from where I stood and it would make an enjoyable splash. But that seemed a shame. A lovely shape and weight, attractive colour – it was good to have something beautiful to keep. I wondered what sort of stone it was. As a hill walker, I can tell a limestone landscape from sandstone, but that's about it for geology expertise. Cousin Malcolm might be useful for this. Rocks was definitely one of the things he'd gone on about at the wedding. Maybe I should send him a pic.

I started off, keeping it in my hand. It felt pleasantly warm. After a few hundred metres, I stopped again. Was it tingling a bit against my palm? Looking at it, the colour seemed to have somehow deepened and brightened, as if it was fluorescing. I remembered the cruise I'd worked on round the Maldives, where the sea fluoresces, much to the amazement of the passengers. But that was bioluminescence, sea creatures, not rocks.

Maybe this was a type of stone that reacted to skin, like those tacky mood rings. Well, not a good moment to investigate it, so I dropped it into the inside pocket of my fleece with my wallet, where it couldn't fall out. It was solidly reassuring against my body.

I spent a good hour wandering the Castle grounds and feeling nostalgic. I located the young oak with low branches that we used to boldly climb. I had grown more than it had. Now it looked small. The Castle itself had been cleaned up, and had a museum and tearoom. I paused on my way back wondering whether to go in. My eye was suddenly taken by a parked van, with its back doors open and a man bending into its load space. A purple van with a red logo on the side, which I could now see had a big F^2 and *Fundamental Forces* in smaller lettering. If it was the same arsehole van, it hadn't taken the midday ferry either. I knew of the company in fact. Malcolm's wife, Bernie – well, mostly ex-wife – worked in their Glasgow office.

I'd paused to read the logo and as I did so, the back doors were suddenly slammed shut. So suddenly they only just missed the face of the man now straightening up. Who looked straight at me. Took a step towards me.

I straightened too, making the most of my height, which was at least the same as his. And he was older than me too, so if push came to shove. Which of course it wouldn't…

'But you're not McMalkin,' he said.

'What? Do I know you?'

He peered at my fleece, with its Alba na Cuan patch.

'You're from the ship! Where's McMalkin?'

'Excuse me, we haven't met as far as I know. What gives you the right to ask me questions?

Then I couldn't resist adding: 'Did McMalkin work for you? And why did you think you'd see him here?'

OK, shouldn't have said that.

'So you do know him. Where is he?'

Well, he'd find out on the evening news, so no harm in telling him.

'Dead. We fished him out of the sea. Go talk to the police if you knew him.'

Odd though, given the police said the name was fake.

His face fell and he looked – what, almost scared?

'But you have something of his. Give it to me!' And he took another step towards me.

'I don't know what you are talking about. I repeat, go speak to the police. And I should tell you that if you threaten me for whatever weird reason, I will speak to the police too.'

I took my mobile out of my pocket.

'I think you should leave.'

He hesitated. Then gave up, and backed off. I watched him as he got into the driver's seat, still holding my phone. And stood there glaring as he drove off.

Well, what was that about, I wondered, as I walked back to town. And should I tell Steven?

Chapter 4

Malcolm – Wednesday 10th September

It was barely light when the phone woke me. Bernie. Who else would it be, so early in the morning?

Bernie was short with me. Why didn't I ever reply to my post? Did I ever actually open it? Was I actually coming to the wedding? Did I actually know the details?

The wedding. I'd pushed it into the corner of my brain, with all the other things I couldn't quite face.

Alison. Our youngest. To Grant. Boring, dependable Grant. Were it up for discussion, Bernie would no doubt say he was a better bet than boring, undependable me.

'Yes,' I said. 'Of course I'll be there. Yes, I knew the details. Thursday the 18th. Lochgilphead. St Margaret's Church. Who's all coming? Richard and Neil, of course. I do hope Uncle David's going?'

Richard and Neil are our sons. Like Alison, they'd taken Bernie's side. It never stopped hurting.

David was my mum's brother. He'd be there, but his children Helen and Donnie wouldn't. I really liked David, and looked forward to seeing him again, but I was relieved Helen wasn't going. Helen had even less time for me than I had for her.

Bernie then reeled off a long list of other people, most of whom were huddling in that dark corner of my brain, along with the wedding. When she finally put the phone down, I rolled over and tried to get back to sleep, but the cat had other ideas.

The phone rang again, as I was feeding the cat. This time it was the office. The Japanese eco-tourists had been rescheduled. Could I meet them at the hut in an hour?

I showered, dressed and breakfasted. Then I grabbed the laptop, and set off in the Land Rover, up onto the moor. It was a fine morning, and the peaks stood proud against the clear blue sky.

The minibus was waiting for me at the hut. Jess was driving, which suited me well. We'd done this run together lots of times before, and she knew my routine: slowly across the moor to the Pass, with a mid-morning break at the National Trust centre, before turning round and heading slowly back to the hut. Geology one way, and history the other. Lots of stops for photo opportunities: sheep on the road, which always charmed the visitors, and maybe the odd deer, or even an eagle.

I parked and boarded the bus. As Jess pulled away, I gave my introductory spiel: safety, comfort breaks, do ask questions. Pausing for the translator, I caught myself rolling the green stone between my fingers. The green stone. I hadn't even remembered pocketing it.

Suddenly I thought about cousin Helen. I wondered what she was up to now. The last time I saw her must have been at the funeral. That had been a disaster. Had she been going to the wedding, I'd really have needed to make an effort. The wedding. I wasn't going to think about the wedding.

The morning was uneventful. Lots of sheep. No yawning. After Jess dropped me off at the hut, I got straight into the Land Rover, and headed back north to the Altnafeadh Hotel for lunch. I'd not had time to make myself anything before I'd set off, and I couldn't be bothered going home to do so, even though it was closer.

The Hotel forecourt was almost empty, apart from Dougie's blue and white police car. Dougie himself was parked at his customary table in the restaurant bay window, munching his way through his customary pie, beans and chips.

I do like Dougie. He can come over all policemanish, as the need arises, but he's basically very decent. Dougie's slightly younger than me, though markedly larger. We'd met when I'd first moved to the village, in the middle of winter, five years ago. His police car had got stuck in a snow drift on our track – the force hadn't quite got around to replacing his saloon with something more appropriate – and I'd hauled him out with the Land Rover.

I called out a greeting and he waved me over.

'Malco!' he said as I sat down. 'How's it hanging?'

'Just fine,' I said, trying not to wince at his egregious archaisms. 'And yourself?'

'All quiet on the western moor,' said Dougie. 'Just the way I like it.'

Jeannie, the proprietor, came over from the counter.

'Hi Malcom,' she said. 'The usual?'

'Hi Jeannie,' I said. 'Yes please. Anything exciting happening?'

'Did you see those two Americans?' said Jeannie. 'Yesterday?'

'If it's the same ones,' I said, guardedly, 'they came by the hut. They wanted directions for the Menzies Stone. New Agers, I reckon.'

'That sounds like them,' said Jeannie. 'They'd booked in here for the night, but something must have badly spooked them. When they got back from their walk, they just jumped in their car and took off. They didn't even ask for their money back.'

'How strange,' I said. 'Did you come across them, Dougie?'

'No sign of them,' said Dougie. 'Like I said, all quiet on the moor.'

'Just the way you like it,' said Jeannie, heading off to the kitchen. 'I'll not be long.'

After lunch, replete, I drove back to the hut. Inside the reception area, things didn't feel quite right. It was as if someone had conducted a search, and put everything back in almost the same place. But why would anyone want to search the hut? Getting in's easy. I don't bolt the door. It's policy: you never know when someone might need shelter in the middle of nowhere if the weather turns nasty. There's never any cash on the premises: why would we need any? And I carry the laptop with me when I'm out. And the local neds are terrified of Dougie.

On a hunch, I went round to the back of the hut and checked the store room. The door opened outwards and was secured with a sturdy padlock. From the marks round the hasp, it looked like someone had tried unsuccessfully to force their way in.

The bicycle. If Patricia Harper hadn't perished by the Menzies Stone, and I'd no good reason to think she had, perhaps she'd come back for it. But why didn't she just wait? Again, I thought about contacting

Dougie, but he was the sort of old fashioned polis who liked actual evidence, not feelings and hunches.

No, I didn't check the store room to make sure the bicycle was still there.

It was another quiet afternoon. Not really the way I like it. I enjoy chatting with people, and finding out a wee bit about where there from and what brings them here. Still, it gave me some time to work on a new display board, presenting local geology. I'd really enjoyed researching that, and it gave me lots of new material for the guided tours. Maybe I could even write a new leaflet.

Then I remembered the green stone, warm in my pocket. I took it out and sat it in front of the laptop. Surfing for serpentine marble, amongst pages of adverts for couthy Scottish jewellery, I found a succinct account of its formation from metamorphised pre-Cambrian limestone. I was right. In the UK, that combination of high pressure on ancient sea beds is only found on the west coast of Scotland.

I put the stone back in my pocket and returned to designing the display. At closing time, I tidied up and headed home. On the kitchen floor, the cat had thoughtfully left me a disembowelled rabbit, but, unaccountably, still seemed hungry. I tidied up the detritus, fed the mighty hunter, made myself beans on toast, and settled down to watch the TV news.

I'd just finished eating when the local bulletin started. I don't usually pay much attention until the weather forecast, but suddenly, in the corner of the screen, there was cousin Helen! Her boat had trawled up the body of a man in the Minch, and landed it at Stornoway. His pockets had been full of stones: perhaps it was suicide. The artist's impression showed an unfamiliar face, but I immediately recognised the next image: a photo of a talisman from the chord around the poor man's neck. It was a stone arrowhead, just like the one Patricia Harper was trying to replace.

What was Helen doing in the Minch? Wasn't she in Sunderland? Oh, right, Helen had retrained as a marine engineer. I should have paid more attention. Still, what a weird coincidence.

The green stone felt warm in my fingers. I knew I needed to talk with Helen about the arrowhead, but I'd no way to get in touch with her. I could phone David, but it was getting a bit late. Tomorrow.

I washed up, and settled down on the sofa, with a book about Scottish prehistoric communities, balanced on the cat on my lap. According to the book, there'd never been much presence in this area. The land had always been marginal and ingress hard. It was far better for Mesolithic hunter gatherers to stick to the coast, and for Neolithic farmers to work the broad river valleys. All the same, Creag Na Caillich was one of the few stone tool factories they'd identified, which did suggest an important role in some exchange based economy.

The lights went out. That's not uncommon in rural Scotland, but more frequent round here since F^2 started up. Goodness knows why a company looking for alternative energy needs so many conventional electrons.

I fumbled my way to the front hall, and found and lit the storm lantern. I should have taken Dougie's advice and bought a generator, but I kept putting it off. Maybe he'd know what was happening, being the polis and all.

I sat the storm lantern down on the hall table and went outside. The whole village was dark, but the sky to the north west was pulsating an unearthly purple.

The telephone rang. One of the few advantages of a land line is that it's independently powered. I went back inside and picked up the handset.

'Malcolm Nicholson,' I said.

'Good evening, Mr Nicholson,' said a voice of indeterminate accent. 'This is a courtesy call from Fundamental Forces.'

'Is this about the power cut?' I said.

'Power cut?' said the voice. 'I don't know anything about a power cut.'

'The whole village is out,' I said. 'And there's a strange light in the sky.'

'Probably the Northern Lights,' said the voice, hastily. 'No, I'm calling about the incident on our boundary fence yesterday evening.'

Blimey! What on earth do I say? I can't tell the truth. And any evasion will doubtless come back and bite me on the bum.

'What incident?' I said.

'The incident by the Menzies Stone,' said the voice. 'You were there, weren't you.'

'I've no idea what you're talking about,' I said. 'And where I go's no concern of yours.'

'But we've got your Land Rover on CCTV,' said the voice. 'Weren't you driving it?'

'There aren't any CCTV cameras round here, as far as I know,' I said. 'And it's illegal to use them without warning signs. Where exactly is this camera?'

There was a clicking nose from the other end. As the line went dead, the lights came back on again. I turned off the storm lantern and went outside. The sky was clear all around.

I needed to talk with Dougie.

I walked down the track to the next cottage, and banged on the front door. After a long pause, the door was opened by a dishevelled looking Dougie.

'Malco, my man!' said Dougie, casually buttoning his trousers. 'What brings you round so late? Is it about the power? There's been a surge on the grid and it crashed the village transformer.'

'Was it F^2?' I asked. 'The sky went a weird colour over in their direction.'

'You think The Force was with them?' said Dougie. 'No, I didn't see anything. You've not been smoking that whacky baccy, have you? It's against the law you know.'

And he winked at me.

'You know I don't smoke,' I said. 'I was wanting to ask you something about F^2.'

'Can't it wait 'til the morn?' said Dougie. 'We're kind of busy right now.'

And he winked at me again.

'Sorry!' I said, backing away. 'Sorry! I'll leave you in peace. Say hello to Glenys.'

'No worries!' said Dougie, going back into the house. 'Stay cool!'

But if Dougie and Glenys had been doing what I thought they'd been doing, how could he possibly know what caused the outage? Unless he knew in advance. So why hadn't he warned the village?

I'd have another go at Dougie tomorrow. And I'd try to locate Helen.

Chapter 5

Helen – Thursday 11th September

I was staring at my Full Scottish breakfast, wondering whether to start on it or not, when my mobile went. Stornoway's pub culture had proved livelier than I thought, and Steven had rustled up more young cousins for a session in the Sea Angling Club. We'd managed a good evening during which I'd managed maybe one more single malt than was wise.

I checked the calling number: Home. Answered it at once.

'Is that Helen? This is your mother.' Mam hadn't really understood mobiles were personal devices or that they displayed the caller's number.

'Hi Mam. Is everything canny?' An unexpected breakfast call was a bit alarming.

'Yes pet, nothing serious.'

'But?'

'Well you know Dad was due a hernia operation?'

He'd told me this a good six months back, stressed it wasn't anything to worry about.

'Yes.'

'Well, the hospital rang yesterday, and there's been a cancellation and so could he come right away, and of course he said yes. Because he's been on the list for so long and it's been getting uncomfortable for him.'

'But why dinnit he ring me yesterday?'

'Well he checked some computer thing he looks at, and it said you were at sea until the evening, and this was the first chance.'

I should have been still at sea the day before, but for the body. Hadn't updated my online calendar.

'Do you have a hospital number? Can I ring him there?'

'They did give me one but it's the nurse's station they said and he's due to have the operation this morning and so I'm to ring mid-afternoon.'

She gave me the number.

'OK Mam, Thanks for letting me know.'

'Well that isn't quite all, pet.'

'Oh?' Calling me 'pet' meant she wanted a favour, as I knew from hard experience.

'You remember your cousin Malcolm's youngest, Alison? And her wedding. Well, it's next Thursday. And your Dad was so keen to go, because you know your Auntie Christine doesn't approve of Catholics, and it s a Catholic wedding, so she won't go, and Dad wanted to make up for it to poor Malcolm, not to mention Bernie was so helpful to you, and there again they separated, so some family support...but of course he won't be well enough to travel then.'

'Oh, Mam. Dinnit tell me. You want me to go?'

'Well your Dad said he was sure you would step into the breach and I know you're on holiday, but it would really help and it's on his mind.'

I doubted it was that much on his mind. Mam is the one for doing the right family thing.

'And Donnie couldn't get holidays at such short notice, and you're already in Scotland.'

One of the reasons I had winkled out of it in the first place was because it would have been a whole day of Mam dropping her usual heavy hints about how I should get married and 'settle down'. At least that was off the agenda. I could see I was cornered.

So I wrote down the details: St Margaret's Church, Lochgilphead. Somewhere in darkest Argyle, according to Google maps, so easily doable from Troon. That's the Alba na Cuan's home port, where I'd left my car. Mam and Dad had planned to travel on the Wednesday and stay in the hotel where the reception was booked. Of course I could have their room.

'Oh Helen, Wilf passed his best wishes on and he hopes to talk to you soon and he's such a nice lad, don't you think pet?'

Ouch. Wilf was my current on-off boyfriend, not yet live-in, though he'd like to be. Trust Mam to raise him. I'd taken the Marine Scotland contract partly to give myself some breathing space and sort out how serious I was about him. All too obvious how serious he was about me. And not something I wanted to talk to Mam about.

'OK, Mam. Got to gan on now. I'll ring the hospital this afternoon.'

I picked at my cold breakfast and decided to stick to the toast.

In fact there was no hurry. When I got back to the hotel the previous day after my trying afternoon, I'd checked where the Alba na Cuan was on the ship tracker. She was nowhere near as far south as she should have been at that point. Looked like they'd had a problem. So no surprise when Steven told me later they'd radioed a message in that there'd been some engine trouble and they were unlikely to be back to fetch me until tea time.

Hmm, most of another day in Stornoway. I'd need to vacate the room by 10, though no doubt they'd look after my kit bag. But the F^2 gowk had freaked me out and I didn't fancy another walk in case I bumped into him again. Or he bumped into me. I couldn't shake off the feeling he'd somehow been following me. Something to do with my pebble? I fished it out yet again and stared at it. It didn't look engineered, just sea-smoothed. But there was that odd glowing behaviour. Was it some kind of Fundamental Forces energy source that McMalkin had stolen?

No, I hadn't told Steven. McMalkin wasn't my problem and becoming part of the on-going enquiry could maroon me here for days. And now I had a wedding to see to as well, biting into the three-week holiday I had awarded myself between contracts. I'd have to decide whether to invite Wilf to the last week. But not yet.

I jumped as my mobile went again, and dropped the pebble back into my pocket. Who was this? Oh – talk of the devil, Steven.

'Hi Helen. Hope the hotel is treating you well. Good evening last night. No sore head I hope?'

I assured him the hotel was fine and I was fine.

'So the car hire interview turned up that our Mr McMalkin asked how to get to the Calanais – you know, the standing stones?'

Of course I knew them. Dad had taken us there more than once, not to mention shouting at me and Donnie for climbing them.

The long and the short was that Steven wondered if I'd like to join him driving over there as he was going to ask locals whether they had noticed McMalkin. Back for lunch he added hopefully.

'That's very nice of you, Steven. I was wondering what to do until the ship gets in. Yes, great. What time?'

I met him an hour or so later back at the police carpark. Yesterday's sun had gone but there was still no wind, and it felt as if a storm might be coming.

The roads had improved since Dad last took us. More than twenty years ago that must have been. New surface and a white line down the middle. Steven drove fast but not recklessly so, and the BMW was a good car. There's a transition – you pass from neat Stornoway suburbia, circumvent the Castle in its green grounds and then you are out onto bare brown land with the glint of water to one side or another and a lot of sky. Which westwards, where we were going, was looking rather bruised and ominous.

There's not much along the road, but we did pass a garage on the right. I noticed a purple van at its old fashioned pumps.

'Well, Steven, it looks like that purple van yesterday didn't leave after all. Unless there are two of them, we just passed it, refilling at that garage.'

Steven glanced in his rear view.

'Oh, the F^2 van, Frank Dooley. I thought so yesterday. They're some mainland research company, doing a project with UHI, the University. Frank's OK, if a bit corporate. Maybe he's having a day off.'

I could have told him then about the day before, but again I didn't. He asked me about places I'd visited working, and I rabbited on.

In half an hour we were there. We got up the narrow uphill access road without meeting a car coming down. I remembered Dad uncharacteristically swearing at some oncoming vehicle that refused to give way the last time I was there.

'Why don't you visit the stones while I visit the houses?' Steven said. 'I'll leave the car unlocked. The weather's looking a bit grim and you might need to shelter. It's pretty safe out here, folk don't lock their doors either.'

The stones were deserted for once, and all the more impressive. I decided to walk right round the whole thing, which makes a kind of big cross, knowing Steven might take some time. I stopped at the far side to admire the view over Loch Roag. It looked very silvery, in what was now rather low light. The sky was darkening, and there were flashes in the clouds westwards.

I got back to my starting point and walked along the long avenue of pairs of stones towards the central circle. Halfway along I stopped. I could feel a very slight vibration against my body from the pocket in which I had stashed the pebble. I took it out. Yes, it had that deep green glow about it. Could it be reacting to charged air from the oncoming storm? Oncoming it was, I could hear thunder now, and feel that sudden wind that sits on a storm face.

Maybe not the storm: the vibration seemed to get slightly stronger as I walked towards the inner circle. It became much more noticeable when I got to the central stone, which was the one me and Donnie had tried to climb. Though the thunder was also louder and closer. The central stone has the remains of a tomb to one side of it, and I noticed a small fresh patch of earth, as if someone had dug a hole and refilled it. McMalkin?

I stuffed the pebble back and was about to investigate further when a quiet voice with that local almost non-accent came from behind me, startling me badly.

'What are you wanting here? *What's given to the stones remains given. When the days balance the worlds balance and then the gate that is open will be shut.*'

I swung round. It wasn't Frank the gowk, but a small woman in a large and shapeless coat down to her knees with a battered green hiking hat jammed down on her head. What I could see of her face was brown and seamed – she was old. Maybe that was why she was coming out with total nonsense. But her eyes were small and dark like a bird's and looked knowing. Round her neck and hanging over her coat, was a chipped arrowhead just like the one I remembered on McMalkin. Amazing!

'I don't mean to be rude, grandma, but I've seen a pendant like yours before. Does it mean something?'

'This?' she closed her hand round it. 'It's the sign of Wicca.'

'What's Wicca?'

She chuckled. 'Some say we are witches. Lucky for us the burning days are gone.'

Before I could ask another question, I caught movement in my peripheral vision, and turning again, realised it was a man, jogging quite fast down the stone avenue towards me. Not Steven. What was corporate Frank doing, pursuing me like this? And what was the best thing to do? Face him or flee him?

But before I could decide, there was a terrific flash of lightning and a simultaneous explosion that felt as if it was just over my head. The world spun and I fell over, stunned. Was this how it felt to be struck by lightning?

I think some time passed, because the next thing I knew someone was shaking me.

'Helen! Helen! Are you OK? Say something?'

Steven. Looking distraught. I struggled up quickly, realising I was still in one piece.

'Steven! The old lady! The F^2 guy!'

'What old lady? Frank Dooley's down as well, stay there, I need to check he's alive too.'

Nice to feel you were someone's first choice.

I leaned against the central stone for a moment. The rain was washing down like a bucket being tipped over my head. Steven had charged back down the avenue to Frank Dooley. I started to totter towards him and saw he was attempting CPR. Maybe the lightning had actually struck Frank. I made myself run.

'Let me help! I have training.' I took over. Steven whipped out his mobile to ring emergency services.

Four long CPR cycles later Frank's face went pink as he started breathing. But he seemed to be out cold.

'There's a helicopter coming,' Steven told me. 'Are you OK?'

I nodded. Hmm, OK-ish at least.

'Go back and sit in the car, get warm. I'll wait with him.'

I trudged back to the car park, soaked to the skin, though the rain was easing off and the storm seemed to have passed. The F^2 van was parked there too. I looked round to see if there was anyone about, and then tried the van back doors. Bingo! They were open.

Inside was some kit I recognised – a box with a screen clearly designed for tracking. I dug out the pebble and brought it close. The apparatus beeped alarmingly and the screen went white. On a whim I touched the pebble to the box. There was an electrical bang and a smell of burning. I seemed to have done to his detector what the lightning had done to Frank.

I could hear a helicopter in the distance so I shut the doors quickly. Feeling a bit of a fraud, I wiped the handles with the end of my soggy fleece. Then I went to sit in the BMW as instructed.

Steven reappeared after about twenty minutes, soon after the helicopter took off again. I had started to shiver – without the keys I couldn't start the car and put the heater on. Steven also looked like a drowned rat and was entirely without his usual bounce.

'Helen, Mrs Morison in the village over there will get us dried and warmed. She doesn't speak much English I'm afraid. The medics think Frank Dooley will be fine. How about you? Shouldn't you be checked over? I'm kicking myself for letting you go up there with a storm coming on.'

'All's well that ends well.' I was very thankful Steven's choices hadn't resulted in Frank dying, but it would be very tactless to say so. And I decided to forget about the dotty old lady too. Clearly she had survived, and it didn't seem a good moment to mention someone raving on about witches.

Boy, was I happy to get back onto the Alba na Cuan when she finally docked around five. I talked Steven out of taking me for a hospital visit. We did get a very late lunch, but before he could become sentimental, I dropped Wilf's name into the conversation, causing a noticeable pause. Nice guy Steven, but not my type.

I checked on Dad too. He was asleep, they said, but all was well.

'Good to see you back, Hulkie,' Bodger told me. 'Sod's law the engines played up with you off the ship. You wouldn't believe the hard work it was getting young Riddle to help me. I'm not sure that boyo knows one end of a screwdriver from the other. One last Scrabble tonight once we sail?'

It's a long haul to Troon from Stornoway, over twelve hours even with the strong forecast following wind. We were starting right after the evening meal was done, and oh joy, I was on middle watch from midnight to four. Plenty of time to think about my eventful Lewis visit and what if anything it all meant. Maybe I should speak to Bernie about F^2?

Chapter 6

Malcolm – Thursday 11th September

An early morning phone call was always far more disconcerting than the nuzzlings of a hungry cat. That morning it was the office. There was a party of school children turning up at short notice. They'd originally booked for early summer, but had had to postpone. Now another of their trips had been postponed, so could we slot them in? There was nothing else in the diary, as the office reminded me. What could I say?

The key thing with school parties was to tire the kids out. So, after a hurried breakfast, I headed straight to work, to allow myself time to run off enough activity sheets. As I neared the Loch Tullock Viewpoint, I narrowly avoided a collision with a purple van with a red logo on the side, which hurtled round the corner, in the opposite direction, on the wrong side of the road. Not so uncommon, sadly. Too many drivers seem to think that the A82's actually the Indy 500.

When I got to the hut, I felt a sudden anxiety about the bicycle. I went round to the store and unpadlocked it. The bicycle had gone.

I knew the padlock hadn't been forced. And there was only the one key. So who had taken the bicycle?

The store had a faint, almost electric, scent. The scent was strangely familiar. As my panic mounted, I felt the walls of the store room closing around me.

I staggered back out into the open, bent over, put my hands on my knees, and drew deep, measured breaths.

Then I remembered.

Just before lunch the day before, the most striking woman I'd ever seen had appeared out of nowhere. Her eyes were of agate, and her face shimmered like feldspar. And she had an arrowhead on a cord round her neck, just like Patricia Harper. I'd known instantly that she wanted the bicycle. Without stopping to think, I went straight round to the shed and tried to lever the padlock off, with the spade that was leaning against the wall. Firmly, but calmly, without making a sound, the woman instructed me to use the key. Then, she took the bicycle from me and disappeared.

Bloody hell! Had that really happened? Was there even a bicycle in the first place? Of course there was! There were oil marks on my jeans where I'd rubbed against the chain, as I'd unloaded the bicycle from the Land Rover.

So who was the woman? Why did I do her silent bidding? And how could I ever have forgotten her until now?

But she wasn't completely silent. As I'd padlocked the door, she'd whispered, or I remembered it as a whisper, '*The gate that is open will be shut.*'

I was still shaken and bemused when the coach pulled up. The coach was packed with kids, but, thankfully, Jess was driving again, and there were two teachers, so there was no need to worry about crowd control. Even better, they'd brought their own activity: a treasure hunt for late summer moorland flora and fauna.

The morning went well. The kids were boisterous but engaged. And I had a decent break at the National Trust centre, chatting with Jess and the teachers, while the kids trekked around the grounds, filling in their questionnaires.

The morning ended badly. Jess had just dropped me back at the hut when Dougie phoned, sounding official. There was trouble at my cottage. I needed to come back now. Right now.

I leapt into the Land Rover and charged down the hill, narrowly avoiding a collision with a purple van with a red logo on the side, which hurtled round the corner, in the opposite direction.

There were two police vans outside the cordoned off cottage. I could see through the kicked in front door that the sitting room had been comprehensively turned over. It looked like every cupboard had been emptied, and every drawer had been upended. The furnishings had been slashed, and the stuffing strewn across the floor.

Dougie leant against his police car, wringing his hands.

'Och, Malco,' he said. 'I'm so sorry. This is just awful.'

'What the hell's going on?' I said. 'Why would anyone want to do this? There's nothing to steal. It's blindingly obvious.'

'It's not a theft,' said Dougie. 'Come on, I'll buy you lunch and tell you what I know. I'd buy you a wee dram, if I wasn't in uniform.'

'Can I go inside?' I said.

'Best not to,' said Dougie. 'Not until the scene of crime team's finished up.'

'Where's the cat?' I said.

'She's safe,' said Dougie. 'She's with the missus.'

My head was bursting as we drove to the Altnafeadh Hotel. What did Dougie mean 'it's not a theft'? And what exactly hadn't he told me?

Jeannie looked very worried, but said nothing, as we sat down at Dougie's usual table, beyond confirming our order. Of course, everyone within twenty miles would have known that my wee cottage had been trashed, long before I did.

The food came quickly. Dougie must have called ahead. We ate in silence. Then, while Dougie fetched us tea and coffee, I phoned the office and told them I'd need the next day off. The secretary was most sympathetic, confirmed that there wasn't anything in the diary, and told me to chill.

Hah!

Dougie returned with two mugs of tepid pale liquid.

'Well,' said Dougie. 'Well.'

'What's going on?' I said. 'What haven't you told me?'

'Why were you so keen to see me last night?' asked Dougie.

'No!' I said firmly. 'No! You're not going to distract me. What's going on.'

'Maybe it's connected,' said Dougie.

'Maybe,' I said. 'You first. How did you know about the power cut? And why didn't you tell me?'

'They tell us in advance,' said Dougie. 'But we're not meant to tell anyone else.'

'Who are "they"?' I said.

'The Force,' said Dougie. 'F^2.'

'What do you mean you're not meant to tell?' I said.

'It's the high heidyans,' said Dougie. 'They get it straight from Holyrood. There's not to be any trouble. They had enough difficulty getting planning permission in the first place. Bloody greenies think the moors are going to be irreparably damaged.'

'What are they worried about?' I said. 'It's just a research centre.'

'It's not just a research centre,' said Dougie. 'It's all our futures. Limitless energy, if they can crack it.'

'Come on! I said. 'They said that about nuclear. Then they said that about North Sea oil. Then it was offshore wind. And we're still burning imported gas and coal.'

'This is different,' said Dougie. 'Really.'

'Like in two hundred years "really"?' I said.

'No,' said Dougie. 'Soon. Real soon.'

'I'm sorry to be so sceptical,' I said. 'But how on earth would you know?'

'See all those briefings I've been going to?' said Dougie. 'In Tulliallan? They're all given by Holyrood and F^2 top brass. Do you really not know anything about this? I thought your wife worked for them. Doesn't she tell you anything?'

'She's in HR,' I said. 'And I'm not even sure if she's my wife anymore, other than legally. Anyway, where are you going with all this?'

'F^2 pretty well have carte blanche,' said Dougie. 'They've had huge bungs from the government and the project's too big to fail. So they have to know about anything involving the site.'

'What's this got to do with me?' I said.

'You were seen up there,' said Dougie. 'Two days ago.'

'And what if I was?' I said, too defensively. 'I'm a moor ranger, for Christ's sake! Of course I go onto the bloody moor!'

'But up by the fence?' said Dougie.

'Come on!' I said. 'The track to Rannoch Station runs along the fence. You know that! Is it suddenly out of bounds? If it is, why doesn't someone say something?'

'We can't stop anyone going up there,' said Dougie. 'Right to roam.'

'What about my right to roam,' I said.

'Of course you've got the same rights as anyone,' said Dougie, hastily. 'But when you act suspiciously...'

'What do you mean "act suspiciously"?' I said. 'What are you accusing me of?'

'I'm not accusing you of anything,' said Dogie, emphasising the "I'm". 'Just be careful, that's all.'

'What's this got to do with my cottage?' I said.

'This isn't to go any further, all right?' said Dougie. 'Two of their experimental subjects are missing.'

'What experimental subjects?' I said. 'They're investigating particle physics.'

'Well,' said Dougie, carefully. 'They're actually investigating how to use particles to somehow tap into energy from their origin. And they need to make sure that there aren't any ill effects, like people think there are with overhead power lines. So they run tests. It's all quite safe. Very low energy.'

'So a couple of people have walked out on them,' I said. 'What's that got to do with me?'

'They took something with them,' said Dougie. 'F^2 seem to think you might be somehow involved. Something about a missing bicycle.'

Oh wow. Patricia Harper. She must be one of the subjects. But how's this connected with arrowheads? I rolled the green stone round my fingers. How much could I tell Dougie.

'There was a woman on a bicycle who came to the hut a couple of days ago,' I said. 'But she was going to Creag Na Callach, to look for a Neolithic quarry. That's in the opposite direction. But you know that. Then there were the two Americans, who were looking for the Menzies Stone. The ones Jeannie mentioned. It's all in the log, down at the hut. You're welcome to check. And, yes, I went up onto the moor. The Americans thought they'd seen something. But they seemed really flaky, so I thought I'd better check it out myself, before I bothered you. And there wasn't anything there, of course. All right?'

Was that enough?

'Thank you!' said Dougie, sounding very relieved. 'That makes lots of sense. It looks like there's no connection with your cottage, after all. Everything's a bit of a mystery, isn't it. Let's head off. The SOCOs should have finished.'

Dougie drove me back down the hill. He seemed happy with my economical truth, but I still wasn't buying his. How did anyone know I'd been up at the Menzies Stone?

The police cars had gone and the only sign of the SOCOs was where they'd dusted for fingerprints. I spent the best part of the afternoon tidying up. The mess wasn't as bad as it first appeared, and they'd mostly spared the kitchen and bathroom. I would need new cushions for the sofa and a replacement mattress, though.

Putting away stuff I hadn't looked at in years reminded me of leaving Glasgow. For sure, life with Bernie hadn't always been great, but I thought we rubbed along well enough, until the accident. I couldn't help my claustrophobia and panic attacks. The psychotherapists said that all I could do was live with it. Why couldn't she?

By early evening, the cottage was liveable in again. There was no sign of the cat. Glenys must have been keeping her inside. I'd collect her later. First, I needed to get in touch with Helen and try to find out what she knew about the arrowhead. Uncle David should be able to give me her contact details.

I found my address book and dialled David's number. Aunt Linda answered the phone.

'Hello Linda,' I said. 'It's Malcolm, your nephew. How are you both?'

'Malcolm!' said Linda. 'It's lovely to hear from you, pet. It's been such a long while and we're both well and how are you keeping?'

'I'm doing away,' I said, not wanting to get bogged down in one of Aunt Linda's endless conversations. 'Might I have a quick word with Uncle David, please?'

'I'm afraid not,' said Linda. 'He's in hospital. He's just had his hernia op and he'd been waiting for nearly two years now and there was a cancellation. Those cuts! They're just criminal!'

'Oh!' I said, concerned. 'I do hope everything went well. Do send him my love.'

'Thank you, pet,' said Linda. 'I'll be sure to do that. Everything's fine, but he won't be home for a few days and he'll not go to Alison's wedding, so Helen's going instead. Was it something I can help with?'

Whoah!

'Well, I'm sorry Uncle David won't be there,' I said, 'but I'm glad, for Alison, that one of you can come. You know, I've not seen Helen since the funeral. What's she up to now?'

'She's on a boat somewhere off the west coast of Scotland,' said Linda. 'She's loving it.'

'That's grand,' I said. 'It's nice to hear that things are going well for her. Oh, did you see her on the TV news last night?'

'Goodness me!' said Linda. 'Our Helen on the telly and she didn't say anything and we were talking just yesterday and I wonder why she didn't tell me. She's not in any trouble is she?'

'Oh no,' I said. 'Nothing like that. It was some news item from Stornoway. She was just on the edge of the picture for a few seconds. I was wondering what took her there.'

'That's all right then,' said Linda. 'Nothing to be bothered with and I must tell David when I'm next visiting. Was there anything else?'

'Well,' I said. 'If Helen's going to the wedding, and she's in Stornoway, maybe I should talk to her about how she's getting there. Maybe I could give her a lift from wherever the boat drops her off.'

'That's very thoughtful of you,' said Linda. 'Very thoughtful. Have you got her number?'

'I haven't,' I said. 'I'd be grateful if you could tell me it.'

'Of course, pet,' said Linda. 'It's in the phone memory and I'll just read it out to you.'

As Linda recited the digits, I tapped them into my mobile phone. Then we bantered away genially for another ten minutes. Aunt Linda did most of the bantering. And she never did ask why I wanted to talk with Uncle David.

I felt a bit guilty after the call. I hadn't exactly got Helen's number on false pretences, but I hadn't been entirely straight with Aunt Linda either.

Time to get the cat. I walked down the track to Dougie and Glenys's cottage and banged on the door. Glenys opened it.

'What a guddle,' said Glenys. 'We're really not used to these goings on. This is a quiet place. And fancy someone breaking in when the polis lives next door! I do hope everything's all right.'

'It's more or less back to how it was,' I said. 'Thank you so much for looking after the cat. I'm sorry to have put you to any bother.'

'No bother at all,' said Glenys. 'She often drops by for a wee chat while you're out. I'll just go and get her.'

Glenys disappeared into the house and returned with the squirming beast. As she leant forward to pass me the cat, a pendant I'd never noticed before swung free from her neck. The pendant was a Neolithic arrowhead, just like the one Patricia Harper sought, just like the one the drowned man wore.

Chapter 7

Helen & Malcolm – Friday 12th September

Malcolm had slept badly. He really needed to talk with Helen, but Helen had been pretty spikey at the funeral. There were a lot of things he wanted to check with her, which necessitated telling her lots of things first. Malcolm knew he wasn't so good at short explanations. And Helen didn't have time for long ones.

After Malcolm had dressed, serviced the cat, and fortified himself, he dialled Helen's number. The phone rang for longer than he'd have liked. He was about to abandon the call, when Helen finally picked up.

She'd just opened the car door when her phone had started ringing, and keys in hand, had been scrabbling in her pockets for it. The number was unfamiliar and she really hoped it wasn't some scammer. Tired and worried, she was ready to bite any scammer's head off on the spot.

'Who is this please?' she asked impatiently.

'Hello Helen,' said Malcolm. 'This is your cousin Malcolm. Malcolm Nicholson.'

'Hello Malcolm,' said Helen. 'Is this about the wedding? I'm afraid not a good moment for a blather, just off the ship and ready to drive on.'

She so wished she hadn't agreed to go to the damn wedding.

'Oh Helen,' said Malcolm. 'I'm so sorry. But I do think it's important if you've got a couple of minutes. Not really about the wedding. Well, yes, maybe we should talk about that.'

'OK,' said Helen, trying to control her irritation, 'so if not about the wedding, about what?'

'I saw you on TV a couple of nights ago,' said Malcolm. 'On the news. About that body you found.'

'Ah yes,' said Helen. 'Bit of a hectic episode really. But the poor guy topped himself it seems. So no juicy murder inquiry. Just as well or I might not have made the wedding.'

There was a chilly wind across the car park, and she started to pace around, trying to keep warm. She wished Malcolm would get to the point or let her go.

'Sounds like a rubbish business,' said Malcolm. 'But that pendant. The arrowhead.'

'The PENDANT!' said Helen, her interest all at once captured. 'You want to know about the pendant? Why?'

'Well,' said Malcolm, patiently, 'to make a long story short, I saw one just like it the same day.'

'Another one?' said Helen. 'That makes three! I saw one just yesterday.'

'Oh wow!' said Malcolm. 'The one I saw was broken. You know I work for Remote Resources…?'

'Yes, yes, yes,' said Helen. 'I know all that!'

'Why is this so hard?' muttered Malcolm to himself.

'Look,' said Malcolm. 'A really strange women came into our centre. She had a broken arrowhead and she wanted to know where to find another one. She was very pushy.'

'That's so weird,' said Helen. 'Well, she probably thinks she is a witch then – someone said they are the sign of Wicca – which is to do with people who claim they are witches. Some old woman I met had one.'

Helen recalled the old woman's seamed face and the small black eyes. And the air of utter certainty with which she'd spoken.

'Anyway,' said Malcolm. 'I sent her off to the Neolithic quarry above Killin where they come from. And then two Americans turned up wanting to get directions to a boundary marker on the moor. And they came back saying the pushy woman was dead. Which seems like a bit of coincidence given your body...'

Christ, another body, thought Helen. This is all too much.

'So why weren't you on the news then?' she cut in.

Malcolm looked up at the ceiling, as if summoning inner strength.

'I went up onto the moor,' said Malcolm, 'and the body was gone. So I could hardly go to the police, could I.'

'Come on man,' said Helen dismissively. 'They were having you on. Wild goose chase. Unless they had a pic or something? Even then it could have been some kind of nasty joke. You never know with Americans.'

'Their camera battery was flat,' said Malcolm, 'but they described her really accurately. And when I went to look I found her bicycle.'

'How do you know it was her bicycle?' said Helen. 'Flat batteries, how convenient. You'll probably appear later on some TV show for practical jokers.'

All this blather for a tall story, she thought crossly.

Malcolm sighed deeply.

'Well,' said Malcolm, 'she arrived at the hut on the same bicycle. And the Americans seemed really badly spooked. I'm sure they weren't putting it on.'

'Sure, they weren't,' said Helen. 'Well, whatever. Oh, before I drive, I was thinking about you the other day. You know geology stuff don't you?'

Might as well get something from the call, she thought.

'Yes,' said Malcolm, recovering some enthusiasm, 'the arrowhead is really interesting. It's a metamorphic rock. Calc-silicate hornfels…'

'Fascinating,' cut in Helen. 'That wasn't what I was going to ask about. I found this green stone, about hand-size, a smooth round pebble thing. It's maybe off a beach somewhere. What sort of rock do you think that is? Does it come from Lewis?'

'Oh wow!' said Malcolm. 'That's crazy! I found one that sounds just like that, near where the body was supposed to be. A wee round stone. It feels really nice to hold...'

'WHAT?' said Helen. 'Are you making this up, man? Pendants and stones – how likely is that? You're having me on again. Pure blather. You aren't setting this up for TV or something? Because I dinnit want to be on one of those shows thank you very much.'

Helen realised she'd walked herself nearly to the edge of the car park, and turned round, feeling the cold invade her belly. This was all wrong.

Malcolm really wanted to put the phone down, but there was more he needed to explore.

'Come on Helen!' said Malcolm. 'It's not like that! Why would I do that? I think there's something really heavy going down. The next day the hut was searched and then my cottage was trashed. Have you heard of a company called F^2 …?'

'Curiouser and curiouser,' said Helen, struggling to control her rising sense of panic. 'Not only have I heard about them, some F^2 gowk called Frank Dooley started chasing me round Lewis in one of their vans.'

'Blimey!' said Malcolm. 'That sounds really threatening. As far as I know, F^2's mostly based in Glasgow, but they have got a plant near here on a remote bit of the moor. They're supposed to be looking at alternative energy sources. It's all very high security. I wonder what he was doing on Lewis. Might you have done something to make them suspicious? I think that's what's happened to me.'

'Funnily enough,' said Helen. 'I think he might have been after that pebble. In fact I found out he had some tracker thing in his van.' She paused. 'You know what, I think it might be an F^2 thing and not a natural pebble at all. Some kind of novel energy source. Does your one glow?'

'So now who's the fantasist?' muttered Malcolm.

'I've not noticed it glowing,' said Malcolm. 'But it does feel unnaturally warm. I'm not sure why. I don't think it's artificial. It's serpentine marble. It's only found in the Inner Hebrides. Iona. You get it in jewellery.'

'Well I dinnit think it's natural at all,' said Helen. 'Normal rocks don't start glowing or start feeling warm – mine does that too. And it sort of vibrates a little bit when it's doing it. There must be some energy coming from somewhere. And I dinnit think it's radioactivity either.'

And how I wish I'd never picked it up, she thought bitterly.

'So what's this tracker?' said Malcolm. 'Where were you when you found about it?'

'Well, it's a long story,' said Helen. 'Let's just say I got a chance to look in the back of the van when Dooley was otherwise occupied. And you know what? There was some kit with a little screen in there that reacted to the pebble, and then when I touched the kit with the pebble, it all went bang and fused. So the pebble must have an energy source of some kind.'

This is getting pretty whacky, thought Malcolm.

'Do you really think the old woman you met with the arrowhead was a witch? The pendant wasn't just some fashion item? They're obviously quite common.'

Christ, this man had a good line in daft questions, Helen thought.

'Of course I dinnit think she was a witch,' she said brusquely. 'I dinnit believe in witches, boggles nor brags. But she thought she was a witch. She definitely said the arrowhead was a sign of Wicca and said that meant witches and just as well they didn't burn them any more.'

'Well,' said Malcolm, 'the Americans I mentioned seemed like crusty old New Agers. And they were trying to find the marker stone where they later claimed they saw the body. When I went up there, there were flowers on the stone as if someone had left them as an offering. So I wonder if there's a connection?'

Suddenly, Helen felt she couldn't take any more.

'Oh, your Americans,' she said, trying not to sound panicky. 'With non-existent dead bodies. Whatever does New Age nonsense have to do with all this anyway? F^2 aren't any New Age thing, they're cutting edge physics. I wasn't being chased by Americans.' She took a deep breath. Time to go before she really lost it. 'Look Malcolm, this is all weird stuff, but we can talk about it at the wedding. I've got to drive and I was on mid-watch so I'm tired, not quite in full fettle. Can we leave this now?'

'Well,' said Malcolm tetchily, 'you did mention Wicca, and that's New Age isn't it. OK. I'm really none the wiser. I can't see how the stones are connected to F^2 unless they're somehow part of the energy process they're looking at. I supposed they could have changed them somehow. Maybe like a pocket energy source? But how come we both found them? Anyway, thanks for talking. See you on Thursday.'

'OK Malcolm,' said Helen. 'No doubt we'll find a moment to go over it all over a drink. All very interesting. I'll be off now, I've to drive up to Loch Lomond. Good to talk to you.'

And Helen ended the call, knowing she had not exactly been kind to Malcolm, the way her Mam had told her to be. She resolved to try and make it up when they met at the wedding. Then got into the car, wishing she could just drive away from the whole mess.

Malcolm put the phone away. That had been about as bad as he'd expected. Still, amongst the squabbling, it had become increasingly clear that there were a lot more connections than coincidences.

Chapter 8

Helen – Friday 12th September

When I drove off from Troon, I was as unhappy as I ever remember being. So much so, I had to will myself to watch the road and the road signs for my route towards Glasgow. I felt even worse than when I broke up with Jed, two years back, after he called me 'a fucking Amazon balls-breaker'. That time I had been furious and heart-broken in equal measures. This time I knew I was scared. And there isn't much that scares me.

I felt completely freaked out by the call with Malcolm. There's coincidence and then there's nightmarishly improbable coincidence. Arrowheads popping up for both of us was bad enough, but that we'd both found green stones that were certainly not normal stones was really creepy.

And what I hadn't told cousin Malcolm, among other things, was that I'd tried to get rid of my pebble during middle watch. I couldn't bank on the shorted-out detector being the only one a company like F^2 had. Or even if it was, of course they could build another.

So I tried to drop the pebble over the stern. And I couldn't.

Holding it in my hand I had broken out in a cold sweat, my eyes went funny, and my breathing speeded up. I think it's probably what people mean by a panic attack. Before I knew it, the pebble was back in my pocket. Just as well I hadn't tried it when people were about. Seemed like F^2 had somehow created an addictive surveillance device.

Was that why McMalkin drowned himself then? What did he think Frank the gowk was going to do to him? Because he must have been after McMalkin, that was the only way to explain the scene in the Castle car park. And was I going to be pursued all round the mainland as well? I did warn Malcolm about the tracking during that call, but it didn't sound like he took it in.

Hang on a minute! Of course there were ways to block electro-magnetic radiation, you just needed to wrap an object in an electrically conducting material. Hence the Faraday cage. And I must have something like that somewhere. Lots of components arrive in bags made of such materials so they don't get shorted out en route. I'd just got onto the A77 so I pulled into the next layby and ferreted in the toolbox I carried in my load space.

Yes, here was one. Taking a deep breath, I grabbed the stone out of my pocket and dropped it into the bag. Quickly, before it could start to glow the way it seemed to when I handled it. Phew, no panic attack. But it went back into my pocket all the same. That made me feel a bit less fraught.

Back into the car, along the A77, and onto the M77 next. Light traffic, easy to think.

Another thing I hadn't told Malcolm was that I'd spoken to Bernie before sailing the previous evening. She'd been pretty scathing about him, so it didn't seem tactful. Bernie is a little bit like a distant big sister. When I finished prenticing at Nissan, I started to get restless. Big organisations don't suit me, and though Mam and Dad both seemed happy working there, I began to realise it wasn't for me. Any more than the 'get married and settle down' idea Mam kept on about.

Dad suggested I chat to Bernie. Maybe he thought F^2 would be a good place for me. But Bernie just asked me lots of questions, over several calls. Talking it over with her made it easier for me to decide what I did want rather than just what I didn't. So that's how I came to retrain in marine engineering. That and volunteering for the Sunderland lifeboat made me a seafarer, and it's suited me well. Bernie's always been so positive about what I do.

After my run-in with Frank the gowk, she was the obvious person to talk to about F^2. She's worked for them all that time, and risen to be in charge of their HR. Of course I didn't go head on into it. First off, we talked about the wedding, which was my excuse for ringing her. I asked about possible wedding presents. That was when I got an earful about Malcolm, who had completely panicked her. She wasn't even sure he was coming until she'd got him on the phone that morning. Awkward if Alison had arrived at the church and he wasn't there to lead her up the aisle.

Still, Mam says Malcolm hasn't been the same since his accident, so to be kind. That was not long before Ganny McIver's burial. Bernie didn't come to the burial, what with being a Catholic and not flavour of the month with Ganny or Malcolm's mam, Auntie Christine. I haven't seen her in a good long while, though I give her a call every so often. She likes to hear about my trips.

'So how's work?' I asked Bernie.

'Oh Helen, such a to-do today,' she said. 'Believe it or not, one of our employees got struck by lightning out on Lewis, poor wee man. That's the first time I've had that come up as an HR problem. He's OK they say, but I had to ring his wife, and she was in a dreadful state. He wasn't even due to be there this week, but something urgent came up at our outreach project with UHI.

'But perhaps you heard about it, weren't you on Lewis too Helen? Didn't I catch you on the local news yesterday? Something about a body? That must have been awful.'

Oops. I really didn't want to talk about the lightning incident and being chased round the island by someone who'd ended up in hospital. So I gave her some stoical stuff about worse body-in-the-water incidents.

'I did see your company's van in Stornoway though. I wondered what it was there for. Cutting-edge physics didn't seem a Lewis thing. So is there a product of some kind emerging? New energy sources or something?'

'Well, we've a big announcement coming up soon, though physics types being what they are, it's all a bit close to the chest, so I'm not sure exactly what it's about, ken? They blether on with their jargon, quantum wave packets, transilience gates, gravitons and goodness knows what else. All Greek to me, but watch this space!'

'Look, I'm landing at Troon tomorrow and I'm coming through Glasgow, on my way to Lochgilphead. I expect you're busy with wedding stuff, but any chance we could grab a quick coffee together? I'm sure there won't be much chance to chat at the wedding. The guests will keep you busy. It's years since I saw you.'

Bernie was too busy for lunch breaks these days she said, but she was in town after work Friday as she was going out with a friend – unspecified. We could have a drink first. And would I like to stay over? I told her about taking over Mam and Dad's booking at the Slockavullin Lodge from the Wednesday, and how I planned to climb Ben Lomond first and had a cottage close by on Friday. She sounded as if not having to put me up was a relief really.

Ben Lomond had been the first step in my original holiday plan, which involved climbing a whole set of Scottish mountains. One every other day I reckoned, with a recovery day in between. Not only had the wedding shot a hole in it, I was beginning to feel I wanted at least as much to know what F^2 were up to and what my pebble was all about. Not to mention Malcolm's stone. And the weird arrowhead pendants. And whether all those coincidences were really coincidental. Well, I was a free agent for three weeks and I could do what the hell I wanted.

I hit Glasgow mid-morning, so the traffic was fine through the various motorway junctions. I planned to get installed and then come back into town to meet Bernie at 6 in a Merchant City wine bar.

The cottage was along the side of Loch Lomond, only an hour further on, but I was really tired after doing middle watch. Once out into the countryside, I noticed a distillery with attached café and stopped for a coffee. As a bonus, I invested in a selection pack of aged malts for the happy couple with a crystal decanter and glasses. None of Bernie's gift suggestions were the kind of thing I could round up in a hurry. Mam and Dad had probably sent something more suitable but there was no way I'd turn up empty-handed. Maybe they liked malts anyway. I bought a bottle for myself while I was at it.

I stuffed the package in my load space and was about to bring the tailgate down when I heard something strange. It sounded like a cat. I looked around and couldn't see one. There it was again. Christ on a bike! It sounded as if it was coming from inside the car. I slammed the tailgate shut. I looked through the back passenger window. I blinked. I could see a large grey tabby sitting on my back seat! It looked like the one in the children's *Mog* books, but more elegant in shape and minus the white bib. Where the fuck had that come from? I pulled open the door and made a grab for it. It dived under the front passenger seat.

Well, it couldn't be local for sure. I'd only had the driver door open to get out and then shut it at once. Ah. I remembered taking the phone call with Malcolm back in Troon. All that pacing around the car park. With the driver-side door left open because I'd been about to get in when he rang. Oh shit. It must be a Troon stowaway.

The long and the short was that I couldn't face trying to dump the animal in the distillery car park. So I drove off with it still on board. I quite like cats – we had a large black called Buster when I was a kid. I could try ringing the Troon harbour office and reporting it, and at some point drive it all the way back. After the wedding. If it didn't wander off in the meanwhile. Which would make it not my problem.

When I got back to Glasgow, I parked closer and quicker than I expected, which made me a bit early. On an impulse I checked Google for the F^2 offices. They were in the Merchant City too, on Queen Street. So I wandered past. Not very flashy from the outside. Their name was the biggest at the entrance, but they shared a building with a set of other high tech companies. Still, when Bernie started with them, they were only a tiny Glasgow University spin-off. Though without products, a bit of a mystery how they balanced their books.

The wine bar was called High Spirits. Groan. I was still early, at least I couldn't see Bernie. The bar advertised 'fifty gins', but I don't like gin and in any case I had to drive back to the cottage. I went for a non-alcoholic cocktail and watched in fascination as the bartender made it in front of me. It came complete with a silver umbrella and a jelly-sweet on a stick. As I turned away from the bar with it, Bernie appeared. Her perfume was running a good three meters ahead of her and she had clearly been primping her make-up. So the friend must be a man – maybe she was dating. Good for her. I told her ages ago her Catholic 'no divorces' thing was a piece of idiocy and she and Malcolm would get along better if they both moved on.

I found us a table and she joined me with one of the fifty gins, in a delicate shade of mauve. I gave her a hug.

'Ooh Helen, you'll crack my ribs. No wonder your Dad calls you Topsy. Is he OK by the way? Aunt Linda told me the op was nothing to worry about.'

'I caught him just after I rang you yesterday, when Mam was visiting. Yes, he's in fine fettle all things considered. This will make such a difference, it was getting really painful.'

And off we went on family stuff, how Donnie and his family were doing in London, what Alison and Grant had planned for the wedding, her brothers Richard and Neil, and their burgeoning careers.

'But what about you, Helen? Not to be nosey, but have you met any nice men? I ken how Jed broke your heart, but he's well in the past now.'

'Well Bernie, I'll tell you about my current bloke if you tell me about your friend for tonight. You're looking far too glam for it to be a girls' night out. Deal?'

Yes, she did blush.

'He's called Thierry – that's Ti-erry, not Terry, he's French. Very much the gentleman, it's early days yet. But we get on so well.'

'Wow, French! How did you meet him?'

Actually this wasn't a recommendation for me. I worked with various Frenchmen in the big cruise company I started out at. They were universally up their own arses, a total pain as colleagues.

'Well, F^2 are a growing company and we needed an occupational health capacity. Recruiting our own seemed a bit over the top, so we looked for someone we could subcontract to. Thierry is a professional psychologist with his own practice and was looking to expand. Of course as head of HR I need to liaise, and we just seemed to hit it off.'

Oh dear. A workplace romance as well. But I could see from Bernie's face she was in that spell-bound state I recalled all too well from Jed. Various people – and Bernie for one – had told me Jed was no good for me. I'd taken no notice at all. So there was no point in saying any of this to Bernie. And maybe he'd turn out to be just what she needed.

'That's great.'

Needless to say, that was when the man himself turned up.

At first glance he looked OK, not too matinee idol, though he did have that Gallic cragginess and brown curly hair. Nice smile, intelligent-looking rather than 'aren't I wonderful?'

'Oh, I am so sorry. Bernie, have I arrived too early?'

'Of course not. Thierry, this is my cousin Helen. Helen, this is Thierry.'

I stood up to greet him and held out my hand. A flicker of surprise, but he recovered well and shook. Firm, warm; not limp, sweaty, or crushing. OK, maybe I should stop being so critical. Just that I wanted this to turn out well for Bernie.

'Helen, enchanted to meet you. Bernie has mentioned you.' A slight accent, but otherwise a very RP voice.

'Nice to meet you too, Thierry. Well Bernie, it's been great to catch up. I'll be getting back to the cottage. See you Thursday!'

This was not, I felt, the moment to hang about. And I was happy I'd been let off talking about Wilf.

As I walked back to the car, I passed one of those city express supermarkets. Oh, the cat. I'd left it in the cottage with a back window ajar so it could go out – I hoped – to do its business. I emerged with a packet of food, a tray and some cat litter. Might as well do things properly until I could return the creature to its native habitat.

Chapter 9

Malcolm – Friday 12th September

I didn't have to go to work, and there weren't any phone calls to disturb me, so I had a lie in. And, for once, the cat left me in peace: Glenys must have fed her better than I usually do.

I took my time getting up, and had a leisurely breakfast. Then I telephoned Helen, who turned out to be every bit as belligerent as I'd remembered. She barely listened to me, and it felt like there was a lot she wasn't telling me. Where did her stone come from? And where did she meet the woman with the arrowhead talisman?

Suppose F^2 really were after Helen for her stone. Were they after me for mine as well? Was it F^2 who'd searched the hut and trashed my cottage? But if they could track her stone, why couldn't they track mine? Her stone glowed, but mine didn't. Was that it? Did they even know about my stone? They knew about the bicycle, though. Did they think my stone was with the bicycle? But you can't hide a bicycle in soft furnishings.

My stone. Her stone. Whose stones were they? Two bodies. Two arrowheads. Two stones. One story? It couldn't all just be coincidence.

To be fair, though, there were things I hadn't told Helen. Like how the bicycle and I had parted company. Or the F^2 phone call. Or about Glenys's arrowhead.

Glenys. Last night was awkward. She probably thought I was tongue tied, staring at her cleavage. Poor pathetic Malcolm. The truth is that I was badly thrown by her arrowhead.

There was a knock at the front door. Of course it was Glenys. Had my day just got even worse?

'Hello Malcolm,' she said.

'Hello Glenys,' I said. 'What can I do for you?'

'I wanted to ask you for a favour,' said Glenys.

'Ask away,' I said.

'I saw your truck was still outside,' said Glenys. 'Are you not going to work?'

'Not today,' I said. 'I've got the day off. I was about to head down to the Tartan Trading Centre, to look for a new mattress and cushions.'

'What a coincidence!' said Glenys. 'Dougie was going to take me there this morning, but they've cancelled his day off. Could I come with you please? I'll pay my share of the petrol.'

'You're most welcome to come!' I said, relieved. 'And you'll certainly not pay anything.'

'Can I at least buy you a cup of tea?' said Glenys. 'How soon are you leaving?'

I looked at my watch.

'Half an hour?' I said. 'And a cup of tea sounds good.'

'Thank you!' said Glenys. 'That's grand.'

And she returned back down the track.

I phoned the insurance company. They were surprisingly efficient, and told me just to go ahead and buy what I needed; the Tartan Trading Post was on their list of approved suppliers. I should send them photographs of the damage, the receipts for whatever I bought, and a case number once I'd got one from the police.

Next, I measured up the sofa and the mattress. I hoped they were standard sizes. Maybe I could reuse the cushion covers. Maybe I should just buy a new sofa.

The Tartan Trading Centre is on the major crossroads just outside Crianlarich, where the A82 linking Glasgow and Fort William meets the A85 due east to Perth. It started out as a roadside van, selling hot drinks and pies to long distant lorry drivers and bikers. The enterprising owner soon made enough to replace the van with a transport café. Then, as tourism took off in the late 60s, the cafe was themed as Scottish Western, with tartan wallpaper, carpets and upholstery, and dirks and claymores on the walls. Hence the name. The new look proved popular, and the cafe steadily accreted ancillary businesses – gifts, local produce, clothing, furniture – all housed in adjacent sheds, a bit like my work place. Just before I'd arrived, the whole site had been redeveloped as an integrated upmarket mall. And the long distance lorry drivers and bikers were banished back to a roadside van, on the far side of the sprawling car park.

Well, that's how Glenys told it, as we rattled along the glen. Glenys herself was delivering knitwear. She was a textile designer and had refined her own brand, using the muted yet vibrant colours of the moor, with a bracken and heather motif. Glenys's cardigans and jerseys were a bit on the pricey side, but warm and very hard wearing. And she did a steady trade in tammys, beanies, scarves and gloves.

When we got to the mall, I parked, and we went our separate ways, having agreed to meet up for lunch at the deli style bistro. I headed straight over to the furniture store, where an attentive young man sold me a new mattress, before showing me far too many sofas. I was rather fond of my old sofa. It folded out to make a double bed, and was one of the few items I had from before Bernie and I got together. Still, things change. I sat and lay on lots of sofas, and eventually plumped for what seemed like the most comfortable, hoping the cat would approve.

Glenys was already waiting in the bistro. We queued for sandwiches, which we munched our way through, in companionable silence. Then, as she'd threatened, Glenys bought the hot drinks. As she re-joined me, my all too male gaze was again caught by the pendant round her neck. To my alarm, Glenys took the pendant off and passed it over to me.

'Here,' she said. 'Have a look. You couldn't take your eyes off it last night.'

I stuttered my thanks and inspected the pendant. It was just like the one that Patricia Harper had shown me.

'It's calc-silicate hornfels,' said Glenys. 'Metamorphic. Very old.'

I laughed and handed her back the pendant.

'You're the first person I've met who could have told me that,' I said. 'You know it's local?'

'For sure,' said Glenys. 'From the Creag Na Caillich quarry, just down the road, above Killin.'

Wow! She really does know about this.

'Have you ever been up there?' I said.

'Oh yes,' said Glenys. 'Every equinox and solstice.'

How strange. Then I remembered the phone call with Helen.

'Maybe I shouldn't ask,' I said, 'but you're not a Wiccan, are you?'

'Indeed I am,' said Glenys. 'And of course you can ask.'

'Gosh!' I said. 'Dougie's never mentioned it.'

'Dougie knows fine,' said Glenys, 'but he thinks it's an excuse to drink prosecco and moan about men.'

'Whereas you dance naked round standing stones by firelight?' I said, regretting it the moment I spoke.

Glenys laughed.

'Only if it's warm enough,' said Glenys. 'Otherwise, we drink prosecco and moan about men.'

'So why the quarry?' I asked.

'It's all in the name,' said Glenys. 'It's a local seat of power. The Cailleach's an ancient divine hag. Caillich's a variant.'

Oh! When I was reading about arrowheads as witch stones in my book of myths and legend, I should have paid more attention to the witch, and less to the stone.

'That must be from some Gaelic myth,' I said.

'It's not a myth,' said Glenys, pointedly. 'Anyway, have you been up there yourself?'

'Well,' I said, 'you know I'm really interested in local geology?'

'We had noticed,' said Glenys.

'So I'd love to visit the quarry,' I continued. 'There should be lots of well exposed vertical rock faces. But I've never quite found the time.'

'We could go this afternoon,' said Glenys, 'if you're not busy. I'd be happy to show you the way. It's the equinox quite soon, and I need to check out the quarry to make sure nobody's messed with anything.'

'That sounds like a good excuse,' I said. 'I've nothing else that's pressing.'

Apart from a pile of unopened post, and a wedding to get ready for. And what looked like a conspiracy that nobody wanted to let me in on.

We cleared the table, climbed back into the Land Rover and set off east. The road followed the River Dochart through the broad glen. On the lower flanks of the mountains, the trees were still green, though thronged with bright red berries, betokening a hard winter. Just as the main road curved south to Loch Earn, we pealed off north east to Killin. Beyond the village, just after the bridge over the River Lochy, we turned back west onto a poorly kept single track road.

'You can pull up here on the left,' said Glenys, as we approached a small house. 'It's all right. The owners are friends. They don't mind.'

I stopped by the house, opened up the back of the Land Rover and found my walking boots.

'It's a bit of a hike,' said Glenys, as I pulled on my boots. 'And a bit wet. Slow and steady.'

I looked at Glenys' feet. She was stoutly shod, as if she'd planned this all along.

Glenys led me across the road, and we started along a steep muddy path up the mountain. Beyond a long abandoned bothy, we followed the fence west, to a burn that ran down the mountain to feed the river. Upstream, the burn led to a cluster of ruined shielings, where we paused to catch our breaths.

'Imagine living here,' I said. 'It must have been really grim.'

'They only stayed for a few weeks in the summer,' said Glenys, 'so the sheep could gorge on the high pasture. I bet they partied like crazy. Lots of music and dancing. Lots of ale and whisky.'

'Let's hope so,' I said. 'How far now?'

'We're about halfway,' said Glenys. 'Let's keep moving.'

The burn split four ways back to its sources.

'This one,' said Glenys, taking the north east fork.

After a slow scramble up the steep slope, we came out onto a plateau, at the head of a narrow defile between the peaks before Ben Lawers.

'We're here,' said Glenys. 'The actual quarry's over to the left.'

I walked across to the rock face. At my feet were piles of debris. Amongst the debris were what appeared to be unfinished axe heads. And arrowheads. Lots of them. I bent over and collected half a dozen.

'What have you found?' said Glenys.

I showed Glenys the arrowheads.

'Nice!' said Glenys. 'Be careful when you try to make holes in them, though. I ruined a couple of Dougie's drill bits, and he wasn't best pleased.'

'Drill them?' I said. 'Surely we should leave them here.'

'Och, no one will ever notice if you keep them,' said Glenys. 'Besides, they might come in handy.'

'Handy for what?' I said.

But Glenys had turned away, and was pacing the plateau, mumbling to herself.

'What on earth are you doing?' I asked. 'Surely not magic.'

'You don't do magic,' said Glenys. 'Magic does you.'

'So does magic do you?' I said.

'Magic does everyone,' said Glenys. 'It's just that most people don't know it.'

'Get away!' I said. 'It's all just sleight of hand. Like rabbits out of hats.'

'Have you got a hat?' said Glenys.

Oh, really? I reached in my pocket and found my woolly beany.

'And one of the arrowheads, please,' said Glenys.

'Here,' I said, handing her the hat, and an arrowhead.

Glenys popped the arrowhead into the hat, and muttered a few words. Then she reached into the hat and drew out a very small grey rabbit. The rabbit twitched, sprang free of her hand, and darted away down the mountain side.

Oh! Really!

'Blimey,' I said. 'Blimey! How did you do that?'

'Do what,' said Glenys, handing me back the hat and arrowhead. 'Now, are you going to show me yours?'

Then she laughed at my confusion.

'The stone,' said Glenys. 'The stone. You've been fiddling with it pretty well all day.'

'How did you know I had a stone,' I said.

'It told me,' said Glenys. 'Come on. Let's see.'

Sheepishly, I reached into my other pocket and drew out the stone. The stone was warm and glowing green.

'This is bad,' said Glenys, looking at the stone. 'Very bad. You shouldn't have this.'

'Could you keep it for me?' I said, proffering her the stone. 'It seems to respond to you.'

As I tried to pass the stone to Glenys, it glowed more brightly, and started to vibrate.

'It's responding to where we are,' said Glenys, backing away. 'I told you this was a place of ancient power.'

'You're welcome to it,' I said. 'Honestly, I've got a strong sense that, for me, it's nothing but trouble.'

'That's as maybe,' said Glenys. 'But it's chosen you. You need to keep it safe, until its rightful owner returns.'

Would that be Patricia Harper? Or the striking woman who'd taken the bicycle? But both had disappeared.

Faint shouting came from below. I looked down back to the road. A purple van was parked in front of my Land Rover. The shouting grew louder.

'Mr Nicholson! Mr Nicholson! Can I have a word with you please?'

I recognised the voice from the phone call.

'I think it's F^2,' I said to Glenys. 'And I think they're after my stone. I need to get away from here.'

I turned and made for the pass.

'No,' said Glenys. 'Not that way.'

Then she started a low, repetitive incantation. And as she chanted, a mist rose from the hillside.

'How will we ever find our way back?' I said.

'Use the stone,' said Glenys.

Without the faintest idea of what I was doing, I held the stone out in front of me. A green path gleamed through the thickening mist.

'The stone knows the way,' said Glenys. 'Come on.'

We made our way down the mountain, trusting to the path. By the time we reached the Land Rover, the mountain was completely wreathed in mist.

'Well, that was truly weird,' I said, as we set off back to Achalladar.

'Thank you,' said Glenys. 'That's high praise.'

'How do you know all this Wiccan stuff?' I said. 'Did your mother teach you?'

'Och no,' said Glenys. 'She'd be horrified. But I must say, I'm surprised at how accepting you are.'

'After the last few days, everything seems pretty strange,' I said. 'So what's a little magic?'

'What magic?' said Glenys.

'The mist,' I said.

'There's always mist,' said Glenys, nonchalantly.

'I wonder what'll become of the F^2 person,' I said.

'They'll be fine,' said Glenys. 'You know the mists clear quickly. But I bet you've not heard the last of them.'

We were soon back at my cottage. As we got out of the Land Rover, Glenys thanked me, and suggested that I kept what had happened to myself, for my own well being. Then, without another word, she headed off home.

My head was reeling. I'd still so many questions for Glenys. And I'd never even asked her if the quarry was in order for her Equinox prosecco.

I went indoors and made myself a pot of tea. Then I sat down at the kitchen table and started to work through the post.

The post was mainly statements for things that were paid by direct debit. Then there was the quarterly mailshot from Geology Scotland, which I put aside for later. That left me with two envelopes: one addressed in Bernie's handwriting and the other in Alison's.

Bernie's envelope was a wad of bumph about the wedding arrangements, accompanied by a perfunctory note. I was booked into the Slockavullin Lodge for two nights, all inclusive. I was to be at the church for 6pm, the day before the wedding, for the run through for the video. And, at the reception, I was to make the father of the bride's speech, and take the second dance with Alison. That all sounded pretty grim. I just hoped I could hold it all together.

Alison's envelope held a letter:

Dearest Dad

I know things haven't been good between us for a while, so I really do hope my marrying Grant can be a new start for you and me as well. I'm so looking forward to you giving me away, even if it is all patriarchal nonsense. And you know you'll always be welcome in our home.

Love ever!

Ali xxxxx

I was very moved. She'd even signed herself with her pet name, with a wee circle instead of a dot over the 'i'. Of course I could hold it all together.

At the bottom of the pile was a flyer from the Community Council. There was to be a public meeting on Saturday morning, in the Altnafeadh Hotel, where representatives from F^2 and the Department of Rural Resilience would present plans for the further development of the plant at Tigh Na Cruach. All welcome. Tea and coffee to be served.

That was tomorrow. What were F^2 up to? And what had it got to do with me and, as seemed increasingly worrying, the stone?

Chapter 10

Malcolm – Saturday 13th September

I'd just woken up when the phone rang. Not, as I suspected, Bernie. Not as I feared F^2.

'Malcolm,' said my mum. 'This is your mother.'

'Hello mum,' I said, most surprised. 'It's been a while. How are you both?'

'I'm calling about the wedding,' said mum.

Straight to the point. Not a conversation I wanted to have.

'What about the wedding?' I said. 'I hope you got an invite.'

'We did,' said mum. 'And we sent it straight back. We'll have none of that Romish nonsense. You're not going, are you?'

'Of course I'm going,' I said. 'I'm sad you feel you can't.'

'Of course we can't,' said mum. 'I'm surprised you can bring yourself to go, after everything that happened.'

'I love Alison,' I said, 'like I love all my children. And I'll support them in whatever they choose.'

'What about that dreadful woman,' said mum. 'She'll be going, I suppose.'

'Of course Bernie's going,' I said. 'She's Alison's mother.'

'And you're still going?' persisted mum. 'Despite how badly she treated you?'

'This isn't about me and Bernie,' I said. 'It's our daughter's wedding. We're both really happy for her. Why can't you see that?'

'You should never have married her,' said mum. 'At least you're free of her now. But look at how she's corrupted your offspring.'

'It's got nothing to do with Bernie,' I said. 'And, as far as I know, Alison's got no interest in religion. But her fiancé's a Catholic, so they're having a Catholic wedding, because that's what he'd prefer.'

'She's weak, just like you,' said mum. 'And she'll end up abandoned and lonely, just the way you have.'

'I'm fine, mum,' I said. 'And we didn't separate because of Bernie's religion. You know that.'

'It's all such superstition,' said mum. 'Men in frocks. Burnt offerings. Even worse than that nonsense my great grandmother was accused of.'

Oh!

'What nonsense was that?' I said.

'I'm sure I've told you,' said mum.

Of course she hadn't.

'So what was she accused of?' I said.

'Malicious gossip,' said mum. 'They said she came from a long line of Godless wise women. But she was a fine upstanding Protestant, like her forebears. It's all in the family Bible.'

Wise woman? Wiccan? That'll be right.

'What was her name?' I said.

'Margaret,' said mum. 'Margaret MacAskill. But that's all a long time ago. And I wanted to ask you a favour.'

'Ask away,' I said, even more surprised.

'We'd like to give Alison a present,' said mum. 'We'll not sanctify her marriage, but your father and I both regret that we've never known our grandchildren. And she deserves a decent start.'

'Oh mum!' I said. 'That's so nice of you! What do you want to give her?'

Mum named a surprisingly large sum of money.

'Oh mum!' I said again. 'That's an awful lot. Are you quite sure?'

'Och yes,' said mum. 'We don't need it. And eventually everything of ours should come to your children, through you. But we don't want that Jezebel to get her hands on a penny, if you pass over before she does. You are still married, aren't you. She'll not let you go. Besides, there are tax advantages if we do it now.'

Principled and pragmatic.

'Thank you,' I said. 'Thank you. That's very generous. I'm sure Alison'll be delighted.'

We discussed the practicalities, and parted on far better terms than I could recall.

I fed the cat, showered and started to dress. Then, on a whim, I tried on my suit. The suit hung off me, as if I were a scarecrow. I'd need to buy another. Had I really lost so much weight? I was certainly more active, and eating and drinking far less than when I was a teacher.

I finished dressing and had a hearty breakfast for a change. Then I bagged up the suit for the charity shop, and set off to the meeting.

So my great granny was one Margaret MacAskill, from a supposed line of Hebridean wise women. Helen's great granny as well. I wonder if Helen knows?

Outside the Altnafeadh Hotel was a small but noisy demonstration. Their banner proclaimed: *RAGE – Rannoch Against Graviton Energy*. I knew most of the protesters. And of course I sympathised with them. Who wants more pylons across the moor? But my employer Remote Resources was a charity, and utterly dependent on local and central government aid, so I'd been gently, but firmly, told to keep my politics to myself in public.

The meeting was held in the Hotel's ballroom: yet another converted Nissen hut, well lit, with a parquet floor and a stage. As I entered the ballroom, I was handed an agenda for the meeting, and a smudgy multi-coloured RAGE flyer titled: *GROUSE NOT GRAVITONS!/ WE ARE NOT YOUR PHEASANT PLUCKERS!* The old ones are the best.

The ballroom was almost full – a good couple of hundred people. Down the front, I could see Dougie in full uniform, hovering nervously. On the stage was a serried rank of dignitaries. I'd met the Convenor of our local authority a couple of times, but I didn't recognise any of the others.

The Convenor stood and called for order. After a pithy welcome, she introduced the first speaker, the Minister for Rural Resilience, all the way from Holyrood. The Minister made a short generic speech from memory, emphasising the government's commitment to clean, renewable energy, and hoping that the forthcoming F^2 announcement would herald a new era of Highland regeneration, if not, indeed, wider Scottish prosperity.

The Minister was followed by the F² Chief Scientific Officer, Dr Sam Crawford. Dr Crawford was garbed in a clean white lab coat, and armed with a slide show. As they worked through the slides, I realised that it was exactly the same set that had been shown three years ago, at the start of the project.

Gravitons. Gravity particles packed with energy. Universe permeated with them. Until now hard to detect. Need for remote location with low electro-magnetic pollution.

At last, there were some new slides. Major, if ill defined, breakthrough. Scalable detection. Need to move from research to pilot system. Hopeful of net contribution to national power grid within two years.

Well, that all sounded too good to be true.

The final speaker was from the F² Outreach Forum. In order to expedite development of the pilot system, over the next few months there would be a marked increase in movements of heavy equipment by rail and road to Tigh Na Cruach. These would be timetabled to minimise interruptions to normal transport flow, and noise. There would then be a period of sustained activity, with minimal effect on the local environment. We were welcome to sign up for a visit to the site if that might help allay fears.

Were there any questions? There were lots. Most were gently batted away with vague assurances. RAGE wouldn't be satisfied; nor should they be.

Avoiding, as I thought, controversy, I asked about the cryptosporidiosis that was killing off the grouse. How wide spread was it? What steps were being taken to control and eradicate it?

The F² Outreach person said that this was really an environmental health question, and nothing to do with the project, but their laboratories and staff would be happy to help in any way they could. The Convenor sat quietly, studying her hands on her lap.

I should have pointed out that the outbreak had first been notified around the time that the F² site was fenced off. I should have asked why particle physics research required laboratories suitable for biochemistry. And why was so much heavy equipment needed?

As the audience dispersed, I made my way down to the front to sign up for the site visit. The F^2 stand was staffed by a younger woman with short brown hair, wearing a grey trouser suit and sensible shoes.

'Mr Nicholson,' she said quietly, when I reached the front of the queue. 'I'm so glad you came. I'm sorry I missed you yesterday.'

The voice from the phone call!

'That was you!' I said, too loudly. 'On the mountain! Why are you harassing me?'

'I'm a friend,' said the woman, gesturing to me to lower my voice. 'I don't like what's happening any more than you do.'

'I don't know what you're talking about,' I said. 'Are you going to sign me up for the tour or not?'

'Of course,' said the woman. 'Just pop down your details.'

She passed me a pad, and I wrote down my name and work email.

'That's grand,' said the woman. 'I'll make sure you're sent confirmation. But I really do need to talk with you. Soon. Not here and now, though.'

Just what is happening? Maybe this would be one way to find out?

'All right,' I said. 'I'll be in Fort William early this afternoon.'

'That works for me,' said the woman. 'Do you know Hernando's Hideaway? How about meeting there at 2pm?'

'That's fine,' I said. 'I'll see you then.'

What had I let myself in for? I had to be extra careful about what I said.

I left the Hotel and drove up the road, through the mountains to the Pass of Glencoe, and down the other side to Ballachuillish. Once over the bridge at the mouth of Loch Leven, it's a straight run up Loch Linnhe to Fort William, nestled under Ben Nevis, at the south-western end of the Great Glen.

I've never been over fond of Fort William, which, for me, has that small town, land-that-time-forgot feel about it. Everyone you see seems markedly younger or markedly older than I am. I'd rather be in the big city, or the middle of nowhere. Still, the town centre has learnt to live with the supermarkets, and it has a certain buzz to it after the moor.

I parked at the south end of town, and walked up the High Street to the Oxfam Shop, where I dropped off my old suit. Then I went further along the road to the gentleman's outfitters. I spend practically nothing on clothes, so I don't mind splashing out on something that'll last. I toyed with buying a kilt, but they'd nothing off the peg in the Nicolson tartan. Instead, I found a well fitting suit, pretty much like the old one: single breasted, dark blue, with plain buttons and enough inside pockets. An undertaker's suit, Bernie would say.

⏣

I paid for the suit, and headed on to the jewellers, where I dropped off four arrowheads to be strung on fine silver chains. Wedding tokens. One for Alison. One for Bernie. One for Helen. And one for spare. Then I set off for lunch.

Hernando's Hideaway, on Middle Street, must be one of the best fish restaurants on the west coast. Started by a former Italian prisoner of war, who was really called Fernando, it's still run by his grandchildren. According to local lore, Fernando was a great fan of post-war Broadway musicals, and wanted a name that stood out from the usual diaspora trattoria.

The waiter showed me to an empty booth by the window, and I ordered their beer battered haddock, and a pot of tea. Then I took out my phone and checked my email. The F^2 woman had proved most efficient. I was booked into a tour of Tigh Na Cruach on the following Tuesday. I was to be at Rannoch Station by 9am sharp, and the tour would last two hours; no photography allowed. I replied in acceptance, and then emailed the office to tell them that I'd be back at work on the Monday afternoon.

My haddock arrived at the same time as the woman from F^2. As she sat down, she said her name was Polly Sharp, she'd already eaten, thank you, and might she have a long flat white, when I'd finished my fish. She came across as self possessed, and we chatted amiably in between my mouthfuls, yet I could sense that she was as anxious as I was.

The waiter cleared away my plate, and brought the tea and coffee. Polly and I eyed each other nervously.

'Well,' I said, finally. 'What do you need to talk about so urgently?'

'What did you take away from the meeting?' said Polly.

'Your lot have had some breakthrough,' I said. 'And there's about to be loads more disturbance. I didn't get why you need all the heavy equipment, though.'

'That's the right question,' said Polly. 'Where do you think gravitons come from?'

'They're all around us, aren't they?' I said. 'Like cosmic rays, or background radiation.'

'Think about it,' said Polly. 'Gravitons cause gravity. So where's the most gravity.'

'You mean our planet?' I said.

'Exactly,' said Polly. 'So what's the best way to free them?'

Then it struck me.

'By digging for them,' I said. 'Is that the plan? Really?'

'Really,' said Polly.

'But Rannoch's on a major fault line,' I said. 'Any serious excavation could make fracking look respectable.'

'Exactly,' said Polly again. 'It's so dangerous. No one's done this before. They've got to be stopped.'

'They?' I said. 'They're your employers. Why can't you blow the whistle? Why come to me?'

'This whole thing's too big to fail,' said Polly.

Dougie had said that, hadn't he.

'Look at the money the government's pouring in to it,' Polly continued. 'It's almost half of the renewables budget. Not to mention the tax breaks. If I speak up, they'll squash me.'

'So why come to me?' I asked again.

'But you know all this, don't you?' said Polly. 'That's why you've been sniffing around the perimeter fence, isn't it? Now I can give you undeniable confirmation, so you can go public. That's what you're planning, isn't it? You and RAGE?'

'This is the first I've heard of it,' I said. 'And I've practically nothing to do with RAGE. I thought it was all about the stone.'

'The stone?' said Polly. 'What stone?'

Oh wow! Has Helen got this all wrong? Maybe F^2 aren't after the stone at all. Unless Polly's bluffing me.

'The stone the plant's built on,' I said. 'We've just talked about it.'

'Ah,' said Polly. 'I thought you meant something else.'

'But it was you lot that turned over my office and trashed my house, wasn't it,' I said. 'So what were you after?'

'I feel really bad about that,' said Polly. 'But I had to go through with it.'

'You did it!' I said. 'You? What on earth for?'

'It was partly to warn you off,' said Polly. 'And partly to look for evidence.'

'What evidence?' I said. 'What am I supposed to have done?'

'They think there's a mole,' said Polly. 'Who's passing secrets through you. You get to read them, and tell RAGE, before you pass them on. One way F^2 get discredited, and the other they lose their lead.'

'This is crazy!' I said. 'I told you, I've got nothing to do with RAGE. Anyway, who am I supposed to be passing the secrets on to?'

'Nobody seems to know,' said Polly. 'But what about those two Americans? The ones who were up at the fence, a couple of hours before you were.'

'But they're tourists,' I said. 'New Agers. All they did was ask for directions. Anyway, how do you know we were there? There aren't any cameras. There certainly aren't any warning notices, apart from for the grouse plague.'

Polly laughed.

'The grouse plague?' said Polly. 'Surely you know that's a hoax, to keep people away from the plant. There's absolutely nothing wrong with the grouse.'

'This really is all crazy,' I said. 'Suppose, just for a moment, that I did tell someone else. All I've got is your word for it. Can I name you?'

'No, of course not,' said Polly.

'But this is like a self fulfilling prophecy, isn't it,' I said. 'Now there really is a mole, and it's you! Anyway, why are you telling me all this?'

'Who else could I tell?' said Polly.

'That's not what I meant,' I said.

'Ah,' said Polly. 'Right. That's fairly easy. I was the golden girl. First class degree. PhD. Postdoc Fellowship. Lectureship.'

'That doesn't sound so bad,' I said.

'And then I got stuck,' said Polly. 'As the cuts bit, I landed more and more teaching and pastoral work, and my research dwindled away. They couldn't make me redundant, as that would have scuppered their gender balance. But all the promoted posts were held by men who weren't much older than me. So I thought science communication would be a good move sideways, and F^2 seemed progressive. Green energy and all. It turns out they're just as bad as all the rest, but, if I go public, I'll never work again.'

'That's pretty rubbish,' I said. 'I'll do what I can, but don't expect too much. And thanks for confiding in me.'

'Thank you!' said Polly.

Chapter 11

Helen – Saturday 13th September

I was up at sunrise the next day for my Ben Lomond climb. Everyone that writes about it says it can be next best to a football crowd, it's that popular. A Saturday in September with a good weather forecast was unlikely to be quiet.

The cat had slept on the other half of the king-size bed. I know talking to cats is daft, but anyway…

'Well Mog, you'll have to stay here while I climb my mountain. That's if you want to see Troon again.'

The cat stretched and gave me a steady look – its eyes were as green as I'd ever seen on a cat. So far it seemed an intelligent animal as cats go.

'And whatever were you doing last night, eh Mog?'

When I got back the previous evening, my headlights had picked out a cat silhouette. It was sitting up with its tail tucked round its feet on the verge outside the cottage staring up into the beech tree at the fence.

I got out and then walked over. It chirruped, without looking at me. I followed its eyes upwards. There was a large owl up there! Staring back. The owl turned its head slightly and blinked at me, then turned its glance back onto the cat.

I went to stroke the cat, to distract it – though an owl that size would challenge the most determined feline hunter. But it ducked its head away under my hand the way cats do when they don't want to be touched. So

I went in, leaving the front door ajar. Ten minutes later it was back inside rubbing against my legs.

Now the cat chirruped again, sounding almost dismissive, and then yawned pinkly.

'OK, Mog, none of my business. But I recommend smaller birds for your breakfast.'

My big advantage was that the cottage was only a mile or two down the road from the car park where the trail up Ben Lomond begins. I didn't bother to shower as I'd need one when I got back, and grabbed a quick breakfast. Then I put my rucksack with its hill walker kit on the front seat.

'Right Mog, I'll be back later,' I told him as he lurked by the car. 'Stay put will you?' Mog stalked back into the cottage with his tail disapprovingly upright. But he could get out through the back if he wanted.

There are two main routes up Ben Lomond: the tourist trail and the trickier Ptarmigan ridge. I planned to go up the Ptarmigan and back down the tourist route. Down is harder than up. It was clear and sunny, but there were clouds off to the west coming in, so no guarantee it would still be clear by the time I got to the top – about three hours from starting they reckoned. Still, walking the Northumbrian hills I'm used to bad weather, and I'm also a whizzo with map-and-compass navigation.

Sod's law said that the weather was fine, with great views over the Loch, right up to the scrambly bit at the end. One minute I could see the actual summit – a relief after several false ones – and the next, a mist had swept over me. I took it carefully, knowing that as long as I climbed upward I'd get there. I was soon at the trig point without any mishaps. It's not a big space and there were a couple of people already there, but they were soon off down. I celebrated with my second bottle of water and the ham sandwich I had saved for the purpose. Sound carries oddly in a mist, so I heard the next two people some minutes before they got to the top – American voices, a woman and then a man.

'Sure, we know what the theorists say about it, but that doesn't mean you can really build the gate. The math says quantum wave packets may jump branches but that doesn't give us a bridge, never mind a gate. Physics sure isn't engineering.'

'Yeah, they said that about atom bombs back in the 1930s. Where there's a will...'

That all sounded rather interesting. But they stopped rather suddenly as they emerged onto the summit from the tourist trail. They probably noticed me, leaning on the trig point.

'Be my guest,' I said, stepping back from it.

'It's a real shame there's no view today,' the woman said. 'Hey, I wonder, honey, could you just take a shot of the two of us by the trig point? Gotta have some evidence we made it up here.'

That's Americans for you, straight to what they want. Of course I took a shot with the phone the woman handed me. Then just for a moment there was a gap in the low cloud. The loch and all its islands appeared below us as if they'd been suddenly switched on.

'Wow', they said. I whipped out my own phone and took the pic before the mist could close on us again. Not a perfect shot because the woman was on the edge of it, but better than nothing.

As Wilf has told me several times, I'm on the monosyllabic side when I'm walking. So I nipped off down the tourist path, dodging the next arrivals, while the Americans were still exclaiming about the view, and moments before more mist blew over. My idea of hell, man, if I had to talk to them all the way down.

It was only an hour to the bottom even with pinch points, where you had to stop and let people coming up get past. I hadn't allowed myself to do any thinking going up, it's better to concentrate. But the tourist path was pretty easy as well as slow after the first steep drop from the summit. Unwelcome thoughts crowded in.

I couldn't spend my life carrying some high-tech surveillance device around with me, even insulated from tracking. I needed to know how to get rid of it. That meant I needed to know more about it. I had to find out what F^2 were really up to. Quantum wave packets, transilience gate and gravitons, according to Bernie. But she'd studied business organisation at Strathclyde, not physics. She probably didn't know any more than I did about what those were, if she'd got them right. And I wasn't sure I wanted to tell anyone, and especially not Bernie, about my pebble. After all, you could say I'd robbed it off a dead body. Hulkie the total fucking idiot.

Hmm, the Americans had mentioned quantum wave packets and some kind of gate. They sounded as if they knew what they were talking about – was there any way I could talk to them? Or maybe cousin Malcolm could help, he was right next to the F^2 plant. Though I'd have to get him off geology and conveniently missing dead bodies. He had a stone too after all. Though he didn't seem nearly as worried as I thought he should be about that.

I got to the bottom feeling my brain was on a hamster wheel and decided to treat myself to a good lunch rather than go straight back to the cottage. There are various restaurants round the loch, all taking advantage of the great view to lure in tourists, but the nearest is a pub that Google said did a mean steak pie. It had a whole wall of slots looking out over the loch. I had plenty of time to read more Google reviews: the ones that said the service was pretty poor were also quite right. Maybe they had to butcher the cow first. I'd been watching the loch for nearly forty minutes by the time my steak pie and chips arrived.

As I dug in hungrily, a group arrived in the slot behind me. American voices. I did not turn round. My lucky day.

'This sure is a cute little place. A real English pub.' Oh yes, that was the woman from the top of Ben Lomond.

I flapped my ears for the next ten minutes, eating my chips slowly. They admired the view, agitated for waitress attention, demanded iced water and put in an order that included the haggis special. Three of them, the woman and two men. Eventually, the man who hadn't spoken before said:

'Turned out to be a busy day, folks. I dropped by the F^2 town hall meeting this morning. Had to scorch it to get here.'

Now I really listened hard.

'We're real sorry we laid that on you, Ethan,' the woman said. 'But after the body incident, we felt turning up was a big risk. Betcha that ranger guy was there, he'd have known us.'

Jesus wept. Malcolm hadn't been conned.

'You guys sure that woman was dead, and not just knocked out or something? Because there's been zero, nil, nada in the British press about it. Believe me, the Embassy gets them all and I've gone through them.'

'What can we tell you?' said the other man. 'Of course we didn't touch anything, but didn't look like she was breathing. We had to report it, we already told the ranger we were going up that way. You told us to keep a low profile, so we hightailed it. Anyway, how was the meeting? Anything useful?'

'I'd say they were heading for some trouble with the locals, there were a bunch of tree-huggers outside whining, and some hostile questions. Well, you guys are the physics experts, but to my ears it was all PR stuff. Here, I took pics of the slides. Oh – and they offered plant tours to the locals, the sign-up email is on one of the slides.'

Silence for a while.

'What d'ya think, Martha?'

'Well, it confirms the rumours we'd gotten of a breakthrough. But nothing on what they're engineering of course. Hmm, heavy equipment coming in, expand the detection pit? Wouldn't you say, Dean?'

'Is it the big one, though? Graviton collection across parallel branches?'

'Dean, give a poor cultural attaché a break. That was pure gobbledegook to me.'

'Come on Ethan, you must have heard of the 'possible worlds' hypothesis? It's one of those things everyone knows about quantum mechanics. The world state splits at every division in quantum state?' Martha sounded impatient.

Oh yes, even I'd heard of that one – though only in SF books. Seemed like Ethan the embassy man had too.

'So the parallel branches are possible worlds? I thought that was just an idea in the math, not a for-real?'

'That's the big question,' Dean said. 'For a lot more than 64,000 dollars. Collecting gravitons from the parallel branches would really up the potential by some. We heard Europeans are snooping around too; from some research project F^2 were involved with last year. We're relying on you to keep them and any other interested parties off our backs. Remember, Martha and I are doing you guys a favour as concerned citizens, not special agents.'

At that point their food turned up, a lot quicker than mine had. American pushiness had obviously worked. Nothing but the clink of cutlery and approving comments on the food.

I wanted to hear more but I couldn't sit there all day. For one thing they might notice I was listening to them. For another, I needed to think about what I'd heard so far. It fitted with Bernie's brain dump but no mentions as yet of stones, portable energy sources or surveillance. So it didn't help with my problem.

I picked up my bill and went off to pay.

I didn't have to go to the loo after that, I was only just down the road from the cottage. But anyway.

I was washing my hands and thinking when a bright voice said:

'Hi, honey! I guess you made better time down than we did with our old bones.' Martha.

'Oh, hello. Bit of a crowd, wasn't there?'

'No kidding! Almost as bad as a Veteran's Day sale. Hey – didn't I see you on the television last week?'

There's the downside of being taller than the average woman. People tend to remember you.

'Yes, to do with the ship I was working on.'

'Fishing out a dead body, wasn't it? Pretty traumatic I guess.'

'It can happen when you work at sea.' Pause. Change the subject. Quickly. 'Now you've been up Ben Lomond, are you doing any others?'

'Oh no, honey. We're just seeing the sights. One mountain is enough. Or maybe too much – see how we are tomorrow.'

'Where else have you been?'

'Touring the mainland so far. You were on Lewis? Do you recommend it?'

'Oh, you have to see some of the islands. But the Inner Hebrides are easier to get at. Mull and of course Iona, the holy isle. They have fabulous green marble there.'

No, she didn't rise to that one, as far as I could see.

'Anyway, enjoy the rest of your tour.' I exited quickly.

So she was interested in Lewis. Had McMalkin worked for the Americans? But surely they'd know about the stones if so. Still, by the sound of it there were other wasps round the F^2 jam pot, so maybe

McMalkin had worked for the 'Europeans' that Martha's friend Dean had mentioned, whoever they were.

Well, if Frank the gowk had been following McMalkin in his showy van, my energetic cousin Steven the bobby would have found out by now. Then if the Americans had an in to the police – and they could – they might have heard about it all. Maybe I should have been more cooperative, I thought, as I drove back to the cottage. They could probably find out stuff a lot more easily than me. But finding out who the 'Europeans' were might be more useful.

After I had showered and changed, I went online and tried out all those science terms I'd heard. *Quantum wave packets* were short bursts of stuff that travelled as a unit. So far, so good. *Gravitons* were the basic unit of gravity, long hypothesised but only recently discovered. Hmm, no complete theory due to 'an outstanding mathematical problem with renormalization in general relativity'. Whatever that meant. *Transilience Gate* flung me into a bit of Google that listed academic papers where even the titles were incomprehensible. The first was 'A coupled transilience model for graviton quantum tunnelling with and without entanglement' from a few years earlier. When I looked at it wondering whether the first paragraph might make sense to me – it didn't – I noticed the lead author was an S.L.Crawford, Fundamental Forces. Hmm. I'd bet the two American physicists had read that and would understand it.

Finally I looked for Martha, physics professor, USA, images. Not so many women physics professors, and I had an image of my own from my Ben Lomond top pic. Yes: Professor Martha Gellman, Institute of Advanced Study, Natural Sciences Princeton. Well – there was her email. I could get in touch. Did I want to?

One thing for sure, I needed to talk to Malcolm again. Well, I had his number on my phone.

Chapter 12

Helen & Malcolm - Sunday 14th September

The bell rang. Malcolm went down the hall and opened the door. It was Helen. He'd forgotten how tall she was. Was she really taller than him?

'Hello Malcolm,' she said. 'Sorry to get you up early on a Sunday, but, like I said last night, I really think we can straighten things out better in person than over the phone.'

'Good to see you, Helen. I was really concerned by your phone call. Come on in. Have you had breakfast?'

'Grabbed a coffee before I left, but yes, if you have some toast or something?'

'I usually have porridge. I'll happily make you some.'

'OK, as I'm in darkest Scotland I'll give porridge a go.'

Helen followed Malcolm into the kitchen. The kitchen felt like it had been furnished from a catalogue, with white melamine cupboards, and pine table and chairs. There was an electric cooker and a traditional Ulster sink, but no sign of a dishwasher.

'Have yourself a seat,' said Malcolm, 'while I get things started.'

Helen sat down at the kitchen table and looked around. Malcolm made up the porridge from oats and milk. Then he put the porridge in the microwave and set it to a low heat for 5 minutes, just the way he liked it.

All in all, Helen thought that Malcolm's cottage was a bit basic but he seemed nicer in person than over the phone. You could certainly tell he was into geology, with the various bits of rock lying around on his windowsills. Well, better get to it.

'Malcolm, you know I was telling you about the problems with my pebble? Can I see your stone? I really want to know if it affects you the way it does me.'

'For sure!' said Malcolm. 'I wonder if they're from a similar stratum. We should be able to tell from the striations.'

Helen fished her pebble out of her pocket.

'You see I've kept it in an insulating bag?'

'What on earth for?'

'It acts like a Faraday cage, which means that F^2 can't track me any more. I have an extra bag for you as well. I'm sure you won't want them tracking you either.'

'Could I see your stone, please?' Malcolm asked.

He held out his hand.

'You can see it from here,' said Helen. 'But I can't hand it over. Just thinking about doing that makes me feel terrible. Did I tell you I tried to drop it off the stern of my ship? I had a panic attack. And I don't get panic attacks. There's some horrible addictive thing going on.'

'That's awful. No, I've not tried to get rid of mine. Here it is.'

He took his stone out of his pocket and held it out towards Helen.

Their stones vibrated in their hands and began to glow.

Malcolm started back.

'What the hell's going on?' he said.

Beams of light emerged from each and joined, linking the stones together. Then the microwave pinged and they both jumped and looked at it. The light darted towards the microwave and there was a loud BANG.

'Jesus wept, man!' said Helen. 'We just shorted your microwave! Or our stones did.'

A thread of smoke drifted up from the back of the microwave, with a smell of burnt insulation. Helen leapt up and yanked the plug out of the wall.

'Just as well the porridge had finished,' she said. 'I told you they had energy sources in them.'

Malcolm looked aghast.

'What just happened? That's totally crazy! How will I ever explain that to the insurance company?'

'Hey,' said Helen, 'it looks like we zapped it because we had the stones together and focused on the microwave at the same time. Is there something else we could try that out on?'

'Absolutely not! Could I have that spare bag, please?'

Helen dug a second bag out of her pocket and passed it to Malcolm. They both put their stones away. There was an uneasy silence.

'Well,' said Malcolm, 'maybe we should eat the porridge before it gets cold.'

He served up the porridge. Helen added several large spoonfuls of sugar to hers.

'So, getting back to things,' said Helen. 'Like I said last night, I wanted to apologise. Apologise in person, Mam always told me. You were right about the body. I'm sorry I was an arse about it.'

'Thank you,' said Malcolm, 'but it's really not like that. It was a pretty crazy thing to tell you, especially after you found an actual body.'

'Hey, I met your Americans. And they were pretty positive about the body.'

'Don't you think they're just New Age tourists?'

'Oh no, I dinnit think so. For one thing they aren't New Age at all, that was all a front. They're physicists, man. Quite leading ones I think.'

'Really? They seemed pretty clueless.'

'Well, I looked them up online. And I overheard their meeting with someone from the American embassy over lunch. They spouted a lot of physics about what F^2 might be doing. They said they were 'concerned citizens' but that's just a nice way of saying 'spies' if you ask me. They want to find out what F^2's "breakthrough" is.'

'Like industrial espionage? Maybe that's why F^2 think I'm working with the Americans.'

Malcolm explained how his office had been searched, and his cottage trashed. Then he relayed what Polly Sharp had told him about the major new excavations.

'I'm really worried about what they're up to,' said Malcolm. 'If they manage to open a fault line, it could be catastrophic. The geology's nothing like as stable as people think it is.'

'What do you think could happen?' said Helen.

'I've got no idea. I don't think anyone's been stupid enough to try it before. Perhaps a major earthquake, like fracking, only worse?'

'F^2 seem like one rogue company to me,' said Helen. 'I looked up *Transilience Gate* online, because Bernie mentioned it and the Americans were going on about some kind of gate. Guess what? There's some physics paper that might be about it that I can't follow. And it's written by an F^2 person! Maybe you could have a look?'

'I'd not take stuff you find on-line too seriously,' said Malcolm. 'You can never be sure where it comes from. I prefer books.'

'Good luck with finding that in a book,' Helen said. 'Anyway, the other reason I came is that I'd really like to see some of this for myself. Can we go up there?'

'What, like now? I suppose so. We could drive across the moor to the boundary fence, where the body was, and take it from there.'

'I can drive us if you navigate.'

'That's nice of you, but it's really remote, and the track's very rough once we've left the main road. We can go in my Land Rover. It'll take a good couple of hours there and back.'

'Can we see their main gate?'

'That's way round on the far side of the moor. It'd take another hour from here just to get to the access road. And I think it'll be heavily guarded. Let's start up by the boundary fence on this side.'

'Sounds reasonable then.'

Malcolm tidied up the breakfast things. Then they climbed into his Land Rover and drove north up the road to the Altnafeadh Hotel. Malcolm turned off the tarmac and slowly followed the track to the Black Corries Lodge. The track condition worsened as they approached the Menzies Stone. Malcolm pulled off the road by the boundary fence, and they both got out.

'Wild landscape isn't it?' said Helen. 'Just right if you're up to no good. Is this where the body was? The Americans weren't sure she was really dead, you know? They said there were no reports of a body later.'

'Well,' said Malcolm. 'I haven't actually told the police anything. Dougie's the local polis. He's a pal, and I wanted to check things out before involving him. And, of course, I never actually saw a body.'

'Maybe F^2 hauled it off. But it's odd nobody's noticed she was missing. A bit too much like McMalkin, the man that doesn't exist. False address and ID, the police say. So I think he must have been a spy too.'

'Dougie reckons F^2 hires people for safety testing. He said two had gone missing.'

'So maybe your woman was trying to get into the plant again? But where is the plant? I can't see it,' said Helen.

'It's one of those green buildings. Low, and covered in turf, so it blends in. It was a condition of the plant going ahead. We can't see it, but it's over there somewhere.'

Malcolm pointed east.

But Helen was scanning the fence.

'Hey, look over there,' said Helen. 'Where that vertical support is. Wouldn't you say that was some kind of gate into the plant?'

'You're right,' said Malcolm. 'I must have missed that the other night. I suppose she could have electrocuted herself trying to get through. But then where's her body?'

'If she was in an F^2 experiment, they might have taken her back into the plant.'

'She's a total mystery to me. And I hadn't bothered to find out anything more about her. All I actually had was her bicycle, which I found over there. I haven't even got that now.'

'What happened to it?'

'It's like a bad dream.'

Malcolm explained how the bicycle had been taken from the hut, and his encounter with the remarkable woman, who'd somehow made him hand it over.

'I don't know what she did to me,' said Malcolm. 'It felt like she'd put a spell on me or something.'

'Weird,' said Helen. 'Sounds like she hypnotised you. Though the arrowheads are supposedly witch things. That's what the old woman at Callanish said. She came out with a lot of wild stuff as well. But I'd no chance to ask her about it.'

Helen told him about the lightning strike and how afterwards the old woman had disappeared.

'For all I know,' said Helen, 'she lived in one of the houses down the road and scarpered when the rain came, but it was odd.'

'I think the arrowheads are maybe important though,' said Malcolm. 'The Wicca thing.'

But Helen had turned back towards the fence.

'Malcolm! Hang on a mo! Look, what's that over there? Just beyond the fence?'

There was a squeaky mechanical sound and a rustle in the heather. A silvery robot-like head appeared at about knee-height. It was mounted on a horizontal metal body supported by four legs, the source of the noise. There were red LEDs where eyes would be and antennae-like ears on either side of the head. The head turned towards them.

Malcolm was transfixed.

'What the fuck?' said Malcolm. 'What the fuck is that?'

'Some kind of a robot, I think,' said Helen. 'And, if I know robots, it has a camera linked to the F2 security system.'

'What the fuck are we going to do?'

'Quick, get your stone out!'

Malcolm and Helen dug into pockets for their pouched stones, took them out and held them towards the beast.

'Focus on the head,' said Helen. 'We need to knock out the camera!'

The luminous green beam from the stones hit the metallic head, which exploded in an unearthly shower of blue sparks. There was a strong smell of burning. The nearby heather began to smoulder as the body collapsed onto it.

'I think we should leave,' said Malcolm. 'Now!'

'Just let me get a pic,' said Helen. 'Cool tech!'

Helen took a photo with her phone. Then they clambered back into the Land Rover. Malcolm circled the Menzies Stone and set back off to the Hotel.

'Bloody hell, Helen! What just happened?' said Malcolm. 'What's the connection between the stones and electrical stuff?'

''Good question.' said Helen. 'F^2 no doubt know the answer, and everyone else would like to. With a bit of luck, they'll think the Americans knocked out their robot.'

'Let's hope so for our sakes. I suppose that's how they knew I was up at the boundary fence. The Americans as well. The robot must have missed Patricia Harper. No one's ever mentioned her again.'

'Maybe the robot zapped her, and then F^2 dragged the body away. And nobody wants to complain, because she was a spy too.'

'That's an awful lot of spies. Are you sure there's not a Wiccan connection? The dead people both had arrowheads, like your woman at Callanish, and the woman who took the bicycle.'

'True. Well, the Americans said there were other factions sniffing around. But come on, witches? No such thing. Though that could be some kind of cover, I suppose.'

'But you know,' said Malcolm, 'the more I see of the stones, the less they seem like something F^2 made. Anyway, I'm glad you were here. That was quick thinking.'

'We should meet up more often. Any time we have someone to zap.'

They drove back along the track to the main road. Clouds scudded across the sky, casting shadows over the purple plain. In the darting sunlight, snow pockets glistened from the high corries.

'Are you staying for lunch?' said Malcolm, as he parked at the cottage.

'I have to get back, man,' said Helen. 'I need to get to the shopping centre back at Loch Lomond to buy some clothes for the wedding. My Rohan keks and a fleece might cause negative comment. But if you've the makings of a sandwich that'll keep me going.'

'Sure! I usually just take a packed lunch to work so I can make enough for both of us.'

'So how do F^2 make that plant function in such a remote spot?' said Helen. 'Are they all in Land Rovers like you?'

'The plant's at Tigh Na Cruach, in the middle of the moor.'

'So how do you get in?'

'The main entrance is at the end of a service road from Rannoch Station. The West Coast main line from Glasgow comes just past where we are, and curves round the western edge of the moor.'

'I'd love to know what's really going on in there.'

'Actually, I'm going to visit the plant on Tuesday. Guided tour. Might be helpful? Maybe you could sign up for one.'

'Oh, the Americans mentioned tours for the locals. Give me the sign-up email, and I'll have a think about that.'

'Come on in, and I'll make those sandwiches.'

Chapter 13

Helen – Sunday 14th September, afternoon

My road back to Glasgow was along the A82, one of the main routes to and from the Highlands. Leaving Loch Lomond soon after seven that morning it had been almost empty. Going back after midday, there was more traffic, mostly travelling at that irritating Sunday speed of people who are admiring the scenery rather than trying to get somewhere. But the real trouble with the journey was too much time to think. And I had a lot to think about.

On the plus side, Malcolm had been easier to get on with than at Ganny McIver's wake. Probably time-the-great-healer and so on after his accident. And I did now have a mobile number for him and not just his stone-age landline. But he was also a bit too laid back for comfort. During my lifeboat days, I'd come across people who'd been through bad experiences. For them, nothing afterwards seemed worth the worry. So maybe I'd have to do the worrying for both of us.

Because on the negative side, zapping things with two stones was pretty serious stuff. Even though it had been fun at the time. First I'd thought my pebble was a portable energy source and then a surveillance device. Now it seemed that in combination with a second stone it was actually some kind of laser-equipped weapon. Where was all that energy coming from? And what would happen if you linked half a dozen of them together?

The Americans couldn't possibly know about the stones, or that's what they'd have talked about rather than gravitons and gates. I could trade what I knew for what they knew but then they'd probably want my pebble to investigate, which was out of the question until I could deal with the panic attack problem somehow. And it might make trouble for Malcolm if they worked out he had one too. Not to mention the downside of Americans with novel weapons. I could keep quiet about the stones and just tell them about the robots. But maybe tangling with them at all was a bad idea.

While I was pondering this, my phone pinged with an incoming message. I'd spoken to Dad the evening before and he was fine, but of course my first thought was news from or about him. I'd just got to somewhere called Tyndrum, which passed for a town in these parts, so I pulled over at the Real Food Café to check.

The text was from Bernie's number, but read:

'Helen, this is Thierry, Bernie's friend. She asks me to chat to you about the wedding. Can we meet later today?'

How odd.

Still, Bernie must know about the text since it was from her phone. She might well be very busy, this last weekend before the wedding. But maybe she really wanted me to give Thierry the once-over?

I was heading for a shopping complex at the bottom of Loch Lomond where I was pretty sure I could buy some posh trousers and a flashy tunic for the wedding. Possibly even a hat, if they had one I could tolerate. Though this was a pain. I hate shopping, but all my dress-up gear was back in Sunderland.

Some quick online search showed there was a Shore Café in the complex, inevitably with a view over the Loch. I texted back to say I'd meet Thierry there at four.

Leaving the car park, I paused as a very shiny BMW, in black, like cousin Steven's, entered it. Then felt a coldness in my chest. Unmistakeably, through the front windscreen, I saw the driver was Martha the physicist. Now how likely was that?

I looked away hurriedly, hoping she hadn't noticed me, and swung out onto the road. Of course there were plenty of tourist options along the A82 and it could just be coincidental. On the other hand…

This addition to my worries had faded by the time I'd spent two hours in the shopping centre. It was unpleasantly crowded and hot. Did I tell you I hate shopping? Even if I liked buying clothes, let me tell you there isn't a lot of women's gear for someone my height. I have to look through the 'outsize' brands, which, along with shop assistants that tut, makes me feel like a freak.

Eventually I managed some tailored navy trousers and a silky tunic in peacock colours. A wide-brimmed hat in black would have been useful for funerals too, but it made me look like a cowboy. Then I found a blue velvet trilby, complete with a pheasant feather set at a jaunty angle. Very Scottish.

I arrived at the Shore Café on time, much in need of a coffee. Of course there was a queue. As I stood in the 'wait here to be served' cluster, I caught sight of a waving arm. Thierry. He had obviously arrived early and bagged a table close to the windows.

'Hi Thierry,' I said, manoeuvring my shopping round to the side of the chair.

'Helen, good to see you again,' Thierry said, betraying a slight twitch of his arm as if he wasn't sure whether to shake hands again. He clearly knew we were not on two-kiss terms.

Ouf, it was good to be sitting down. Thierry acquired the attention of a waitress and I ordered a large cappuccino. He recommended the scones with jam and cream, and I went for those too. Malcolm's porridge and two cheese sandwiches had only gone so far. The service was excellent and my order arrived almost at once.

'OK, Thierry, how can I help? Does Bernie want me to do something specific at the wedding? I'm sure Alison doesn't need any more bridesmaids.'

Hmm, from his puzzled look he didn't know that was a joke. Perhaps they don't have bridesmaids in France.

'Helen, I have to apologise, and Bernie also. She asked me to talk to you about something else. Not Alison's wedding. But it is confidential. Not for a text message.'

Oh god, were they going to get married?

'It is about F^2. She is worried. I am also worried. But Bernie is a very loyal person. She did not want to express her worries directly.'

'So what exactly are you both worried about? And what do the worries have to do with me?'

'The man Frank Dooley, who was at Lewis, when you were at Lewis too. Who was injured by lightning.'

'Bernie said he was visiting some project at the University there.'

Thierry shrugged, the way French people do.

'Bernie spoke to the team there because she thought they needed to know he was injured. They had not met with him. They did not expect to see him.'

Interesting. I put my coffee down.

'And?'

'She had a call from a Lewis policeman yesterday. To her home. Steven McIver. The same name as you.'

'Yes, he's a cousin. I met him when I was there.'

'He enquired about Frank Dooley. In the context of the body your ship found. He said that this Frank was twice seen close to the victim, McMalkin.'

Thierry looked straight at me.

'He also said, maybe he should not have said, that you were there when the injury took place.'

I tried not to splutter a mouthful of scone.

'Come on, he was struck by lightning! Nothing to do with me.'

'Of course not. McIver said you provided medical attention. He thought Bernie might want to send you some thanks. But you did not tell Bernie about this in your phone call when you spoke of Lewis.'

'So why is that a worry?'

'It made us wonder whether Frank had spoken to you about McMalkin. And how he came to be in the same place as you that day. We cannot ask Frank as he has little memory of the last week according to McIver.'

'So are you worried about me or worried that F^2 are employing a possible criminal?'

Thierry looked as if he wasn't quite sure what to say. Then:

'We are both worried about F^2 itself. Bernie feels something has changed in the last year. There are more secrets. F^2 were involved in a big European project collaborating on new power sources, something they were very proud of. Then this year, they suddenly withdrew. Bernie never found out why, though the other partners were upset and F^2 had to pay some money back. And there was an incident at the plant in the summer.'

'What happened?'

'It is one of the secrets. And what I know of it I cannot tell you for professional reasons.'

I thought that one through.

'OK, you do occupational health. The workplace shrink. So you have a patient who has told you something in confidence.'

'I cannot say.'

Which was as good as an admission I felt. Well, as Thierry had told me something new, it seemed fair to tell him something back.

'Yes, you're right that Frank talked to me. I'd go so far to say he seemed to be pursuing me. Very strange behaviour for someone in a company van. He thought I knew about something McMalkin supposedly had.'

'And do you?'

I looked straight back the way you do when you are not telling the whole truth.

'McMalkin had almost nothing on him. Except pockets full of stones.'

Thierry was undoubtedly better at keeping a straight face than I was, but when I said 'stones' I could see a definite reaction. He knew something about stones. Did Bernie as well?

But this was as much cut-and-thrust as I could take after the rigours of an afternoon shopping, so it was time to change the subject.

'You know I think a lot of Bernie. She's like a big sister to me. I can see that she thinks a lot of you. I want her to be happy. I hope you do too.'

'I am fond of Bernie.'

Oh dear, that didn't sound anything like the look on Bernie's face had told me she felt. I may have glared at him, he certainly looked away.

I got to my feet.

'How much do I owe you for the coffee and scones?'

Thierry rose to his feet too.

'Oh no, nothing. You were my guest.'

'Thanks, good scones as you said.'

I collected my shopping bags.

'If your patient should ever want to talk to me about what happened in the plant, please do pass on my number.'

I could feel him watching me leave.

When I got back to the cottage, the cat seemed rather pleased to see me. Maybe he was used to more company than I was giving him. He'd looked all ready to jump into the car with me for my early start up to Rannoch that morning until I'd shooed him away.

'Well, Mog. Sorry to leave you on your tod all day. Maybe you should have stayed in Troon.'

He rubbed against my legs and chirruped at me as I unpacked the new clothes and put the bags into the recycling bin. I refilled his food bowl.

Looking out, I could see the evening was unexpectedly bright. Earlier clouds had blown over and the low sun gave the spectacular scenery of mountains and loch a stage-set effect.

'Back soon, Mog. Time I gave my legs something to do.'

It was at least an hour until sunset so I walked up the road along the loch, stretching the muscles, admiring the view, and beginning to feel things couldn't be so bad. Maybe I should forget all this F^2 stuff and just go for my next mountain. By the time I got back, the landscape was in the evening shadow of the mountains and I was ready for one of the microwave meals I'd picked up the previous day.

The first thing I noticed was an agitated cat. His fur was on end, his tail was thrashing, and he was making the low whining growl of a seriously annoyed animal.

Just as well really, as otherwise I might not have understood so quickly that someone had been in the cottage. Tidiness and seafarers go together, and I am very particular with my stuff. My new clothes had been refolded, my laptop and kindle were not quite stacked the way I had left them. The top drawer of the chest was fractionally open and my kitbag on top of it, slightly crooked. I remembered Malcolm telling me how his place had been trashed.

The cat stalked under the coffee table and there was more growling and a scratching sound. I tipped the table onto its side. Attached to its bottom surface was a silver object about the size of a watch battery. OK, there was something I could try that might dispose of that. I slipped my pebble out of its bag, touched it to the bugging device and there was a satisfying 'pop'. I felt it was a toss-up as to whether F^2 or the Americans would be put out. Things were getting personal.

Chapter 14

Malcolm – Sunday 14th September

I'd too many thoughts to collect, after Helen left. And not enough lunch, before the phone rang. It was Henry Craig, the de facto, if not titular, head of RAGE. Henry was too young for Rock Against Racism, too old for Black Lives Matter, and too self-opinionated for any mainstream group. Instead, he repeatedly threw himself into local campaigns: his energy fuelling them towards their inevitable implosion, as his co-conspirators tired of his dogmatic certainties.

Although his heart was in the right place, Henry was the last person I wanted to talk to. After attending a presentation I'd given about enhancing environmental diversity, he'd tried to involve me in a scheme to promote the reintroduction of bears into the Central Highlands. Luckily, head office had warned me off. While I'd done my best to avoid him ever since, he'd been prominent at the front of the RAGE demonstration outside the F^2 meeting. Come to think about it, though, I hadn't seen him inside.

Long before I'd encountered him, Henry was a not very published poet, who topped up his tiny private income by running writing groups. Along the way, he'd had five children with his long suffering partner Megan, by far the better writer. After the success of their *Preacher Man* series, they'd bought a cottage at Port Appin, which wasn't exactly on Rannoch Moor.

Preacher Man was originally a one-off novel, set in the 18th century Hebrides, in the lawless period following the Forty Five rebellion. The eponymous preacher was, for reasons hinted at obliquely, estranged from his Lowland family, and toured the isles on horseback, solving crimes, salving souls, and breaking hearts. Though the book was written jointly, it was largely based on Megan's doctoral research, long postponed by child care. A surprise hit with airport and railway station bookstores, a new volume now appeared every other year. There was even talk of a TV series.

I barely knew Megan. She often went to events with Henry, and rarely said much, but everything she did say was always to the point. She was patently very smart. And she was patently very patient. Goodness knew what she saw in Henry.

'Henry,' I said, cautiously. 'How can I help you?'

'Malcolm,' said Henry. 'How are you? It's been such a long time. I blame myself, of course, but I've been so busy with the writing, that I've little time for anything else.'

'I'm fine,' I said. 'How's the family?'

'Booming!' said Henry. 'Well not literally. Megan put her foot down, and packed me off for the snip.'

'Good for her,' I said. 'Look, I've had a trying morning, and I'm in the middle of lunch.'

'It'll not take long,' said Henry. 'I'd really like to pick your brains about stopping F^2.'

'Come on, Henry,' I said. 'We've been over this before. Remember the bears? You know I can't get involved in anything in an official capacity.'

'How about unofficially?' said Henry. 'You must have heard something about what F^2 are up to.'

'Just what was said at the meeting,' I said. 'You were there, weren't you? I saw you outside.'

'None of us went in,' said Henry. 'We didn't want to legitimise their phony consultation.'

Right on.

'So what are you planning?' I said.

'We're discussing direct action,' said Henry. 'Non-violent, of course. But we've no idea how the plant's organised.'

'There are public tours,' I said, instantly regretting it.

'That's interesting!' said Henry. 'You don't know anyone who's going on one, do you?'

'There's a web site,' I said, evasively. 'You could sign up yourself.'

'Oh no,' said Henry. 'I couldn't possibly do that. I'm far too high profile.'

'Well,' I said, 'if I hear anything, I'll be in touch. I've really got to get going now.'

'Thanks anyway,' said Henry. 'Do let me know what you can find out. We're totally in the dark. Anything would be helpful.'

'We'll see,' I said. 'Cheerio.'

'Stay in touch,' said Henry. 'Cheerio.'

I put the phone down and returned to my half eaten sandwich, brain buzzing.

I really didn't want to believe that the green stones had unearthly powers. The path through the mist, on Creag Na Caillich, could have been a trick of the light, like some sort of Brocken Spectre in reverse. But combining Helen's and my stones had indubitably trashed the microwave, and taken out the robot hound. I really needed to find out more about these stones. And what they had to do with the body Helen found. And the one I hadn't. And how it all connected to F^2. If it connected to them at all.

I stood up, and tidied away what had passed for lunch. Then I realised that I'd not seen the cat since I got back from the moor. When I ate at home, she usually pestered me for food. Maybe she was round at Dougie's? She seemed to have taken to Glenys. Glenys seemed to know how the stones worked. I needed to talk with Glenys again.

I went out of the cottage, and went up the lane to my neighbours. Glenys was outside, headphones muffling her ears, chopping wood. The cat sat on a log, watching her. I walked across to the cat and stroked it behind the ears.

'I've been expecting you,' said Glenys, taking off the cans.

'I'm sorry if it's being a nuisance,' I said picking up the beast.

'Not at all,' said Glenys. 'You're both always welcome. But that wasn't what I meant.'

'Well,' I said, putting the squirming cat back onto the log, 'I guess you want to talk about the stone.'

'That as well,' said Glenys.

'As well as what?' I asked.

'The arrowheads,' said Glenys. 'What's your real interest in them?'

I felt a bit shifty. I no longer really knew who I could trust with what. But she had asked me straight out.

'It's complicated,' I said. 'Really complicated.'

'Everything's always complicated,' said Glenys. 'Cup of tea?'

'Yes please,' I said.

'Let me load you up,' said Glenys.

I stretched out my arms and Glenys stacked them with kindling. Then she led me inside.

Dougie and Glenys's cottage, like mine, had been built for estate workers, ostensibly to a standard layout, of thick walls and high eaves. So I was always impressed by what they'd done with it, opening the kitchen into the sitting room, and squeezing two more rooms out of the pinched attic.

'Stick it by the fire, please,' said Glenys. 'In the basket.'

I dumped the wood, and browsed the shelves, while Glenys pottered at the sink. Dougie and Glenys didn't have so many books, but well made up for it in DVDs, mostly of films I'd never heard of.

'Here you go,' said Glenys, coming across the room bearing two mugs. 'White, no sugar, isn't it?'

'That's right,' I said, taking a mug. 'Thanks.'

We sat on the sofa, looking out through the French windows at Beinn a'Chreachain.

'So what's going on?' said Glenys.

She listened quietly, as I told her about Patricia Harper and the broken arrowhead.

'I know they're called witch stones,' I concluded. 'But I really don't know their significance.'

'I suppose they're a bit like Rotary Club badges,' said Glenys, fiddling with her own arrowhead. 'They're a way for Wiccans to recognise each other. But they're far more than that. It would be a big deal for Patricia Harper to have broken hers. I'd hate to break mine.'

'Can men be Wiccans?' I asked, thinking of the arrowhead on the corpse Helen had dredged up.

'Everyone's a Wiccan,' said Glenys. 'It's just that they mostly don't know it yet.'

Really? Let's not go there.

'You know,' I said. 'I've just discovered that I've got some connection with what I suppose what must be Wicca. I've told you my family's from Lewis. According to my mum, my great great granny was a wise woman.'

'What was she called?' said Glenys, suddenly very interested.

'Margaret MacCaskill,' I said.

'Margaret MacCaskill?' said Glenys. 'Get away!'

'You've heard of her?' I said.

'Of course I've heard of her!' said Glenys. 'She's really important. She's one of the earliest wise women there are any written records for. Her sayings were recently rediscovered, in a Victorian collection of Hebridean folklore.'

'Her sayings?' I echoed. 'Really? What exactly did she say?'

'Don't scoff,' said Glenys. 'She was a prophetess, who could see the future.'

Really? What is this?

'Look,' I said. 'I'm not at all into this stuff.'

'It's obviously into you,' said Glenys. 'That's why the stone's attached itself to you. How exactly did you come by it?'

In for a cent, in for a euro. I quickly explained how I'd found the stone when I was looking for Patricia Harper.

'The stone must have been hers,' said Glenys, when I'd finished. 'And it's more than a coincidence that someone like her would show up now.'

Someone like her? Now?

'What are you getting at?' I said.

'It's the second prophecy,' said Glenys, looking very serious. 'Margaret MacAskill's. *When the days balance, the worlds balance.*'

'What on earth does that mean?' I said. 'It could be anything.'

'It's the equinox,' said Glenys. 'What else could it be? That's why we celebrate it at the quarry, at a seat of power. But it looks like this one's going to be extra special.'

This sounds utterly implausible. And yet, maybe there's something more than meets the ear.

'Have you got a copy of the prophecies?' I said.

'I haven't, I'm afraid,' said Glenys. 'But I'll tell you who has. Do you know Megan Craig?'

'Henry Craig's wife?' I said.

'That's right,' said Glenys. 'She's a real expert on Highland folkways. Shame she let Henry boil them down into those awful novels.'

'You know,' I said, 'I can't see what she sees in him.'

Glenys laughed.

'Maybe he's good in bed,' she said. 'It certainly looks that way.'

Goodness! Is that the prosecco talking?

'Is she a Wiccan?' I said.

'You'll have to ask her yourself,' said Glenys.

I might just do that.

'I'd best get going,' I said, standing up. 'Thanks for the tea.'

'Thanks for trusting me,' said Glenys. 'I know this all seems a bit weird, but there'll be a good reason, you'll see. If you like, I can ask around about Patricia Harper.'

Around? Do I want to know? Of course I do.

'Thanks,' I said, yet again. 'That might be helpful. Now, where's that cat?'

'Och, just leave her be,' said Glenys. 'I'm sure she'll head home when she's good and ready.'

I left Glenys chopping wood, the cat crouched on the log, watching warily.

Chapter 15

Helen – Monday 15th September

I woke the next morning in a thoroughly bad mood. I'm not the jumpy type, but I had locked the front door and shut the back window before I went to bed. And the day's events had left me with another night of weird dreams.

The pebble on my bedside table glowing green, a dream version of Mog crouched close up to my face with glowing green eyes, and me narrating a complete rerun of the day's events. The whole thing full of that anxious feeling of being pursued. I felt tired and scratchy. Needless to say Mog was curled up on the other side of the bed with his tail over his face and not a care in the world.

I was still worried about, or rather for, cousin Malcolm. He ought to know that Bernie was troubled about what was happening at F^2 and that something had happened in the plant over the summer. I could have rung him I suppose, but I felt paranoid about that. Didn't people who left bugs also tap phones? And I'd bet good money he had no encrypted messaging app on his ancient mobile.

So I had looked up his organisation – Rural Resource – online. I found an email address for 'the Rannoch Ranger', which made Malcolm sound like the punch-line to a joke.

Then I wrote a very cautious email about what I'd learned from Thierry, and my own worries about the Americans. I hoped that Malcolm would interpret my indirect language. Though sod's law said he'd just think it was a thank-you email. I didn't mention Thierry at all, that was for Bernie to tell Malcolm about, or not. I didn't even know for sure Thierry would be at the wedding. If Bernie had any sense she'd leave him out of it. Not that falling for someone left you with much sense, as I'd discovered.

Yesterday's taster of porridge hadn't impressed me, and I crunched through my usual cereal. My original plan said I should be doing a mountain today. Ben Vorlich was only half an hour or so back up the A82 at the other end of the loch. And why the hell not? Did all this stuff have to wreck my holiday? Though a quick look out showed that it was a grey and murky day. Not encouraging.

So I opened my laptop again. I wondered about the European project F^2 had been in and then left so abruptly.

It was easy to find. Called ENERGISE, which was some complex acronym that started *Exploring New Energy Resources* blah blah. Eight partners from five countries over five years, starting two years back. F^2 were the only UK partner, but the set included the huge French state electricity company, a big German energy engineering firm, and an Italian research institute. Research funding of millions of euros. A programme about exploiting novel green energy resources through leading-edge physics, blah blah. These must surely be the Europeans that Martha and Dean had been on about.

Then I decided to check out Thierry. First the F^2 website to see if I could find his family name. Easy, their website said their Occupational Health Officer was Dr Thierry Caussard. Then I just searched on his name and *occupational health*. Bingo. Formerly a Senior Medical Officer in the French state electricity company. Private practice in Glasgow from the previous year.

Christ almighty, that stank. Was he just taking Bernie for a ride? And in reality just another of the wasps around the F^2 jampot? I was so angry I got up and walked around the cottage swearing, almost kicking Mog, who appeared out of the bedroom looking surprised by the noise I was making. He made for the front door and I let him out.

'Never believe a Frenchman, Mog.'

The worst of it was that I could see I'd have to keep my mouth shut. Certainly until after the wedding. Bernie would never believe it was fishy, there'd be some smooth-tongued explanation. But just let that man try to talk to me on his own again and I would give him several pieces of my mind. At least he knew I had him in my sights. Oh, poor Bernie.

Hmm, what did that mean about his mysterious patient? Was this an invention, or were his professional morals a cut above his personal ones? I hadn't put anything about that in my email either, it would have to wait until I saw Malcolm again at the wedding.

I jumped as my phone pinged with a message. Who or what was this? Bernie? Thierry? Someone complaining I'd broken their bugging device?

No, in fact cousin Steven. Whatever could he want?

'Hi Helen. The boss asked me to give you a heads-up. We need to talk to you again. Let me know where you are right now and then he'll ring shortly to fix it up. Piseach!'

'Happy to help. Currently in Loch Lomond,' was what I replied. 'Fucking hell, just what I need,' was what I said. I checked Steven's last word on the assumption it was Gaelic.

Yes. It meant 'Good luck'.

I gloomily made myself another coffee. Didn't look like Ben Vorlich was on the agenda, weather-wise or time-wise. Surely they weren't going to drag me over to Lewis again?

It was a good half an hour before my phone rang, and as it was 'number withheld', just as well I was expecting it.

'Helen McIver. How can I help?'

'Hello Ms McIver. This is DI Sinclair of the Lewis police. Thank you for your assistance last week. We have however some supplementary questions to ask you concerning the death of Mr Gray McMalkin.'

Couldn't resist: 'I thought you said this was not a suspicious death?'

'As sometimes happens, new information has come in that needs to be assessed.'

'OK. Do you want to ask your supplementary questions now?'

'Unfortunately we have to follow procedures which do not allow me to do so. I appreciate that travelling back to Stornoway would be inconvenient, so it would help us immensely if you would agree to attend a police station closer to your current location.'

Basically they had to record people 'assisting the police with their enquiries', and that meant I'd to go to a Glasgow Police station where Mr Tweed Jacket would do a video interview with a local helper. At 3pm.

'Yes,' was the expected answer.

It was now mid-morning. I decided to drive to Milngavie, on the Glasgow outskirts, and catch the train into the centre. Bound to be something I could do there, if only eat a posh lunch. Mam's a Weegie, as Dad calls her when he wants to tease, but we hadn't stopped much with her family as kids – her parents lived in a tenement and by the time I came along there was no room for us all there.

So I wasn't very familiar with the city and felt happy to explore it for few hours. One of the perks of my jobs has been walking port cities, though mostly ones with better weather than Glasgow. It stayed grey and murky, but at least the rain held off. I walked over to the West End, near the University, and ate in a very decent 'New Scottish' place, avoiding anything with haggis in it. No sign of my American friends, to my relief. I thought about the coming interview and what I would and would not say.

Then I walked in Kelvingrove Park and stuck my head in their art gallery. I vaguely remembered being dragged round it as a kid at some point. It has everything from stuffed animals to a Spitfire, which I'd like to have looked over more closely, only it was hanging from a ceiling.

After that I walked further west through Partick to where my phone told me I'd find the specified police station. The building was on a different scale from the Lewis station, though it had a similar institutional smell. It came from the same bricks-and-glass epoch as my secondary school back in Sunderland. I was rapidly installed in a conference room with a big screen at one end, alongside a youngish detective with a strong local accent. He failed to hide his surprise at my height, but at least did not comment.

The screen came to life, and after an interminable 'connecting' icon, cleared to reveal my old friend Mr Tweed Jacket.

'Ready to record, sir?' said my local guy. And at a 'Yes please' from the other end, he hit the keyboard in front of him, and a red recording button appeared at the top of the screen.

'This is Detective Sergeant Erskine recording an interview between Detective Inspector Gordon Sinclair and Ms Helen McIver on Monday 12th September at 15.20 pm.'

'Thank you for agreeing to this interview, Ms McIver,' said Sinclair. 'We have a few supplementary questions relating to the death of Mr Gray McMalkin on September 9th.'

'Fire away,' I said.

'When the body of Mr McMalkin was recovered, all of his possessions were catalogued and handed over? Nothing was omitted?'

'Nothing,' I said. 'He had very little. An amulet, that we left round his neck; a driving licence and credit card, and pockets full of stones that had weighed his body down. We handed everything over.'

'You were kind enough to take a photograph of the stones you mention. Are you sure every last one of them was passed to us?'

'Yes, I think so. They looked like they had come off a beach, but we boxed them up and sent them off with the body.'

'So you would be surprised to hear that your photograph shows nineteen stones of varying sizes, but we seem to have eighteen? The missing one is round and green, a pretty thing.'

'Well, yes. I packed them all myself and the box was left with the body, in our cold store. I'm afraid I didn't actually count them, and I didn't notice any in particular. They looked like they were just beach stones.'

Like I said, I have no confidence in my ability to lie with a straight face. But my hope was that Sinclair had no idea what had happened to the missing stone or even whether it was important. Though someone else might. This guess was rewarded when his next question went on to something else.

'On Wednesday 7th September, and Thursday 8th September you were in Stornoway?'

'Sure.'

'Did you come across a man called Frank Dooley?'

'Not until he was struck by lightning on the Thursday. I applied CPR to him at the Callanish. But I only knew who he was afterwards.'

'Is it the case that when DC Steven McIver found you in the middle of the Calanais stones after the lightning strike you said 'The old lady. The F^2 guy'?'

'I may have done. I was knocked over by the lightning strike, so I was feeling pretty dazed.' Damn Steven and his policeman memory.

'So if you didn't know Frank Dooley, how did you know who he worked for?'

'I saw his van arrive at the car park earlier when I was walking around the site. It's pretty noticeable. He was the only other visitor around.'

'And how did you know it belonged to the company F^2?'

'When your colleague picked me up at the quay on Wednesday morning, the van nearly hit us as we drove onto the road. As a result I recognised it at a petrol station when we were driving over to the Callanish. I commented on it and your colleague told me it belonged to F^2. I think he may have mentioned the name Frank Dooley as well.'

'Have you any idea what Frank Dooley was doing at the Calanais stones?'

'I assume he was visiting them like I was. Is he OK? He was alive when he was taken to hospital.'

'You'll be pleased to hear he is recovering, yes. Could you tell me about the old lady you mentioned. Where did you meet her? Did you speak to her?'

'Only briefly. I was in the centre of the circle, just before the lightning strike. She was small, had a big long coat and a hat, and a wrinkly face. She said something about the stones being impressive and then there was a terrific bang and I was knocked over. She wasn't there afterwards so I assumed she had gone back to the village. It was very wet.'

'We haven't been able to locate anyone in the village who can confirm what you say. And it does seem unlikely that if the lightning strike knocked you over, Ms McIver, a little old lady was able to leave the scene so quickly. Are you confident that was a real interaction?'

'Oh. You think I might have imagined it when I was dazed? I suppose I might have. I don't really know.'

I was pretty sure I hadn't. Why would I imagine someone telling me they were a witch. With an arrowhead amulet? But damned if I was going into all that with Mr Tweed Jacket. His questioning was so different from our Lewis sessions that there had to be something going on in the background. Might the Americans have poked their noses in? I bet a cultural attaché could pull some police strings if he wanted to.

There was a pause. I smiled in what I hoped was a guileless way.

'Can I help you with anything else? Do you think McMalkin's death was suspicious after all?'

Yes, I know you aren't supposed to ask the police questions. I just thought being nosey would seem in character.

'These are just routine clarifications, Ms McIver. Thank you for your time.'

My nearest railway station was Partick, which was on the line back to Milngavie. I spent the time going back over the interview in my mind, wondering what the police really wanted to know. So far it seemed nobody had clocked my altercation with Dooley in the Castle car park, though if that did come out, my keeping quiet would look very suspicious.

But suspicious of what? I only knew for sure what the police also knew, which was that Dooley seemed to be pursuing McMalkin, and McMalkin had apparently killed himself rather than be confronted. They must have looked in the back of Dooley's van by now as well, and found the fused tracker. Hopefully they'd blame that on the lightning. If they wanted to know what Dooley was up to and he couldn't tell them, then no doubt Dooley's boss could.

Kudos to police thoroughness for counting all the stones in my pic. If Tweed Jacket was good at his job – and I assumed he was – he might well feel I had failed to tell the truth at that point. But so what? True, I did have a theory about why Dooley was after McMalkin: that he'd had made off with an F^2 experimental product, possibly for 'the Europeans' and that I was now its lucky owner. But that was only a theory. As Malcolm had pointed out, it didn't account for the arrowhead amulet. That linked McMalkin to the old woman the police hadn't been able to locate. As mysterious as McMalkin himself.

I had just got back to the Milngavie car park when my phone pinged ominously. And before I could check what it was, it pinged again.

The first message was Steven once more.

'Hi Helen. I've been flown over to do some interviews. Passing through Loch Lomond midday tomorrow – do you fancy lunch? Just to chat, no interview!'

And the second was Bernie.

'Helen, I have to do a police interview tomorrow. Have they spoken to you? Any chance you could come round tonight for a meal and a chat?'

What it is to be popular.

Chapter 16

Malcolm – Monday 15th September

Spies. Wiccans. Gravitons. Arrowheads. Green stones. What I needed was a gentle day of familiar routine. Some hope.

The morning started without any phone calls. But when I got to the hut, and sat down to check the email, top of the list was a message from Helen:

> Hi Malcolm
> Good to see you this morning and thanks for the hospitality. Thought you'd be interested to hear I keep seeing your New Age friends around. Maybe they think I can lead them to long-lost Scottish treasure! The moor is very impressive, I'd never seen it before. It must be close to your heart as a ranger. I do hope your local industries will care for it, though I gather some of them are a bit lax and one of them had some big H&S incident in the summer.
> Anyway, thanks again, see you soon.
> Helen

That really didn't sound like Helen at all. So formal. So indirect. What was she trying to tell me? The local industry must be F^2, but that was the first I'd heard of a major Health and Safety incident. Polly Sharp certainly hadn't mentioned it. Maybe Helen wanted me to find out more? Maybe Dougie knew something?

And what did those Americans want with Helen? Dougie had said that F^2 were concerned about them as well. If they were spies, they seemed singularly inept at staying hidden.

Next, I worked through the rest of the emails. There was nothing pressing, apart from another message from F^2 about the site visit: please could I confirm my attendance?

So I telephoned the office, and told the secretary that I'd not be at work on Tuesday, until the afternoon. They said that was fine, and reminded me, not that I needed to be reminded, that I'd be away Thursday through Monday, at Alison's wedding. Would I like any more time off? I'd a huge backlog of untaken leave, which I couldn't carry over into the New Year. Not right now, thanks.

I spent the rest of the morning, pottering around, trying not to think too much about the past few days. At midday, I set off for the Altnafeadh Hotel, in search of lunch.

As usual, the Hotel forecourt was almost empty, apart from Dougie's blue and white police car. And, as usual, Dougie himself was parked at his customary table in the restaurant bay window, munching his way through his customary pie, beans and chips.

Taking comfort in the ordinary, I placed an order with Jeannie, and joined Dougie.

'Malco!' he said as I sat down. 'How's it hanging?'

'Just fine,' I said, for once enjoying his egregious archaisms. 'And yourself?'

'A wee bit busier than I'd like,' said Dougie. 'F^2 have just given us their schedule. There's going to be a series of small power outages over the next few days, and something big's going down on Sunday.'

Noted. I bet Henry Craig would be interested.

'Any idea what?' I asked.

'Not really,' said Dougie. 'Just that they'll be using a lot of power, so there might be lengthy supply interruptions. At least they've told us a bit more in advance than usual.'

'I wonder what they're up to,' I said. 'They're supposed to be generating power, not stopping everyone else from having any. Have they said when?'

'They're pretty vague,' said Dougie. 'If I hear anything more, I'll let you know.'

'Thanks,' I said. 'I don't suppose your lot ever found out who did over my cottage?'

'Afraid not,' said Dougie. 'The SOCOs said the place was clean.'

That'll be right.

'What about those missing F² people,' I said. 'Did they ever turn up?'

'Not that I've heard,' said Dougie.

'And the people I told you about?' I said 'The two Americans, and the bicycle woman?'

'Sorry,' said Dougie. 'I didn't think it worth passing that on.'

Noted. I bet Helen would be interested.

'Has there been any other trouble at the plant?' I said. 'I'd be the last to hear anything, of course.'

'It's all dealt with from Pitlochry,' said Dougie. 'We'd only get involved if something spilled over our side, like people up at the fence.'

I was about to ask how he knew F² had known that I'd been there, but Jeannie arrived with my food.

After lunch, I returned to the hut and phoned Henry. He was most excited when I told him I might have some new information about the moor, and invited me to dinner that very evening. Very pleased with how this was working out, I told him that I'd come by at the back of six. I didn't tell him that I hoped Megan would be there, as it was really her that I wanted to talk with.

I spent the afternoon working on the new display board. At five, I shut up shop and headed home, for a quick wash and brush up, and to select a bottle of wine. Having fed the cat, who I was pretty sure was routinely getting double rations from Glenys, I set off for Port Appin.

Port Appin's more or less due west of Rannoch Moor, as the crow flies. And, as always round here, there's a certain amount of mountain in the way that doesn't trouble crows. The quickest route from my cottage is back up over the moor, through Glencoe to Ballachulish, and then south down the coast towards Oban, instead of north to Fort William.

I'd never visited the Craig's before, and had some difficulty finding their home, largely thanks to the gross inadequacies of digital mapping.

It turned out that they actually lived outside the township, in an isolated row of five fishermen's cottages, above a beach, looking out across a bay to the Firth of Lorn. *Preacher Man* had clearly proved lucrative.

The single story, solid stone buildings, hunkered down against the westerlies, looked like they were to a typical linear design: three rooms wide and one room deep, entered through a porch, which let onto a connecting corridor running along the back wall. Once thatched, the roofs now were insulated with solar panels.

Henry, who must have heard the Land Rover, was waiting for me in the yard.

'Welcome!' said Henry. 'I hope we weren't too hard to find. Come and see the garden.'

I followed Henry round one end of the cottages. What would have been individual plots, each large enough to feed a family and maintain a sheep, had been merged. Now, close to the cottages, there was a lawn with flower beds. Beyond, was a vegetable patch with a greenhouse, and an orchard of fruit trees. A small windmill stood to one side. The whole was bordered by a drystone wall, broken by a gate down to the beach.

'Good timing!' said Henry, when he'd finished showing me round the garden. 'We're just about to eat.'

Henry led me back round to the front, and into the fourth cottage. Once through the porch, I found myself in a large open-plan space, lined with deep cupboards and racking full of boxes, yet still littered with family stuff.

'Sorry about the mess,' said Henry. 'This is what passes for the hall. We all live in the three cottages to the left. The first one's now the living room. Our bedrooms are in the other two. Megan and I have offices in the cottage on the right, well away from the kids. Do hang up your coat. And please take your shoes off.'

I sat on a stool and hauled off my boots.

'Excellent!' said Henry. 'Come on through.'

The living room, like the hall, was two rooms knocked together. At one end, Megan stood at the worktop.

'Hello Malcolm!' she said, turning round. 'Glad you could make it. Nearly ready.'

At the other end of the living room, the children were sprawled round a large television.

'Say hello, kids!' said Henry.

The children grunted politely, and returned to their programme.

'I blame the parents,' said Henry. He looked pointedly at the bottle I was clutching. 'Would you like a drink to be going on with?'

'Not just yet, thanks,' I said, handing Henry the wine. 'Maybe with dinner. I hope this goes with whatever we're having.'

Megan proved a well-intentioned, if disappointing, chef. Still, it was nice to eat someone else's cooking, even if the food was largely beige mush. And it was good to be with a family again, the children paying little attention to the adults, as they squabbled amiably. As for adult conversation, Henry did most of the talking, mainly about the next volume of *Preacher Man*. I didn't say as much, but supposed I really should read one.

'Right!' said Henry, when we'd finished eating. 'Time for grown-up stuff. Bugger off, kids.'

The children cat-called, and returned to the television.

'Lazy little bastards,' said Henry, cheerfully.

'Oh Henry,' said Megan. 'Really.'

'No,' said Henry, 'you're right, that's not fair. They largely pull their weight. And today's an adult shift, so we do everything. You're lucky you missed one of their cooking nights, though.'

I helped Henry clear the table, and stack the industrial sized dishwasher, while Megan made a large pot of tea.

'Let's go next door,' said Henry. 'It's quieter.'

Next door proved to be a snug sitting room, with a glass case of china, and family photos on the sideboard. Henry and Megan sat on the sofa. I sat in an armchair opposite them.

'Well,' said Henry. 'What gives.'

I told them about how F^2 were ramping up activity, culminating in something big on Sunday. And I told them of my fears for how F^2's plans could go very badly wrong. Of course I didn't mention Dougie or Polly. And they didn't ask.

'Right,' said Henry. 'Sunday's the day, then!'

'For what?' I said, anxiously.

'Showing that we won't stand for it, of course,' said Henry. 'We've been planning to invade the plant. Stage an occupation. But we really need to know how it's organised.'

'What about the site plans?' I asked. 'They must have lodged some, when they got permission for the project.'

'We've tried to get them, of course,' said Henry. 'But they're all embargoed. They claim it's in the national interest.'

I thought quickly. Maybe some well deserved media attention might make a difference? So, maybe RAGE going into the plant could prove positively advantageous.

'You won't hurt anybody?' I said. 'You won't do any damage?'

'We might have to cut through the fence to get in,' said Henry. 'And we'd have to make our presence felt. Presumably there's some sort of administrative block. We might spray some slogans, or hang a banner from something tall. But, I told you, RAGE isn't about violence.'

'What about your profile?' I said. 'You didn't want to go to the meeting.'

'It's all about social capital, isn't it,' said Henry. 'I don't mind spending it. But I need to be sure it's worth it.'

Henry looked at me expectantly.

'Well,' I said, 'I actually am going on their tour. Tomorrow. I'll let you know if I find out anything useful.'

'Good man!' said Henry. 'Good man! I'll expect a full report.'

I stood up.

'I really ought to get going,' I said. 'I've an early start the morn'. All the way to Rannoch Station. Thank you both for your hospitality.'

'You're most welcome,' said Henry.

We all went back through the living room, to the hall.

'Henry,' said Megan, as I pulled on my boots. 'Go and wrangle the kids. The wee ones need baths. I'll see Malcolm out. I could do with some fresh air.'

'For sure,' said Henry. 'You'll be in touch?'

'That I will,' I said.

Megan and I left the house. The night was clear and the quarter moon was rising.

'Well Malcom,' said Megan quietly. 'I know you've been talking with Glenys. You need to be really careful. You could be in a lot of danger.'

Tell me something I don't know.

'Why do you think I'm in danger?' I said.

'Margaret MacAskill,' said Megan. 'She's your great great grandmother. So her prophecies will apply especially to you.'

'Glenys said something about the equinox,' I said. '*When the days balance, the worlds balance.* What's that got to do with anything?'

'Sunday's the equinox,' said Megan.

If the wedding's on Thursday, and that's the 18th, then Sunday's the 21st. Oh fuck. Oh come on! This is all nonsense!

'But I wasn't thinking of that one,' continued Megan. 'There's another: *What's given to the stones remains given.*'

I fingered the green stone in its protective bag.

'Why do you think that involves me?' I said.

Of course she knew.

'Your green stone,' said Megan. 'It's really powerful. If you found it, someone lost it, and they'll be looking for it. Other people might be as well.'

That fits Helen's tale. Oh fuck.

'You've got some of these, haven't you,' Megan continued.

She reached down into the neck of her Fair Isle jersey, and pulled out an arrowhead on a leather thong.

'I picked up half a dozen,' I said. 'In the quarry.'

'Good,' said Megan. 'You should always keep one on you, and give one to anyone you think might be in danger, especially blood relatives. And, if anyone mentions the stone, show them the arrowhead, and see how they react.'

'What about Henry?' I asked. 'Isn't he in danger as well?'

Megan laughed.

'Och no,' said Megan. 'Nothing bad'll happen to him.'

'Is that in the prophecies as well?' I said.

But Megan had already turned away, and disappeared into the house.

Chapter 17

Helen – Tuesday 16th September

The sun shone in through the kitchen window as I made my breakfast coffee. Sod's law. It was a much better day for climbing mountains but with Steven due at lunchtime, there was too little time before or after. And the next day I had to drive over to Lochgilphead for the wedding, so that was out too.

I'd told Wilf I wanted a month to myself, which after my three weeks at sea meant I was due to get in touch with him soon. He hadn't mithered me at all, which spoke in his favour. Though he'd clearly been chatting with Mam from what she'd said. I found myself wishing I could talk over my increasingly tricky situation with him. I knew he was no gowk, and he could take a detached view. On the other hand, the amount of explaining involved put me off. And I couldn't completely rule out a white knight reaction in which he'd feel he had to dash over and help me out. Then I'd have him to worry about as well. Maybe I could give him a quick call during the wedding and keep it short and vague.

In the past, I'd relied on Bernie for this sort of advice. But it was clear she was much too involved in whatever the situation actually was.

The previous evening, I'd replied to her text, and then driven over straight from Milgarvie, because she was just down the road in Bearsden according to my phone. Mam and Dad might have hauled me off for a visit or two as a kid; I vaguely remembered a small house, small children, and a much younger Malcolm as a rather hapless dad. As I navigated

Bearsden I decided they must have moved since then. I drove down roads overshadowed by large mature trees, with impressive detached houses half-hidden by substantial front gardens. A different city from the one I had walked earlier.

Bernie was in what probably counted as the down-market end, with 'only' glossy white semis and manicured front lawns. I parked on the road, but I could see there was no car in her drive and assumed she hadn't yet got back from work. I walked around for a while taking in the affluence on display and thinking of Sunderland, where believe me, there isn't much of that.

By the time I got back her car was there, and I went to the door.

'Come in, Helen. I'm just now back. Sit yourself down while I get cooking – do you want the TV news on? I usually listen to it when I get back. Can I get you a drink of something?'

I asked for some tea, thinking I could allow myself one glass of wine when we ate, if wine was on offer. The lounge looked newly decorated. It had large sofas in floral fabrics, pictures of the kids in silver frames, expensive-looking ornaments, and patio doors out into a neatly organised back garden. I settled down in front of the news.

We'd missed most of the national news, so we soon got into the Scottish section. After some not very interesting headlines there were a series of features. One was on Orkney and its archaeological heritage, and focused on the Standing Stones of Stenness, and the Ring of Brodgar, which seemed even more impressive than the Callanish. The feature talked about rituals held there at different times of year by self-styled pagans, the most recent at the start of August. There was a close-up of a guy in robes leading the event, and then the camera swung slowly round a watching crowd in civvies.

'Christ Almighty!' I shouted.

Bernie rushed in. 'Helen, what's the matter? Are you OK?'

'I'm sure one of the people in that Orkney feature was McMalkin! Back in August!'

Of course Bernie wondered if I was mistaken, and I wondered too. But no, I'm good at faces and his had been distinctive, even in death. And given he'd been to the Callanish, he could have visited the Orkney stones too. I could probably rerun the footage on Watch Again later and take a screen shot. I confess though I played it down with Bernie and said I could have been mistaken.

She'd gone for a fairly quick steak and salad option, with some fancy supermarket smoked salmon and shell-fish combination as a starter, so we ate quite soon after that. And there was wine.

I gave Bernie a blow-by-blow of my own interview with Mr Tweed Jacket.

'The thing is Bernie, they don't know that you are married to my cousin and that we have known each other for donkeys. And it's what you don't tell them that comes back to bite you if or when they find out. So I'd mention that right away, especially if it's young Steven you are talking to. Say you were too surprised to go into it on Saturday on the phone. You never know, given Steven is also my cousin he might have to call the whole interview off. Conflict of interest or something.'

I told her to be upfront about meeting me in Glasgow too, but to say that we hadn't talked about Lewis, just the family stuff. Which was true. I explained that I'd told Tweed Jacket I only met the hapless Frank when I was giving him CPR. We hadn't talked about him at all, had we?

'You're right Helen, it's what you don't say. I'd already discovered he wasn't visiting the project by Saturday though, and I told them he was.'

'But you're not his manager, Bernie.'

'And I don't actually know what he was dong there either. That's true too. His manager is over in the plant, he's not someone I know. The plant is a world of its own, they keep a very firm lid on what they are up to. But oh Helen, I am worried that something bad is going on. I just don't know what. But I can't say that to the police.'

She said that in the last year there'd been an uptick in complaints about senior managers bullying people, sudden job reallocations, some managers seemed to be in-people, and others did not.

It didn't seem fair to make her feel even worse by telling her about the Americans. But what if they started after her and I hadn't warned her? So I told her the full story: Ben Lomond, the pub lunch, the encounter in the Ladies, seeing them the next day in their car, the mysterious bugging device. Though I had to add that the last item could be her F^2 colleagues for all I knew.

'That's terrible, Helen. It's not as if you have anything to do with the company.'

'It's to do with McMalkin. Find out why Frank Dooley was pursuing him and it might all become clearer.'

I didn't mention that Thierry might already know. Nothing I could say was going to help there.

Now I sighed as I drank my first coffee of the day, staring out of the kitchen window. I had a horrible feeling Bernie was heading for heartbreak.

We'd puzzled over the physics the Americans had come out with together, and Bernie told me there was possibly over-hyped talk of endless energy. There was a big announcement due in October after one final experiment, so she had heard.

'Well, Mog,' I told the cat, who was rubbing against my legs, 'where's it all ganning, eh?'

Wasn't endless energy, like perpetual motion, an impossibility? If there were such things as possible worlds, sucking their energy into ours sounded like a kind of theft. Maybe there would be a set of parallel world F^2 plants all wondering where their energy was going. This would make a good SF novel really, if it hadn't already been done.

Breakfast and then a walk, I thought. It was hours until Steven was due, assuming that Bernie's bombshell didn't put him off his visit altogether. No point in wasting all of a sunny morning.

I was feeling much cheerier by the time Steven arrived, very promptly, at midday. It's hard to feel gloomy when you have autumn sun on the hills and the loch and that bracing autumn air. I saw him arrive and went out to meet him.

He opened the driver door of his hire car – a decent saloon – but didn't get out.

'Hi, Helen. Get in and we can whizz off for lunch back round the loch a ways. I have to drive off to Rannoch Moor afterwards, so I'm in a bit of a rush.'

I got in the passenger side.

'Good of you not to cancel then, Steven. How's it going?' I asked, as we pulled back onto the road.

'Well, I promised not to talk business, didn't I? But imagine my surprise when I find out the F² HR Manager I was sent to interview in the McMalkin case is married to your – and my – cousin. Small world eh?'

He didn't sound terribly amused.

'Oh, Bernie Nicholson? I didn't realise that's who you were seeing. Yes, I've known her for years. In fact we met up in Glasgow Friday – her youngest is getting married this coming Thursday at Lochgilphead, and I'm a stand-in guest for my parents.'

'So she said. And invited me to the wedding as a cousin into the bargain. But the boss isn't going to be happy about all this – well, incestuous relationships stuff. Not happy with me, and not with you either. You didn't mention it to him.'

'He never asked me about it. Anyway, it's a family wedding thing, nothing to do with your investigation.'

At this point we arrived at a rather nicer place than Saturday's pub. But it sounded like I was going to pay for the lunch, if not in hard cash.

Once we were installed and had ordered, I played my best card.

'Steven, I have found out something that will please you and your boss too.'

I told him about my glimpse of McMalkin on the news the previous night. Then fished my phone out and showed him the freeze frame I'd later extracted. Yes, that was a bit of a game-changer for the lunch. The sun came out from behind the clouds.

'Helen, I take it all back. You are a star! I must tell the boss. Excuse me while I send him a text.'

While he was doing that, our food arrived. This place was definitely better than Saturday's pub. I had a substantial Caesar salad with grilled chicken, and it was good.

'So,' said Steven, his usual bouncy self again, 'have you climbed any good mountains?'

I'd told him about my holiday plans on my last day in Lewis, so that was a reasonable question he must have assumed would take us away from heavy business items. But of course, not so.

Now Steven got the tale of the Americans' doings from Ben Lomond onwards, minus the physics details, but including the bugging device.

'It did occur to me, Steven, that when I got the summons to another interview on what I'd been assured was not a suspicious death and for which I'd been given a death certificate to boot, that they might just have something to do with it? Maybe American Embassy people have a hot line to the police in this country?'

'A Thighearna mhor! Heavy stuff, Helen. I don't know what to say. Maybe we are both of us out of our depth here. The boss didn't say why he wanted to talk to you again, but yes, pressure from on high could be a reason. I was just pleased my tracking Frank Dooley round the island turned out to be useful.'

'I assume you thought to ask Frank what he was up to?'

'We're not total idiots you know. But the lightning seems to have fried his recent memory, at least for now. He was surprised when we told him he was in a Stornoway hospital. He thought he was on the mainland, maybe in Fort William. I'm off to see his manager at the plant next. He must have some answers for us.'

We both focused on the food for a while after that.

'Good choice of eatery, Steven, I enjoyed that,' I said. 'Hey, if it's not pushing the business angle to destruction, what was that about the old woman at the Callanish? You really couldn't find her down in the village? I've thought about it again and I don't think I dreamt her when I was stunned.'

'Nobody down in the village admitted to being up at the Calanais stones in the storm or knowing anyone else that was. But it's an odd thing. Because there are a lot of local stories about an old woman and the stones.'

There was another pause while our plates were cleared away and we ordered coffees.

'What sort of stories, man?'

'Well, you remember we went into the house of Mrs Morison to dry off?'

'Yes, and when you said she didn't speak much English, you meant she didn't speak English at all.'

Mrs Morison had been a bustling woman who produced towels and a fan heater as well as tea in short order, and rattled away to Steven in

Gaelic much too fast for me extract even the small number of words I knew.

'I asked her about the old lady, and she put it down to the ghost, or something more like 'the surviving form' of Margaret MacAskill. She's a legend round there.'

'Who was she, man? A real person or just a myth?'

'You'll find this hard to believe I think, but in fact an ancestor of yours, though not of mine. The grandmother of old Mrs McIver that we buried. Your great great grandmother. Lived by the stones. Said to be a bana-bhuidseach. Hmm, a female sorcerer, a witch I suppose you could say.'

Our coffees arrived. Which was just as well since I was temporarily speechless. I felt as if the temperature had dropped ten degrees and shivered. Took a mouthful of the hot coffee, and then a deep breath.

'If she's a legend like you say, anyone could pretend to be her. A great way to scare the tourists.'

'Oh, I'm not sure they talk about her to tourists. Some of them think she's still around in some way. Sorcerers are said to live on in some other form when they die. I'm surprised you don't know about her. Old Mrs McIver was always having people mutter about it, it's why I suppose she was so particular about the religion. My grandfather thought his brother, your grandfather, had married badly. I heard about it when I was a small child.'

'My Dad isn't into that kind of thing.' Neither religion nor superstition, and not a lot to choose between them, he'd say. I didn't know whether Steven was religious himself so I didn't give him the quote.

'You really think I met a ghost, man? Come on Steven!'

Steven shrugged.

'There are more things in heaven and earth as Hamlet once said. In your shoes I'd leave it, Helen. I'm sure it's not a police matter.'

It certainly sounded like a can of worms a sensible policeman would leave unopened. That might be why DI Sinclair was so keen for me to have imagined it.

We finished with pleasantries and Steven drove me back to the cottage.

‘So will I see you at the wedding?’ I asked.

‘Up to the boss I guess, it’s strictly speaking a working day. Do you really want a detective there? I know I said we’d just chat today, but it’s hard to turn it off, you know.’

‘Ach, don’t blame yourself man. I’m just as guilty. This whole thing seems to have a life of its own. Anyway, I’ll see you there or not. Hope this afternoon goes better for you than this morning.’

He smiled, gave me a wave, and off he went.

Chapter 18

Malcolm – Tuesday 16th September

I'd set the alarm for 6.30, as I needed to get to the station at Bridge of Orchy for the 8.15 train to Rannoch Station. But I was whacked after my visit to the Craigs, and slept through the buzzer. So, for once, I was grateful when the cat woke me around 7.30. I'd just enough time to feed the beast, and shower and dress, before jumping into the Land Rover, and heading the short distance south.

The F^2 plant at Tigh Na Cruach was about as remote as you can get on Rannoch Moor. The former lead mine sat on the north-west shore of Loch Laidon, roughly midway between the Altnafeadh Hotel and Rannoch Station. Originally, F^2 had wanted to run a road straight east across the Moor from the Hotel, tarmacking over the track past the Menzies Stone. Thankfully, our local authority successfully blocked this at the planning stage, volubly supported by RAGE, driven by an energetic Henry Craig.

For me, it would be a good two hour drive, round the bottom of the moor, up the eastern side, and then back west to Rannoch Station, to access the plant along a private sealed road down the loch side. Going by train was far preferable.

I left the Land Rover in the park and ride, bought a return ticket from the machine, and checked the departures board. The north bound train was running late. So I paid a quick visit to Petra's Pie Van, outside the station, where I picked up a cup of tea, and a roll and a sausage – not to be confused with a sausage roll, which involves no roll and little sausage. Then I settled down on a platform bench for an al fresco breakfast.

The West Highland line services the west coast between Glasgow and Mallaig, where the ferries leave for Skye. The distance is only 150 miles or so, but the terrain's rugged, much of the line is single track, and the whole journey takes over five hours.

Apart from the sleepers, the trains were pretty small by Inter City standards: ageing 156 Diesel Multiple Units, back to back, much more suited to suburban railways than long haul. And the service could get really busy in the high season, as there are only three or four trains a day.

Still, this train was quiet, apart from one carriage full of veteran cyclists, heading, I guessed, for Skye. Maybe they'd stop by the hut on their way back south.

I found a table to myself, and settled down to watch the Moor go by. As we passed Achallader, I spotted Glenys, hanging out the washing. On a whim, I waved at her. To my surprise, she waved back. You don't need bushes for the bush telegraph. Maybe Petra was another of the sisterhood.

Thirty minutes later, the train rattled into Rannoch Station. Polly Sharp was on the platform, waiting to greet me. As she walked me across to the F^2 service bus, she quietly told me that there wouldn't be much opportunity for us to talk during the tour, but she would try to point out features of the plant that I might otherwise miss.

The tour timing didn't seem well chosen: most people would be at work. A cynic might suggest that F^2 wanted to show willing without inviting too much attention. So I was surprised that there were already half dozen visitors on the bus. I didn't recognise any of them. F^2 must have been running public events on the eastern side of the Moor, in the wee towns off the Great North Road, like Aberfeldy and Pitlochry.

The new two-lane road ran along the old Forestry Commission track, through the woods beside the loch. Between the trees, I glimpsed goose gaggles, recently arrived from the Arctic, feeding and squabbling amongst the rushes. Two thirds of the way down the loch, the woods ended at the plant entrance, and we were waved through a security barrier by a guard.

It suddenly struck me how much land F² had enclosed. The plans showed only a very small huddle of buildings. There must be considerably more activity underground.

⬠

The bus drew up on a forecourt outside a long low building, covered in heather and bracken. Here, at least, F² had been as good as their word.

We went inside, and were shown into a cloakroom. Polly reminded us that there was to be no photography, and instructed us to put our cameras, and mobile phones, into a locker. They'd be perfectly safe. No doubt we'd noticed the CCTV cameras everywhere.

Polly then told us to pick up hard hats, and visitor identity badges, which doubled as radiation detectors. One of the party expressed alarm, and Polly reassured us that this was standard safety procedure, and we were all perfectly safe.

I was amused by the specious aura of scientificity. There was no way F² would have got a licence to deploy significant amounts of radioactive material. And if any one got in the way of a serious quantity of gravitons, a hard hat wouldn't be much use.

Polly next led us across the corridor into a presentation area, and, after we'd sat down, handed round glossy brochures about F²'s development programme. Most conveniently, the brochure had a map of the plant on the rear cover, though its veracity was anyone's guess. I put a copy in my pocket with a view to passing it to Henry.

We were joined by a harassed looking Dr Sam Crawford, who welcomed us, and apologised for not being able to stay for longer. They were building up to a major experimental phase, which was taking far more of their time than they'd have liked. The audience applauded politely.

Polly then ran a video presentation, which was substantially the same as the live ones I'd already attended.

After the presentation, there was a short round of questions. We then returned outside, put on our hard hats, and boarded a chain of golf buggies, strung together like the wee trains that take people round tourist attractions. I was in the lead buggy with Polly.

Polly drove us round the back of the main building, past smaller buildings that she identified as the stores, garages, the infirmary, and the cafeteria. These at least corresponded to the map.

At the far end, we stopped at what looked like the entrance to a very substantial tunnel, going down into the Moor. The entrance was shuttered with a pair of large steel doors.

Polly told us that this was the main access to the experimental area. She was sure we'd understand that, for safety reasons, we couldn't visit it. But there was nothing sinister. The tunnel followed the old lead mine workings, down into a series of galleries that currently housed the graviton detectors. The next phase involved further extending the galleries, and installing new equipment that would actually return, rather than consuming, electricity: first to make the plant self-sufficient, and then to feed the National Grid.

As we circled round to return to the main building, Polly surreptitiously nudged me. Turning to face her, I saw what looked like a pair of mangled tunnel doors, leaning against one side of the entrance. The doors seemed to have been reshaped, as if they'd been melted and forced outwards. It must have taken a huge amount of energy to warp them. Could gravitons do that? Was that the event last summer that Helen had mentioned, in her all too proper email?

Coming back past the garages, we saw two robot dogs, setting off onto the moor. Polly told us that these were an effective way of patrolling the perimeter. The dogs had stereoscopic cameras as eyes, just as Helen thought, and used advanced image processing, and pattern recognition, to look for changes in the environment. It was most unlikely that anyone would try to get in, but the dogs occasionally spotted herds of deer beyond the electric fence, and could emit ultrasound to scare them away.

That'll be right.

The dogs were fully autonomous, and didn't transmit a live feed back to their handlers, as that used too much power. When they sensed their batteries running low, they returned to the garage, and plugged themselves in, to recharge, and download their data.

That was a relief. I was now sure that nobody could have known about my and Helen's escapade: our green stones must have erased anything on the dog that spotted us.

When we got back to the building, Polly, looking pointedly at me, asked if any of us wanted to visit the rest rooms. Nobody else reacted. I said I did, and she gestured down the corridor, and told me to turn left at the end.

Unsure of what to expect, I followed her instructions, nonchalantly checking the signs on the doors that I passed. Most were marked as offices, but one was labelled *Security*, and the next *Systems*, which, I guessed, was probably a hub for the plant communication and computing infrastructure. I made a mental note of their positions, so that I could alert Henry.

I turned the corner and went in to the Gents, which was empty. I had a quick pee, for form's sake, and washed and dried my hands.

Just as I was leaving the toilet, I was passed by two technicians in white overalls, pushing a large trolley laden with electrical devices. At the far end of the corridor, they opened double doors, with an illuminated radiation warning sign above them. As the technicians wrestled the trolley through the doors, I could see banks of monitors on the far wall of the space beyond. Most of the monitors displayed flickering coloured dials, graphs and tables, like a control room in a cheesy Science Fiction film.

However, in the centre of the wall was a huge monitor, which showed a view into what looked like a vast, well lit cavern. And, in the centre of the cavern, tended by more people in white overalls, was an enormous skeletal rhombic dodecahedron, its struts pulsating an unearthly purple: the same weird purple I'd seen in the sky, during the power outage earlier in the week.

What on earth was that? All the particle detectors I'd read about involved huge tanks of liquid. That looked like something to focus particles, not detect them. But where did they get enough particles to work with?

As the doors closed behind the trolley, Polly appeared from round the corner.

'There you are!' she said, brightly. 'You better get a move on. We're just about to return to the station.'

'What the hell is that?' I asked, sotto voce.

'Not now,' said Polly.

When then?

Polly ushered me back to the cloakroom, where I collected my phone from the locker. As I was pocketing the phone, she nudged me again, and gestured towards a frame of coat hangers that I'd not noticed before. The frame was empty, apart from a grey cape of loden, on the last hanger.

I quickly walked over to the cape and lifted it up. Hanging underneath the cape were a leather aviator's helmet and goggles.

They had to be Patricia Harper's. So she hadn't vanished, well, not from the Menzies Stone, at any rate. Helen was right again. F^2 must have retrieved her, and brought her into the plant. So where was she now? If her things were still here, was she as well?

'Come on!' said Polly. 'Or you'll miss your train.'

I joined the others on the bus, my brain bursting with uncompleted inconsistencies.

'Thank you all for visiting us,' said Polly, as we disembarked at Rannoch Station. 'We hope you've found your tour interesting. Shortly, we'll email you a follow up survey. We value your opinions, and welcome your suggestions for how we might communicate what we're doing more effectively.'

I was the last off the bus.

'Here's my card,' said Polly, proffering it to me. 'We know our activities are important for Remote Resources, and we'll be happy to discuss anything of further interest with you.'

I turned the card over. Polly had written what looked like her private mobile phone number on the reverse.

The train for Glasgow was standing at the platform. As I was boarding, I spotted Polly greeting two familiar looking people. The Americans. What a good thing we weren't on the same tour. I hoped they hadn't noticed me.

The train was as empty as the one I'd come in. Half an hour later, I was back in Bridge of Orchy. I walked round to the Post Office, where

I bought an A4 envelope, and enough stamps for the brochure, first class. Then I drove back to my cottage.

In the kitchen, I laid the brochure out on the table under the central light, and photographed it from cover to cover with my phone. Then, I sealed up the brochure in the envelope and addressed it to Henry. Finally, I picked up the laptop, and drove up the road to the Altnafeadh Hotel for an early lunch.

Jeannie was at the reception. I handed her the envelope, and asked her to post it for me. She looked at the address, and raised an eyebrow, but said nothing. I suspected that she supported RAGE, and I knew that she and Glenys were pals, so she most likely drank prosecco with Megan as well. Then I settled down at Dougie's table, and watched through the window for his police car to arrive.

'Dougie!' I said, as Dougie sat down. 'How's it hanging?'

'Not brilliant,' said Dougie. 'I'm getting hassle from Major Crimes in Lewis. Did you hear about that body that was dredged up south of Stornoway about a week ago?'

Oh! Oh!

'For sure,' I said, guardedly. 'It was all over the news.'

'I've had one of their detectives on the phone,' said Dogie. 'There seems to be a link with F². You're from round there aren't you. Maybe you've come across him?'

'That seems unlikely,' I said. 'My family left the islands way before I was born. I've barely been there. Last time was five years ago, for a funeral.'

Then a wee warning note sounded in the back of my brain.

'What's the detective called?' I said.

'Steven McIver,' said Dougie. 'Ring any bells?'

McIver. That's Helen's name. Must be one of the cousins.

'There aren't so many Hebridean family names,' I said. 'So I suppose he could be related. But I don't think I've met him. What was he asking about?'

'There's some connection with an F² employee called Frank Dooley,' said Dougie. 'Have you come across him?'

'Not round here,' I said, truthfully, if evasively. 'I suppose Bernie might know him. That's my wife. Ex-wife, I suppose. She works for F^2 in Glasgow, in HR. I've told you about her, haven't I.'

'I expect he's been in touch with her,' said Dougie. 'He said he was coming down this way to visit the plant. I wonder if he'll turn up here?'

Jeannie came over to the table to take our order, pad in hand, not that she really needed it.

'Aye well,' said Dougie, as Jeannie disappeared into the kitchen. 'That's enough shop. Anyway, how are you? All psyched up for the wedding?'

'Not so you'd notice,' I said. 'To be honest, I'm dreading it.'

'It'll be fine,' said Dougie. 'It's your daughter, man! Just enjoy her big day.'

'I'm sure you're right,' I said, 'Oh, while I remember I'll be away from tomorrow afternoon until Friday. Do you suppose you could feed the cat?'

'Not a problem,' said Dougie. 'I'll ask Glenys. I'm sure she won't mind.'

Steven McIver. I wonder if he's talked to Helen. He must have done, surely. I need to warn Helen that he's sniffing around here. Well, I'll catch up with her tomorrow evening.

Chapter 19

Helen – Wednesday 17th September

After the previous day's warmth, there was a sharp wind ruffling the loch into motion and glitter as I loaded up the car. Steven's lunchtime words were embedded in my mind:

'Maybe we are both of us out of our depth here.' Woman overboard, I thought, floundering in the sea, with no rescue in sight.

But I've never wasted my time in life moaning about its obstacles, and I wasn't going to start now. There'd be a way through if I kept going.

The previous afternoon I'd chatted to Dad. He was home, though signed off work for another full week. He'd wanted to know how the holiday was going, and my attempt at an upbeat response wasn't all that convincing.

'You sound a bit low, Topsy. You know we're not nebby, you're a grown up person. But if there's anything your Mam and I can do to help, just say the word.'

For a moment I'd wanted to jump into the car and drive all the way back to Sunderland, and leave the whole mess of F^2, the stone, the Americans, the Europeans and Uncle Tom Cobley and all behind me.

But no. That was kid's stuff.

'I'll be fine, Dad. Just looking forward to the wedding.'

'Sure you are!' He'd laughed. 'Well, sorry to have landed you with standing in, Topsy, but very happy you are doing it. Say something nice to them all from us. Your Mam has sent off a present.'

That chat had been just before another of my warm-up meals, eaten under the steady green gaze of Mog, curled up on a chair next to me.

I'd finished eating and was clearing up, when my phone rang again. Not a number I knew, and I'd hesitated before I answered it.

'Hello, who's this?'

'Is that Hulkie?'

Goodness me, that had to be a work colleague from somewhere.

'Yes. Who are you, please?'

'This is Riddle. Jimmy Baillie. The deckie off the Alba na Cuan.'

'Hello, Riddle. Can I ask how you got my number?' I was not in the habit of handing it out to colleagues, whether senior or junior.

'My brother Jackie got it from his doctor, Dr Caussard. The doctor said you'd be OK with him getting in touch. But he's not terribly well, ken, so I said I'd do it for him.'

What! Riddle's brother was Thierry's patient?

'Oh. Your brother works for F^2? Yes, Dr Caussard mentioned him to me though I didn't know his name. Professional confidence and all that.'

'He does work for F^2. More's the pity. Though he's been signed off since his accident back in June. He wants to talk to you about it, ken.'

It turned out that Riddle's family lived over near Killiecrankie, which was commuting distance from the F^2 plant main entrance, in an area with not much work. Jackie had been working in operations there for just over a year until an accident in June. No, they none of them knew what accident exactly. He'd been taken to hospital unconscious with severe bruising, but that wasn't the problem. When he came to, he wasn't himself. He still wasn't.

'You'll see,' was all Riddle would say.

I wasn't sure meeting him was such a brill idea in that case, but Riddle was emphatic. Jackie needed to talk about it. His doctor thought it might help. His family thought it might help. Jackie wanted to meet me. No, it couldn't wait. So that was that. For a young man, Riddle was very firm. Very different from the ever-obliging deckie.

The main problem was working out where to meet. Killiecrankie was in the opposite direction to the wedding, but Loch Lomond was a long drive for them – Riddle was going to bring Jackie over by car. In the end, after I'd scrambled round some maps on my laptop, we picked

Crianlarich. I'd passed through on my way back from visiting Malcolm. It was about halfway between us, and didn't add too much distance to my route to the wedding venue. There was a bar/restaurant called The Leaping Fish which did coffees and bar lunches.

So here I was on a windy morning packing things into my car and feeling distinctly nervous about the meeting.

'Well, Mog, time to go time.' As he always did when I went to the car, Mog had come out to watch. I opened the back passenger door and motioned. He jumped in. A canny creature. I put the litter tray on the floor. I could feel I was getting a bit too fond of the animal. I still had not rung Troon about him, where, for all I knew, some bereft owner was putting up 'Missing' posters on every lamp-post. That was what happened back at home.

I couldn't keep him though. The days of cats on ships were long past, and who would look after him when I was away? It would be unfair on Mam and Dad. And then I found myself thinking *but if I let Wilf move in…* Ridiculous. I couldn't make a big decision like that over a cat. It was bad enough having to take Mog to the wedding. He'd have to lurk outside. The hotel would never allow a cat in a bedroom. And then maybe he'd decide to stay there. He really wasn't 'my' cat.

I was due at The Leaping Fish at 11, but I arrived a little bit early. I parked at the back of their car park and put Mog's scran behind the car where it wouldn't be too obvious. He jumped out and stretched, first head-down, front legs forward, then head-up back legs back. I could almost feel my muscles stretching in sympathy.

'Don't get yourself run over now Mog,' I instructed him, wishing that he could really understand.

The wind had dropped, and it was a pleasant morning. Maybe we were sheltered by the mountain behind Crianlarich, Ben More. It had been on my original list, though near the end of the holiday as it was one of the tougher ones to climb. I looked at it longingly. I might yet get to it.

There were picnic-style tables outside The Leaping Fish, so when my coffee was ready, I brought it back outside. I also got myself what the Scots call 'a tray bake' – a sticky tart-like rectangle, which I hoped wouldn't spoil my appetite for a sandwich. I might buy Riddle and his brother lunch, but I wasn't sure how long they planned to stay.

'Hi, Hulkie'.

Riddle had appeared from the car park, followed by his brother, Jackie.

'Hi Riddle. Nice to meet you, Jackie.' I stood up to shake hands.

Jackie Baille was noticeably older than Riddle, also taller and broader. His guarded and apprehensive face was very different from his brother's determined look. His eyes darted around as if he was afraid something or somebody might attack him any moment.

It felt strange meeting Riddle off-ship like this, and awkward too. We were no longer in the familiar on-board pecking order, making it hard to know exactly how to behave.

'What can I get you guys?' I asked. The good thing about male environments is that there are standard ways of dealing with awkwardness. As a frequent cause of such things I know all about them.

I returned with teas and more tray bakes.

'Jackie,' I began. 'Your brother here said both you and your family thought it would help you to chat. I'm keen to help, but I don't want to cause you pain or upset you. So you're in charge here.'

My med training had included almost nothing on mental issues, just a bit on PTSD relevant to people fished out of the sea alive rather than dead. Not putting sufferers under pressure was the main take-home.

'Aye,' said Jackie.

'Don't worry, I'll stop things if it looks too much, ken,' said Riddle.

'I saw you on the television,' Jackie said slowly, with evident effort. 'And I saw, I saw…'. He stopped, took several breaths, but didn't continue.

'Our mither said he reacted to that drawing of the man we pulled out,' said Riddle.

'McMalkin?' I pulled out my phone and found the screen shot of McMalkin at Orkney, showed it to Jackie. 'This man?'

His head twitched slightly as if he was trying to nod.

'Was he involved in your accident?' I asked.

His head twitched again and he tried and failed to speak. I could see that whatever the accident had been, he found it impossible to talk about it.

'They,' he said. 'They.'

'They? How many?' I asked.

He struggled to speak yet again and then banged the table in frustration. Oh, wait a minute, banged it three times.

'Three?'

He arched his arms outwards above his shoulders. Opened his mouth wide as if he was shouting something, but made not a sound. Christ, this was hard work. And was it helping or making things worse for the poor man?

Then he said 'Stones. Stones, stones.'

Oh, this was what Thierry had meant. If it had been just the two of us, I might have fished the stone out right there and then to see what happened. But Riddle would guess for sure where I'd got it and it would make me look terrible. So I hesitated.

'Maybe something to do with all those stones that poor man had in his pockets?' Riddle said helpfully.

'Could be,' I said.

Jackie swivelled round and pointed at the door into the bar. Looked at me, pointed again.

'Door?' I said. Then 'Gate?' Everyone said F^2 were working on a Transilience Gate, whatever that was.

Jackie looked pleased. Then pointed at the door again, flung his arms out again.

'They came from the gate?' Jackie beamed. Now I was getting somewhere. Not that it made any sense. The Americans said that the gate was intended to extract gravitons from parallel worlds, not people. But what if the stones interacted with the gate?

At this point, there was a feline chirrup and Mog jumped right onto our table, only just missing the tea things. What a wazzock. Talk about a badly timed distraction.

'Sorry guys,' I said. 'I found this cat. It seems quite attached to me.' I was about to lift the animal back off the table when Mog turned towards Jackie, put his front paws on Jackie's chest, and stared into his face, purring very loudly.

Riddle laughed. 'Now it seems attached to you,' he said to his brother. 'I never had you down as a cat person, ken.'

But something really weird happened. Mog gave Jackie a cat-kiss – touched his nose to Jackie's nose. The man's face changed right in front of our eyes. Hard to describe, but it was as if all the muscles relaxed and then came back to life again.

The cat gave him a steady look and then jumped off the table.

Not as much as we jumped when Jackie said, in a totally different voice: 'So d'ya think it's too early for a half, Jimmy? I could do with whetting ma whistle.'

Then looked at me as if he didn't know who I was.

'How d'ya do Miss. I'm Jackie Baillie, dinnae think we've met.'

'We were talking about your accident,' I said.

'Oh, Jimmy will tell you I have them all the time. Clumsy is ma middle name. But nae harm done.'

'Jackie! You're back!' said Riddle. 'Hulkie, that cat of yours is a miracle-worker!'

Well, I'd heard of pet therapy where animals were taken into old folks' homes to cheer people up, but this was a whole level up. Had I really seen what my eyes told me I had?

Riddle and Jackie were now joshing each other. Riddle looked as if Christmas had come early. He turned to me.

'Hulkie, I can't thank you enough – or your cat anyways. I hope this is going to last, but I must take Jackie back so our mither can see how much better he is.'

I'd like to say I was as happy about it all, rather than deeply worried. But I forced cheerfulness.

'Well, Riddle, Jackie, good to see things are on the up again. I guess I'd better make a move too, I've a family wedding tomorrow and I've to drive to Lochgilphead this afternoon. All the best now to the two of you.'

When I got back to the car, Mog was sitting by the back door, giving himself a good wash. Looking like any other cat. I opened the door.

'Gan in.'

To be honest, I was tempted to leave him in the car park. But something told me that wouldn't be easy. He might not be my cat, but it looked like I might be his human.

Yet again it was too late in the day to climb a mountain. Even the closest ones took more than five hours and then I had to get to the hotel. I fiddled with my phone until I found a 2-3 hour walk round the edge of Loch Fyne, on my route to Lochgilphead. Not very challenging, but scenic, and hopefully calming. I nipped back into the bar to collect some sandwiches, which they put in a bag for me. Then off we went, with Mog soundly asleep in his usual furry doughnut on the back seat.

I ate my bait in a Forestry Commission car park, brooding. People coming through the F^2 gate? Was that for real and not just Jackie's imaginings? One of them McMalkin? It would explain why F^2 were so keen to track him down of course. But assuming it was physically possible, why would anyone risk life and limb by what – jumping into a parallel world?

And McMalkin was dead, but were there others still on the loose?

Still, the walk worked its magic. It was a mixture of forest and loch-side, and at one point I saw two black bobbing heads in the water that turned out to be otters play-chasing each other. And there were deer in the forest, vanishing into the dapple from the sun and moving clouds. I felt better afterwards.

When I got to Lochgilphead, I checked out the Catholic church. It was just round the corner from the Parish church. Hopefully that didn't have a wedding on at the same time – embarrassing to turn up at the wrong one. The reception hotel was another ten miles up the road northwards along the coast. This was gentle country after the mountains and glens further back, pretty flat, with fields and woods. You'd hardly know you were in Scotland.

The hotel was visible in the distance before I got there, on a small junction off the main road. It was called the Slockavullin Castle, and though it didn't look much like a castle, it was much older than the Lewis one. Built in what must be local stone and only a couple of storeys high, the central building had expanded into wings either side of a courtyard. I left the car round the side. Mog was awake and looked as if he planned to exit as soon as I let him.

'Haud yer pash,' I told him. 'Back in a mo.'

Then I crunched over the gravel to the main entrance where I was greeted by a youth in a kilt. He took my kit bag before I could stop him and followed me into a foyer carpeted in a dark blue and green tartan.

I gave my parents' names and explained they should have already notified someone that I was taking over their booking. That was all fine, the woman behind the desk assured me. Gave me a room key, and a slip with an internet password on it.

'One more thing,' I said, after she'd finished. 'I have a cat with me. I know you won't want him in the room. I can leave his food outdoors. But I don't want him chased off. He's a large grey tabby.'

'Yes Madam, I'm afraid we do have a no pets rule. But I'll make sure staff know about your cat.'

The kilted youth was still holding my kit bag so there was nothing for it but to let him follow me up to the next floor with it. I fished out a couple of pound coins in the certainty he'd want tipping for his unwanted service. He didn't scowl but neither did he smile. Which meant – I hoped – that I'd judged it right. I much prefer the cruise ship approach where a single service charge is collected from passengers before they leave and then shared out.

OK, time to get back downstairs, let Mog out and put his food down. Canny animal wasn't the word, I felt. He'd be fine. Maybe he'd like it here and adopt the place.

I took the sweeping central staircase back down. It felt like I needed a ball gown to do it justice. At the bottom I found cousin Malcolm at Reception, looking a bit harassed. He must have just arrived.

I told him I was off to feed the cat and we could meet in the bar later. He muttered something about wedding rehearsals. Poor gowk, father of the bride and all that. Thank goodness I was only a spectator.

Chapter 20

Malcolm – Wednesday 17th September

Another morning, another phone call. Bernie. Not really surprising, I suppose, given how close the wedding loomed.

'Hello Mal,' said Bernie.

'Morning Bernie,' I said. 'All set for the wedding?'

'That's why I'm calling,' said Bernie. 'You haven't forgotten the rehearsal this evening, have you?'

'No Bernie,' I said, patiently. 'Lochgilphead. St Margaret's Church. 6pm.'

'That's good,' said Bernie. 'Not that you've a lot to do. Just walking Alison down the aisle.'

'I'm not sure that needs to be rehearsed,' I said. 'I won't be chewing gum.'

'You need to take this seriously,' said Bernie. 'For Alison's sake. She wants to make sure everything's set up for the video.'

'The video?' I said. 'What video?'

'It's what young people do,' said Bernie. 'To keep a record of the special day.'

'We were happy with photos,' I said. 'But if that's what Alison wants. Anyway, I'll see you there this evening.'

Why had Bernie phoned? This degree of friendly banter was unusual.

'Mal,' said Bernie, 'before you go, I don't suppose you're bringing anyone, are you?'

'To the wedding?' I said. 'Why would I bring anyone? It's just family and friends, isn't it?'

'So there's no one special in your life?' said Bernie. 'No one you want to introduce to everyone?'

Pennies are for dropping.

'Look Bernie,' I said. 'I know things aren't good between us. But we are still married. And I did offer you a divorce, and you said no. What I do is my concern, but, if I'd met anyone special, as you put it, you and the kids would know all about it.'

There was what felt like a long silence.

'Look Mal,' said Bernie, finally. 'I think I have met someone special. It's all happened very suddenly. And I'd like them to come with me to the wedding.'

'Just like that?' I said. 'Have you told Alison? What does she think?'

'She says all she wants is for me to be as happy as she is,' said Bernie.

This isn't happening. Is it?

'So who is this special person,' I said.

'Oh Mal,' said Bernie. 'Don't be like that. He's called Thierry. He's a colleague, though he's obviously become a lot more than that.'

'A lot more than that?' I said. 'You're not...'

'No Mal, we're not sleeping together,' said Bernie, sharply. 'Not that it's any of your business.'

'Well Bernie,' I said. 'You do what you like.'

'Honestly Malcolm,' said Bernie. 'It's at an early stage. But it feels right. So I'd like you all to meet Thierry.'

'I'll try to be civil,' I said. 'But this has big implications for both of us.'

'Of course,' said Bernie. 'Thanks for being so understanding. See you this evening.'

'See you,' I said.

And put the phone down.

So understanding? Why am I so upset? I don't really want to be with Bernie, any more than she wants to be with me. But so long as we're supposedly together, I don't have to think about what, if anything, happens next. Well, I suppose I've now spent the best part of five years not thinking about it. But why today, when everything else is so crazy?

Hang on. If Thierry's a colleague, then he works at F^2, obviously. So, I wonder if he's involved in whatever's going on at the plant? I should have asked Bernie. Bastards!

I got up and fed the cat. I was just about to have a shower, when the phone rang again. It was Henry Craig, thanking me for the brochure. Could I give him any more details?

I told Henry I thought that entering the plant unobserved from the Rannoch Station side would be pretty well impossible. They might gain access from the loch side, but they'd have to get past the electric fence. Their best bet might be through the gate up by the Menzie's Stone. Whatever they did, they'd need to contend with the robot dogs. I also quickly described what I knew of the layout of the main building.

Henry thanked me, and said that maybe the best way would be to march in publicly through the main gate. I wished him luck with that, and rang off. Loony tunes.

I didn't mention the purple dodecahedron. If it could blast its way through heavy steel doors, then goodness knows what it could do to unwary intruders. Maybe I should have mentioned it.

I dressed, had breakfast, made myself some sandwiches, and packed a holdall. Then I went up the road to Dougie's and banged on the front door.

'Come in!' shouted Glenys.

I went through to the front room. Glenys was seated at her knitting machine.

'Hey Malcolm,' said Glenys. 'Dougie said you'd like us to feed your cat. That's fine. We've got your keys.'

'Thanks,' I said. 'I'll leave the food out. Please just give her a measure of the dry stuff, morning and evening, and keep the water topped up. I've fed her this morning and I should be back on Friday afternoon.'

'That's fine,' said Glenys. 'She's a nice wee soul. So where's the wedding?'

'Didn't I tell Dougie?' I said. 'Lochgilphead.'

'Nice!' said Glenys. 'Where are you staying?'

'Some swanky place up the road,' I said. 'Slockavullin. I think it's near Kilmartin.'

'Kilmartin!' said Glenys. 'That's a major centre of power.'

'Power?' I said. 'Like the quarry?'

'Like Callanish and Brogdar,' said Glenys 'There are significant standing stones all around. If you've time, go to Nether Largie. But, to be safe, wear an arrowhead, and take your green stone.'

To be safe. But she is feeding the cat.

'Thanks for the tips,' I said, checking that the stone was still in my pocket. 'I'll do that.'

'I know you're sceptical,' said Glenys. 'Just try to keep an open mind.'

'Thanks again,' I said. 'See you in a couple of days.'

'Have fun!' said Glenys.

And turned back to her knitting machine.

There were no hut visitors all day, like the previous afternoon. I'd half expected Steven McIver to turn up, but was frankly relieved that I didn't have to face him.

In the morning, I finished off the new display board design, and sent if off to the office for them to arrange the printing. After lunch, I tidied up the public area into the back office. Just before 3pm, I went round checking that the building was otherwise secure, and I drove up to Fort William.

I left the Land Rover in the roundabout car park on the edge of town, and went up the High Street in search of the arrowheads. The jeweller recognised me as I came through the door.

'Here you go,' said the jeweller, handing me four clear sealed bags. Each held an arrowhead, but they were all strung on leather thongs.

'Thank you,' I said, 'but I'd asked for silver chains. Could you restring them, please?'

'The ladies generally prefer the leather thongs,' said the jeweller, winking at me.

The ladies? How many Wiccans are there?

I checked my watch. I really had no time to hang around, if I was to make it to the wedding rehearsal on time. Without arguing, I paid the jeweller, returned to the car, and set off south, down the coast road to Oban.

One of the advantages of living somewhere remote is that there aren't so many roads. And one of the disadvantages is that there are only a small number of routes, and it's easy to become familiar with them. I suspect that most rural accidents aren't caused by visitors, who seem to drive everywhere in 1st gear, especially on single track roads, but by over-confident locals, especially young ones. I learnt to drive in the city, defensively, so lots of my friends find me over cautious. But I've yet to prang the Land Rover. Well, I have bogged it down in ditches a couple of times. More than a couple.

The road was quiet, and it only took ninety minutes down to Oban. Unfortunately, I got stuck behind a very slow tractor, on the narrow windy road all the way to Kilmartin. By the time I was parking outside the hotel main building, my phone was pinging more and more frequently.

Lots of text messages. All from Bernie. Where was I?

I replied curtly, claiming I'd be another twenty minutes, knowing I could make it in less. I rushed into the hotel and registered. I was trying to persuade the concierge that I really didn't need anyone to garage my vehicle, when I saw Helen coming down the stairs.

'Malcolm!' called Helen, hurrying past me. 'I've got to feed the cat. See you in the bar?'

'Later,' I said. 'I'm really late for the wedding rehearsal.'

But she'd already gone.

I leapt into the Land Rover, and drove down to Lochgilphead, far faster than I'd usually dare. I so hoped this Thierry wouldn't be there. I got to the church with five minutes to go. Bernie was standing in the porch, wringing her hands.

'Oh Mal!' she said, pulling me to her. 'Thank goodness you're here. It's total chaos. I do so wish Alison had let me organise things.'

Grudgingly, I gave her a quick peck on the cheek, and went into the church, trying to avoid the festoons of cable down the aisle. I was relieved that there was no sign of anyone who might be a Thierry.

'Hello Dad!' shouted Alison, from in front of the altar, in confabulation with the priest, and what I guessed was the film crew. 'Better late than never!'

Alison bounded up the aisle and gave me an enormous hug. I was completely disarmed. My wee girl. Getting married. My anger and upset melted away.

'What's happening?' I said when we finally disengaged.

'The lights are all set up,' said Alison. 'We just need a sound check, and then we're good to go. You know Grant, of course.'

Alison's swain joined us, and gingerly held out his arm.

'Grant!' I said, shaking his hand. 'Good to see you.'

'You too,' said Grant. 'God, I could do with a drink.'

'Later!' said Alison, cheerfully. 'Now, has everyone got their scripts? Here's yours, dad.'

She handed me four pages of double sided A4, stapled together. I quickly scanned them. Thankfully, my role was minimal. I'd forgotten how involved a church wedding is, though. I hadn't actually been to one since my own.

Grant and I sat down in a nearby pew, while Alison bustled around.

'All set?' I said.

'I've got a colossal hangover,' said Grant. 'The stag night was a blast. I'm sorry you weren't there.'

I'd found the invitation far too late to do anything about it. Of course I couldn't say that.

'I'm sorry too,' I said.

We sat in an awkward silence. What do you say to your son-in-law about-to-be? Words of wisdom? But what the hell did I know about a successful marriage.

'Are your family here?' I asked, finally.

'Back at the Hotel,' said Grant. 'I'd really like you to meet them.'

'That'll be nice,' I said. 'Do you know if Alison's brothers have got here yet?'

'I'm not sure,' said Grant. 'It's all been a bit crazy. Alison's got everything planned in fine detail. As far as I can tell, all I have to do is agree to marry her...' I laughed. '... which I'm really happy with, of course!'

'Don't worry!' I said. 'You'll both do just fine. She is a wee bit of control freak, though. Gets it from her mum.'

I felt in my pocket, and took out one of the arrowheads, still in its bag.

'Look,' I said. 'I'd really appreciate it if you could give this to Alison. Maybe she could wear it tomorrow. Discreetly of course. But it would mean a lot to me. It's a wee token of where I am now. But not if it's a bother.'

Grant took the bag and looked at it.

'Of course,' said Grant. 'What is it? It looks really old.'

'It's a Neolithic arrowhead,' I said. 'Calc-silicate hornfels. It's metamorphic rock, from Creag Na Caillich.'

Now it was Grant's turn to laugh.

'Ali said you were into geology,' said Grant. 'I don't have a clue what any of that means, but I'm sure she'll treasure it.'

'Thank you,' I said. 'Thank you. Oh, there's some money for you both from Alison's grandmother. We can work out how to get it to you later.'

'That's very decent of her,' said Grant. 'I know she doesn't approve. Please thank her.'

'Of course,' I said.

Bernie came bustling towards us.

'Now then,' she said, officiously, 'if you two old men have finished gossiping, Alison says we're to get started.'

Alison came and grabbed my arm.

'Come on Dad,' she said. 'Time to dispose of me.'

'I'll never do that,' I said as she propelled me back out to porch.

The rehearsal went remarkably smoothly. Of course there were only half a dozen or so of us. And all I had to do was follow the script, and sit down and stand up at the right moments, once I'd handed Alison over to Grant.

Around seven thirty, I was feeling pretty peckish. I couldn't see there was any need for me to hang around any longer, so I made my excuses and left. The sun was setting but the moon was well risen. It would be full by the weekend: a moon for a harvest.

At the Slockavullin junction was a sign to the Nether Largie stones, the ones Glenys had mentioned. This was far more tangible than the quarry where I'd found the arrowheads. But stones are stones. I don't mind at all how people interpret them; for me they're nothing more than reminders of a past that we really can't grasp.

As before, I pulled up at the front of the Hotel. This time, I was happy for the porter to take my bags and the Land Rover keys. I picked up the swipe card for my room from the front desk, and found my way to the bar. Helen, sitting at the counter, hailed me as I came in.

Chapter 21

Both – Wednesday 17th September

'Hi, Malcolm. You well rehearsed?'

'Hello Helen,' said Malcolm, sitting on the bar stool beside her. 'I've just got a bit part, thank goodness. You got here all right then?'

'I'll tell you about getting here in a mo. Can I get you something to drink?'

'That sounds great! A pint of the Druid's Ruins, please. I see they've got it on tap.'

Helen waved at the barman and ordered the beer. When it arrived Malcolm took a deep draught.

'Ah, that feels better. So, tell me about your journey. Mine was really straightforward, until I got stuck behind a tractor.'

'First I need to tell you something else,' said Helen, looking around carefully and dropping her voice. 'My cousin Steven, well, your cousin too, works for the Lewis police. I met him when I was over there. He's investigating McMalkin. To cut the story short, he had to go and see Bernie and she invited him to the wedding!'

'Really? My mate Dougie, the local polis, told me he'd been phoned by a Steven McIver from Lewis, about some Rannoch connection with the body you found. So he's our cousin? Don't think I'd heard of him before. And he's coming to the wedding? This is mental! What do we say to him?'

'Oh, he's Ok, man. Just remember he's a bobby. He did warn me if he came he wouldn't be able to turn the detective bit off, but. He was at the Callanish stones when the lightning struck. He found out that Frank Dooley, that F^2 man, was following McMalkin,' said Helen.

'You're joking! So your dead body's linked to F^2 as well? How often have you come across Steven? How much does he know? If he knows about Bernie, does he know about me?'

'He didn't know about you, but after meeting Bernie, now he does. So he's bound to want to chat with you. Just be careful what you say! He doesn't know about our stones, and let's keep it that way.'

'Jesus Christ, Helen! This is the last thing we need!'

'Tough cookies. It is how it is,' said Helen. 'So what was the plant like?'

'I think I've found out what happened to the woman the Americans were after,' said Malcolm. 'When I went into the plant yesterday, I saw her cycling gear in the cloakroom. You were right. F^2 must have collected her and taken her through the fence.'

'Did you find out what happened back in June?'

Malcolm told Helen about the buckled doors, and the pulsating dodecahedron in the underground cavern.

'At least we've got someone friendly on the inside,' finished Malcolm. 'Nice woman called Polly Sharp. Works in PR. She's a whistle-blower.'

'Does she know anything about people coming through that dodecahedron gate into the plant from somewhere?' asked Helen.

'That thing's a gate? Didn't look like it went anywhere, to me. Who said it was a gate?'

'I told you about that on Sunday? The Americans, and my online search.'

Helen went over Martha and Dean's physics discussion again, and what a Transilience Gate might be.

'They were talking theory so they didn't say what one would look like. But I'd bet on your purple glowing thing being it.'

'But you said it was a graviton machine,' said Malcolm. 'How can anyone have come through it? Where did you hear that?'

'Well, Thierry has a patient who was injured in June...' said Helen.

'Thierry?' said Malcolm, cutting her short. 'What the hell's he got to do with anything? What are you on about…?'

Helen was about to reply, when she was cut short again as Steven came into the bar.

'Hello, Helen. You'll see I've made it to the wedding.' said Steven.

'Hi Steven,' said Helen. 'This is my cousin, Malcolm Nicholson, who's married to Bernie. So he's the father of the bride. Malcolm, this is our cousin, Steven McIver, all the way from Lewis.'

'Hello Steven,' said Malcolm, holding out a hand. 'Good to meet you. Yet another cousin, eh? Can I get you a drink? The Druid's Ruin's nice.'

They briefly chatted about exactly how they were related. Then when Steven's drink arrived, they all moved to a table.

'Bernie didn't tell me there'd be a Lewis contingent,' said Malcolm.

'To be honest, I was only invited yesterday,' said Steven. 'I am working on the McMalkin case – that body Helen was involved with.'

'What a strange coincidence,' said Malcolm.

'Well, I was sent to interview Bernie, as the HR manager for F^2,' said Steven. 'Imagine my surprise when she told me she was as good as family. My boss was surprised too, which is never good. But Helen saved the situation for us all when she told me McMalkin was seen in Orkney in August. With a screenshot to prove it. A whole new area of investigation.'

'There's an actual picture of McMalkin?' said Malcolm. 'I only saw the artist's impression on the news. Have you got it on you, Helen?'

Helen found the image on her phone and passed it over to Malcolm.

'Bloody hell!' said Malcolm, staring at the screen. 'That's Patricia Harper! Behind McMalkin!'

'Who is Patricia Harper?' asked Steven.

Malcolm and Helen looked at each other.

'Well…' started Malcolm.

'Hello you lot!' called Bernie, entering the bar. Thierry followed her in.

'I'm glad you're all together,' said Bernie. 'That makes introductions so much easier. This is Thierry Caussard, my good friend. Thierry, I think you know Helen. This is Malcolm, and his cousin Steven.'

'Enchanted to meet you all,' said Thierry. 'And especially you, Malcolm.' He inclined his head. 'Can I buy everyone some drinks?'

'While I've got the chance,' said Malcolm, as Thierry went over to the bar, 'I'd like to give each of you a small wedding token. I've already given one to Alison.'

He reached in his pocket, took out two bagged arrowheads, and passed one to Helen and one to Bernie. Helen looked at her arrowhead as if she thought it might bite her.

'How thoughtful,' she said.

'Oh Malcolm!' said Bernie. 'Ever the geologist. What a strange present. What's it supposed to be?'

Thierry returned to the table.

'The drinks will be here in a short moment.'

'Look at what Malcolm's just given me,' said Bernie, passing the arrowhead to Thierry.

'That is so interesting" said Thierry. 'Calc-silicate hornfels metamorphic rock. It is very old.'

'Goodness!' said Malcolm. 'How do you know that? Are you a geologist? Is that why you're with F^2?'

'Oh no,' said Thierry quickly. 'I am a medical doctor and a psychotherapist. But in childhood I wanted to be a geologist and I maintain my interest in the field.'

'How curious,' said Malcolm. 'You'll know it's a Neolithic arrowhead then.'

'But naturally,' said Thierry. 'And it's a most appropriate wedding gift. It symbolises an association with the ancient earth. And also with the female-male coupling. In the archetype, the point represents the male organ, and the piercing for the thong the female.'

There was a silence.

'So how did the wedding rehearsal go then?' asked Helen.

'It wasn't how I'd have organised it,' said Bernie. 'But Alison seemed happy, and that's the main thing.'

A young waitress arrived with a tray of drinks. While she handed them round, her green eyes seemed fixed on the arrowheads. She touched her throat lightly, where a leather thong was just visible.

'Were you and Grant doing man talk, Malcolm?' continued Bernie. 'You seemed very tight together.'

'Just getting to know each other a bit more,' said Malcolm. 'I've barely met him. He seems all right. I hope they get on better than we have.'

There was another silence.

'So Thierry, what brings you to Scotland?' asked Steven. 'From your name, you are French?'

'Ah, this is a long story of unhappy family circumstances,' said Thierry. 'There was a need to start a different life. Scotland has a connection with France in history and a strong medical tradition. I decided to set up a private practice in Glasgow. It was thanks to Bernie that I come to do some work for F^2.' He smiled at her warmly, and she smiled back.

Helen rolled her eyes at Malcolm. Malcolm shrugged.

'So what work do you do for them, exactly?' asked Steven.

'I am in charge of occupational health,' said Thierry. 'So I help any employees who have work-related stress or any psychological problems from the pressure of their lives.'

'Are there many of those?' asked Steven.

'Not so many,' Thierry replied. 'This is why I can do this work alongside my private practice.'

'I heard there was a big accident there in June though,' said Helen, brightly. 'Did you get any patients from that?'

'In my profession, confidentiality is fundamental,' Thierry said. 'So perhaps we should find a different topic.'

'I'm really hungry,' said Malcolm. 'I assume the restaurant's still open. Have you all eaten?'

'That's a great suggestion,' said Steven. 'I'm starving.'

Chapter 22

Malcolm – Thursday 18th September

I'd found it really hard to get to sleep. It was partly not being in my own bed. And it was partly anxiety about the wedding. But, mostly, I felt utterly lost in labyrinthine confusions. I'd follow the left hand wall, if only I could locate it. But it seemed like every time I thought I'd found a causeway, it led me into another ditch.

I finally dropped off around 5am, but I'd barely slept for an hour when I was awakened by sustained rattling on the windowpane. At first, I thought it was an autumnal hailstorm, but the noise was far too regular. I got up and drew back the curtain. The owl stopped pecking at the glass, sat upright, and stared directly at me.

Surely not the same owl?

Half asleep, I felt in my coat pocket, found the pouch, took out the green stone, and held it up to the glass. The owl winked and flew away.

Why did I do that? Too tired to care, I put the green stone away, curled up under the covers, and went back to sleep.

At 8am the alarm on my phone woke me. I showered and dressed. Then I went down to the breakfast room. I'm not usually keen on hotel buffets, but this one was top notch, with a sous chef, in a tall white hat, wrangling the frying pan.

I'd had more than enough company the previous night. I'd finally met Grant's parents. And I'd caught up with the boys, and their partners. So I found a table to myself on the far side of the room.

I was tucking in to Loch Fyne's finest kippers, when I realised that Steven was hovering near me, brimming plate in hand. Reluctantly, I asked him to join me.

'That is very nice of you Malcolm,' said Steven. 'I'd hoped to find Helen but she's not here. You are the only other person I really know.'

'That's an impressive plateful, Steven. I hope you're leaving space for the wedding breakfast.'

'As wedding breakfasts go it is a fairly late one, and weddings take energy, don't you agree?'

'Lots of psychic energy for me, as I'll mostly be sitting down. Are you a dancer?'

'Oh, ceilidhs are a vital part of the skillset in Lewis. No doubt I can work the food off on the dance-floor, yes.'

'I don't suppose Helen has much time for dancing on that boat of hers.'

'It sounds as if they had other things on their mind on her latest voyage. It's certainly a plateful of work for us following up on McMalkin. He seems to have left hardly any visible mark on the world until his body turned up. That's why Helen's discovery was so important and also why I was so interested that the two of you recognised someone else in the picture. "Patricia Harper", I think you said?'

Here we go.

'I don't think Helen recognised her, strictly speaking,' I said. 'But, yes, I did.'

'So where did you come across her,' said Steven, 'if you don't mind my asking? I'm not being official here, but of course you know it might get official later.'

I explained that I'd already talked with Dougie, and I repeated what I'd told him.

'It's hard to credit,' said Steven, 'that you would remember so instantly a random visitor that you only saw for a few minutes?'

'Well,' I said, 'she was very distinctive. And she was looking for a local geological site. So I gave her directions.'

'So did she say why she wanted to visit the quarry?'

Careful now.

'She had a broken arrowhead,' I said. 'Like the ones I gave Helen and Bernie, last night. She wanted to find a replacement. I recognised the rock. Calc-silicate hornfels. Metamorphic. Very old. And it only comes from one place near the Moor.'

'So,' said Steven, 'I suppose that Helen may have mentioned to you that McMalkin had exactly the same sort of arrowhead round his neck. Our local experts say the same as you about its composition.'

'I saw that one on the TV news, before I talked with Helen. There aren't so many places where the arrowheads were made, so it is likely there's a connection.'

'And have you any idea what the connection might be?'

'It's almost certainly nonsense, but there may be a link with pagan beliefs. The arrowhead is an ancient symbol of power. I suppose they could both have been adherents.'

'That's interesting,' said Steven. 'And do you know if she went to the quarry, or anything else about her movements?'

That is the big question, isn't it.

'Well, this is going to sound crazy,' I said, 'but two Americans reported seeing a body up on the moor that looked like hers. I went up to check but there was nothing there.'

'And did these Americans seem reliable folk?' said Steven. 'Can you tell me any more about them?'

'How would I know? They seemed pleasant enough. An older couple. Well dressed. The details are in the book back at the office. We log everyone that drops by. But Patricia Harper only left her name.'

'Why would these Americans think a body was Patricia Harper's?'

'They didn't think that. But, as I said, she was very distinctive. They claimed the body they saw was dressed in a poncho and a flying helmet. Patricia Harper was actually wearing a cape. But she also had a flying helmet and goggles.'

'Yes, Helen's picture seems to show her in a cape. When you went to the location the Americans had told you about, was there any other sign of her? For example, you said she was riding a bicycle.'

No avoiding it now.

'Yes, I did find her bicycle,' I said, 'but there was no other sign of her. It's strange, actually. I took the bicycle back to where I work, but the next day it looked like someone had broken in and stolen it. I didn't bother reporting it. It was probably bored teenagers. Happens all too frequently. I'm sure it's the same where you are.'

'Well, it's a pity you didn't report finding the bicycle,' said Steven. 'Where exactly did you find it?'

'Haven't you talked with Dougie, our local polis? Anyway, it was up by the Menzies Stone. It's on the old boundary between the counties. Just on the edge of the F^2 plant, up by the fence, where there's a gate. Maybe you should ask F^2 if they know anything?'

'Maybe I will. Thanks Malcolm, this has all been very useful. Away from business now, and onto the fun, as they say.'

And Steven commenced an energetic consumption of his full Scottish.

When we'd finished eating, I went back to my room. That was difficult. I hoped I hadn't dumped Dougie in it.

I had a wash and brush up, and clambered into my suit. Then I went downstairs to the hotel lobby, and sat on a sofa under a potted palm, well away from the heaving throng. The men seemed evenly split between suits and kilts: Steven looked like a porridge oats advert, in what I presumed was the McIver tartan. The women were a curious mix of posh frock and business suit. Helen really stood out in her feathered blue hat, which struck me as an odd choice for someone already so prominent.

A young waitress came across with a tray of bubbling drinks in tulip glasses. I asked for something alcohol-free. I've never been a great one for drinking before sunset. It makes me charismatic for half an hour, and then I get a headache. The waitress seemed strangely familiar, but she'd vanished before I could place her.

The lobby cleared, leaving Alison alone by the entrance, waving off her guests departing for the church. I stood up and joined her.

'Hello Dad,' said Alison. 'All set for my big day?'

'I should be asking you that,' I said. 'I think I'm also meant to ask if you're sure you want to go through with it, but I know the answer.'

'Och, dad, you're so sweet,' said Alison. 'Of course I'm sure. I love Grant and he loves me. You do like him, don't you?'

'I barely know him,' I said, 'but he seems very fond of you, and that's all that matters. Of course, I told him that, if anything happens to you, there'd be a horse's head on his pillow.'

'Excellent!' said Alison. 'I'll remind him of that if he ever gets grumpy.'

'To be honest,' I said, 'I'm quite nervous about getting this right. I don't want to let you down.'

'It's me that's supposed to have nerves,' said Alison. 'You'll be fine. It's all just pantomime. But it's got to be done properly. Here, I've got something for you.'

Alison went over to a small table, picked up a buttonhole, of a single red rose dressed with forget-me-nots, and pinned it to my lapel.

'There,' she said. 'Now you're almost as bonnie as me.'

A large and shiny black limousine drew up outside.

'This is our cue!' said Alison. 'Off we go!'

The wedding felt interminable. Once I'd walked Alison down the aisle, just as we'd rehearsed, I sat quietly at the front, with Bernie and our sons, while the priest droned on. After an age of bobbing up and down, the happy couple kissed, and we all retraced our steps to the church porch, for a combinatorial explosion of photographs. Luckily it didn't rain.

We were late back to the hotel, but the wedding breakfast turned out to be a stand up buffet, so there was no further delay. I did my best to be convivial, but I'd soon had enough of the wisdom of crowds, and, as soon as was polite, I slipped away to my room.

There was still a fair wait before the reception, so I fired up the laptop, logged into the hotel Wifi, and checked my email. One new message. From Polly Sharp. Starting with her mobile number. Might we talk?

Polly had been growing on me. I rang her then and there.

'Hello?' said Polly. 'Who is this?'

'It's Malcolm,' I said. 'Malcolm Nicholson. You asked me to call you.'

'Oh Malcolm,' said Polly 'Thanks so much for getting back to me. I'll add you to my contacts.'

'I'll do the same,' I asked. 'So how can I help?'

'I wondered if we might meet, please,' said Polly. 'Maybe this evening?'

'Sorry,' I said, 'But I'm away over night. How about after I'm home tomorrow?'

'That should work,' said Polly. 'But well before Sunday, please. What are you up to?'

I don't want to have this conversation.

'I'm at a wedding,' I said. 'Near Lochgilphead.'

'That's a bonnie part of the world,' said Polly. 'Not your own, I hope.'

And laughed nervously.

'No,' I said. 'Certainly not my own.'

'Well, I hope it's fun,' said Polly. 'I'm not a great one for weddings. All that family. All that hanging around.'

'You're right there,' I said. 'But needs must.'

'Someone close?' said Polly.

I really don't want to have this conversation.

'My daughter,' I said.

'Goodness!' said Polly. 'I didn't realise you were married.'

'It's complicated,' I said.

'Surely it's simple,' said Polly. 'Either you're married, or you aren't.'

'Well,' I said, 'technically we're still married, because she doesn't do divorce. But we haven't lived together for five years.'

'Oh!' said Polly. 'I'm so sorry! I didn't mean to pry.'

'That's all right,' I said. 'It is what it is, I suppose. I just wish I knew what it was.'

'Oh Malcolm,' said Polly. 'I guess this isn't exactly your happy day.'

Now it was my turn to laugh.

'I need to grin and bear it,' I said. 'Literally. Anyway, how about yourself?'

'Still single,' said Polly. 'As my mother keeps reminding me.'

'Oh!' I said. 'That wasn't what I meant at all!'

'Sorry,' said Polly. 'Too much information. No, I'm fine, but I've got some concerns we should discuss face to face. Call me when you're free?'

'I'll do that,' I said. 'Catch you later.'

'Hope it goes well,' said Polly.

And hung up.

Goodness me! Most unexpected.

I lay back on the bed and thought about my father of the bride speech. What should I say? What could I say? Pithy anecdotes about the young Alison? Weak puns about granting permission to marry? Of course he hadn't asked me. Nor had she.

The words wouldn't come. I was whacked. I dozed off. Then Bernie was hammering at the door:

'Mal! Mal! Come on! Everyone's waiting for you!'

Of course I was the first speaker. I quickly spruced myself up, and followed Bernie downstairs into the ballroom, to ironic, if friendly, applause. Bernie led me to the top table, and sat me down, in the glaringly empty place, between her and our eldest son.

The serving staff brought everyone champagne. Then, after quite unnecessary nudging from Bernie, I stood up and banged a spoon against my glass to get everyone's attention. Without really knowing what I was doing, I launched into an affectionate address to Alison, which was surprisingly well received, perhaps because it was so short. More toasts were followed by a very decent three-course meal. Bernie was beaming. I could tell that she'd had her way here.

Too long after everyone had finished, the serving staff cleared away the tables and chairs. Then the band struck up a hot Latin number. Grant and Alison took the floor, and went into an astonishingly agile routine that they must have been practising for months.

I was frozen by nerves. There was no way I could follow that. But, as Alison mock-dragged me from my chair, the band started to play *The Tennessee Waltz*, and we managed two whole circuits of the room without falling over each other's feet.

'Good stuff, Dad!' said Alison, as the music died. 'I'm so glad you've done all this. It means everything to me.'

I felt happy for Alison, but overwhelmingly glad that I'd run out of script.

I spent the rest of the evening avoiding Steven and Thierry, and also Helen, even though we'd so much to discuss. There'd be time enough after the wedding, and I didn't want to draw attention to our sudden mésalliance. Bernie was surprisingly affable. It wasn't the drink, though we'd both had far more than usual. Rather, there was a sense that our wee girl had grown up, and that we both needed to as well.

It was the back of eleven when I finally returned to my room. I was taking off my shoes when there was a knock at my door.

I opened it to find the young waitress bearing a tray. On the tray was a large tumbler of whisky.

'Room service!' she said, in an accent I couldn't place.

'But I haven't ordered anything,' I said.

'On the house,' said the young waitress. 'For the bride's dashing father.'

I picked up the glass and sniffed the whisky. I didn't recognise the aroma.

'What is it?' I asked.

'It's the hotel's own brand,' said the young waitress. 'From a local distillery. Single malt. *Creag Na Caillich*. Have a good evening!'

Chapter 23

Helen – Thursday 18th September

I woke early on the day of the wedding after another night of disturbing dreams. No Mog on the other side of the bed.

I lay there for a bit while the last dream faded wondering why anyone put themselves through these events. Bernie was terminally stressed, Malcolm was utterly miserable, and Thierry looked as if he wished he hadn't agreed to come. Even Alison seemed more interested in her video than the real-world event. Oh, Steven was having fun, but that was because he was in policeman mode and people had to answer his questions or be rude to a wedding guest. If I ever got married – a big if – it would be down the Registry Office with my parents and then an evening in the pub with me marras.

But I was here as a stand-in for Mam and Dad, so I needed to make an effort. 'Be nice' was what they wanted, and I hadn't really lived up to that the previous night. Deep breath. More effort.

The service wasn't until eleven, so I decided to have a short walk before breakfast. It seemed that every day since we'd fished McMalkin out of the sea there was some more stuff to think about. I found thinking easier when I was walking. And according to my laptop, the whole area was chocka with stone-age stuff, with a couple of stone circles under a mile down the road. There and back would be an hour at most, and maybe a later breakfast would save me from another round of conversational effort.

The sun was only just coming up when I got outside, with long autumn shadows across the landscape. But clouds moving in from the west suggested the sun wouldn't last the day. I wanted to cut across the field opposite the hotel but the low stone wall had barbed wire along the top. So I walked down the narrow road to a junction where a rusty metal field gate was open and resting at an angle on the mud. There was a sketchy path across the field. It passed along the edge of a small wood and got very boggy, making me regret coming out in my trainers. Still, I had some brogues for the wedding and the trainers would dry out later.

So if I'd got the hang of what Jackie Baillie couldn't quite say, he reckoned McMalkin had come through the Transilience Gate. A wild idea. And Jackie might not be at all reliable. I really did need to talk to the Americans and see if they thought their theories could cope with this. But if you did go with Jackie, lots of things made more sense. The F^2 pursuit of McMalkin. Him being a man that apparently didn't exist. Maybe even drowning himself rather than be captured?

Then what if Malcolm's Patricia Harper had also come through the gate? We knew there was some connection because they both had green stones and arrowheads. My screenshot confirmed it. So was she dead too? Or was she somewhere in the F^2 plant?

And here was another wild thing. If they had come from a parallel world then maybe they had brought the green stones with them. Perhaps, like Malcolm said, they weren't F^2 things at all. Not a reassuring thought really. I fingered the pebble in my pocket, as I realised I often did.

Maybe Malcolm could find out more from the whistle-blowing woman he mentioned the previous night. I'd had no chance to get him on his own to ask about her – Polly, he'd called her. If she really was a whistle-blower. In his shoes I'd be very careful in case she wasn't what she said she was. But the chances of talking to the father-of-the-bride in the middle of the wedding didn't seem good.

Past the wood I could see the stone circle, spread out over much of the next field. It was not nearly as impressive as the Callanish stones, nor the Orkney ones I'd seen on the TV. Maybe they had just lasted less well here on the mainland and were once the same sort of thing. If

McMalkin hadn't drowned, would he have visited this stone circle too? What was it about stone circles?

As at the Callanish, I decided to walk round the whole site. When I bent round at the far end to walk back I realised that someone else had appeared on the field. A tall man in a bright red anorak who looked somewhat familiar. My path took me towards him and soon my first thought was proved right. Thierry, also on an early morning walk. Well, I couldn't avoid him without being ostentatiously rude. Time to be nice.

'Hi, Thierry. So you're into fresh air as well. Shall we walk together?'

'Hello, Helen. I am delighted to. Yes, it seemed to me that some small exercise would clear the head before the day's events.'

'How's Bernie? She looked a bit stressed last night.'

'Ah, she finds it difficult I think. The marriage of your last child is always important, and then it is inevitable that she and Malcolm both feel pain from a broken relationship.'

I could feel my blood pressure going up at the thought of Thierry making Bernie feel even worse at some future point.

'I hope you are able to give her some support.'

'Bernie made a strong request for me to attend for that reason and so I am doing my best. Although I had worried that my presence would be felt as an imposition by other family members. Perhaps also a statement about our own relationship, open to misunderstanding.'

Hmm, that was an invitation to discuss it if ever I heard one. I hesitated. I was trying to be nice after all. But I might find out something useful if I put Thierry on the spot.

'Thierry, I'm going to be blunt with you. You and Bernie told me that F^2 were in a big EU project and left suddenly last year, and Bernie doesn't know why. I checked it out online. One of the partners was the company you worked for until sometime last year, the French national electricity company. Then someone else told me that Europeans were trying to find out what F^2 were up to. And then you become close to Bernie. So am I misunderstanding your relationship with her?'

We had carried on walking slowly round the site. At this point Thierry stopped for a moment and I briefly wondered if he was going to walk off in a strop. But no.

'Helen, you are, as you say, blunt. But I know you are close to Bernie and so I respect your reasons for asking this question. And the answer, it is both yes and no.'

He started walking again.

'It is true that I was asked to move to Scotland and to find out about F^2. Our project was to find new sources of green energy. In France this would substitute for our many nuclear stations, which are becoming problematic. We all have an interest in this. When F^2 left it seemed they wanted to keep work, to which all had contributed, for themselves. This did not seem right.'

He stopped again, and turned, gesturing to emphasise what he said.

'But I assure you, there was no plan to become as you say "close to Bernie." This was just how it happened. And I think you see it is perhaps a little more on her side than on mine, though I admire and respect her. You cannot be so angry about that. These things do not always function in balance. I am as she said last night, her good friend. Does that answer you?'

OK, I'll give you he seemed sincere. I even felt a twinge of sorry-for-him. Because I knew he was right. Wilf seemed much more stuck on me than I thought I was on him. It happened. And it was tricky.

We had by this time got back round to where the path entered the field.

'Fair enough, Thierry. I appreciate your frankness.' Customer service Hulkie in action. 'I don't know about you, but I'm ready for some breakfast, so time to go back. In return I can tell you something I think will interest you.'

And as we walked back, squelching through the mud again, I told him all about the Americans. I also told him what they said a Transilience Gate might actually be – like Bernie, he'd heard the term without knowing what it was. Free information for him, but I felt I might need some allies in the near future.

After a quiet breakfast I went to feed Mog. No sign of him at first, but as I was filling the bowl, he slunk out of the undergrowth behind the car park and rubbed against my legs. I stroked that soft fur a cat has just below their ears and he purred at me. His miracle cure of the day before seemed less important and worrying.

A sudden skittering of small birds out of a big tree behind the hotel caught my eye and I wondered what had alarmed them. I could just make out a large hunched brown form up there. Another owl?

But it was time to go back in and get dressed up for the main event. The mirror suggested I would pass, though my blue velvet hat with pheasant feather was not exactly inconspicuous on someone as tall as I am. There again, a woman of my height is always going to stand out, as they say.

As I came down to Reception I could see Steven lurking in a rather lurid red and black kilt, which just had to be the McIver tartan. It was clear he was waiting for me. Give him credit, he blinked a bit at my transformation, but still came out with the right sort of words.

'Helen, you look very elegant. Could I hitch a lift to the service with you? I'm not sure where to go in Lochgilphead and I don't know anyone else except Malcolm and Bernie.'

But naturally he still wasn't going to turn the policeman bit off. As soon as he was in the passenger seat, my blue hat sitting on his red and black knees, he was at it.

'I was talking to Malcolm about Patricia Harper over breakfast,' he began.

'Steps back in amazement, man. So now you'd like to ask me what I know about her?'

'Well, yes.'

'Not a lot beyond her name when push comes to shove. I drove up to see Malcolm on Sunday, chat about the wedding, see the moor. He told me about her.'

'So what did he tell you?'

Ooh, police craftiness here. I had no idea how much of the story Malcolm had passed on.

'He blathered about her looking memorably weird, and then some Americans claiming they found her body up by the F² plant. And the funny thing was, man, they were my Americans, the ones I told you I met up the top of Ben Lomond. Who then started following me around. If they are why your investigation has sprung into life again, good luck with getting them to tell you anything. Anyway Malcolm said there was no body when he went to look.'

'But there was a bike?'

'So he told me, but then it got stolen from the outhouse at his work. And he said he felt such an idiot at having zero evidence he didn't report any of it.'

'And did he mention an arrowhead to you, like the one he gave you last night?'

'Yes.' And I gave him Malcolm's story on the broken arrowhead.

'By any chance did the old woman you thought you saw at the Calanais stones have one too?'

Clever Steven. Lucky for me we'd just got to the turning off the main road through Lochgilphead that led to the church. My surprise was hopefully hidden by gear changes and turning.

'Yes, she did, Steven. She said it was the sign of Wicca. And then the lightning struck. Policeman off duty for the wedding service now, I hope?'

I parked us up and Steven followed me thoughtfully into the church.

This was the first Catholic wedding I'd been to. Probably the first church wedding of any kind since I was a kid in fact. Most of my friends don't marry, and those that do, either go down the Registry or pick somewhere exotic. This version seemed rather energetic: stand, sit, kneel, in rotation. None of the hymns were the ones I knew from school assembly and there were call-and-response things for which I didn't know the responses. Steven, next to me in the pew, tried harder than I did.

Endless photos outside afterwards, but mostly of the bride and groom and immediate family. I soon extricated Steven, and we drove back to the hotel for the wedding breakfast, in fact a lunchtime buffet. This started well for me when one of Alison's brothers asked me who I was and then said 'Oh, so you are from the Geordie branch of the family.' And my late breakfast meant I wasn't that hungry. I also stayed off the drink – plenty of time for that later. As soon as I could, I excused myself and went back upstairs.

I'd decided I ought to ring Wilf, so I did that next. It was kind of nice to hear how pleased he was to speak to me. I told him about us fishing out McMalkin: I'd only been on the Scottish News, so he hadn't seen me. Of course I had told Dad but I'd also asked him not to spread it around or I'd never hear the last of it when I got back to Sunderland. I said the same to Wilf. He does understand that sort of stuff. I also explained there'd been some police knock-on that had messed up my holiday plans, apart from Ben Lomond anyway. That I'd ring again Sunday and let him know whether it was a good idea to come and join me for the last week of my hols.

'Love you, Hulkie,' he said by way of goodbye. As he does. 'Gie ower, man,' I said, as I do.

I wasn't sure how I felt after that. Which was the problem.

To take my mind off it, I bit the bullet and composed an email to Professor Martha Gellman. A cautious one. Reminding her how we met, suggesting there were topics in which we had a common interest; if she was still in the Highlands Friday, maybe we could meet up briefly. At The Leaping Fish in Crianlarich, midday.

That would wipe out another climbing day and this was probably a terrible idea. Like baiting a bull maybe. My finger hovered over the Send button. But how else could I find out what the odds were of my own theories being correct? And if my stone had come through the gate, maybe it could go back that way and I would be free of the damn thing. Not that I was going to mention that to them if we did meet. I pressed Send.

After that I lazed around and read some swords and sorcery until it was time for the next wedding thing downstairs. Speeches, cake-cutting, reasonable sit-down meal. Except I got sat at the top table next to Alison's other brother. 'Oh, you must be the Geordie branch of the family,' he started. Then looked as if he wished he hadn't as I set him right. Which gave me a pang of conscience about failing on niceness once again. So I went into Customer Service Hulkie mode with lots of questions about his job, partner, family and so on and so forth. Along with much smiling and nodding on my part.

The meal was followed by dancing, which is not my thing. After some show-off stuff for bride with groom, and bride with Malcolm, there was an inevitable ceilidh session with a guy shouting out the moves. Steven was in his element with lots of fancy footwork. I just about managed one or two of the easier dances without knocking anyone over. Then I found some of Alison's friends from Uni who were reasonable fun to chat to. Sank a few single malts. By eleven I'd had enough. I reckoned that was my family wedding quota done for the next five years at least.

I was in the bathroom, just about to clean my teeth, when I heard a knock at the door. I opened it to find a young woman with a tray, possibly the waitress from the night before. On the tray was a tumbler of whisky.

'Compliments of the house,' she said. Odd, I thought, but one more wouldn't hurt. So I thanked her and took it. It tasted pretty good too.

Chapter 24

Malcolm – Friday 19th September

I'd slept solidly and awoke with a muzzy head. I didn't think I'd had that much to drink. The nightcap must have helped, though.

I got up and showered. Then I dressed in my usual clothes. It was a relief to be out of the suit. I wondered if I'd wear it again.

As I pulled on my shoes, I noticed the soles were caked in mud. But I'd barely been outside since I'd arrived.

There were two messages on my phone. The one from Glenys said:

Were you at Nether Largie?

What a strange construction. Not '*have you been to*' or '*are you going to*'. I replied:

Not yet.

The other message was from Megan. Henry must have given her my number. This message said:

Please contact me.

Later.

I checked my email. Nothing from Polly. Why was I disappointed?

I went downstairs to the breakfast room. There was no sign of Helen, who I wanted to talk to, or of Steven, who I didn't. Bernie and Thierry were at a table by themselves. I'd no reason, nor desire, to join them.

I was helping myself from the buffet, when one of the hotel staff came into the breakfast room, and rang a hand bell.

'The happy couple are about to depart,' he announced.

I joined the guests outside, and queued to hug Alison: my wee girl no more. Everyone cheered and waved as they drove off, strings of tin cans rattling beneath the car. Fare forward, voyagers.

I suddenly felt sad and hollow. I needed to clear my head. Without having breakfast, I went straight upstairs and packed. Then I returned to reception to check out. I was about to leave, when the young waitress approached me.

'Mr Nicholson,' she said, holding out an arrowhead on a leather thong. 'I'm sorry to bother you, but I think you wife must have left this in the bar. Might you return it to her, please?'

'Of course,' I said, feeling cross with Bernie. 'Thank you.'

I pocketed the arrowhead, and stashed my gear in the Land Rover. Then I set off on foot to Nether Largie. I'd picked up a brochure from the reception desk, and followed the map on the back. The site was a short distance away, along small roads round three sides of the field that enclosed the stones. From the entrance, opposite a car park, a wooden walkway led to the central stones.

As I got closer to the stones, I had a growing sense of déjà vu. And, as I walked round the central stones, I had a nagging feeling that there should have been more of them, and that they should all have been bigger. But I was pretty sure that I'd never been to Kilmartin before. Perhaps I was recalling some long forgotten childhood trip to Callanish.

I still felt muzzy. This wasn't helping. It was time to go home. I walked back to the hotel, fired up the Land Rover and headed north. The single track road that traced the east bank of Loch Awe was empty, which suited me well. The last couple of days had involved intensive doses of other people, in far too close proximity.

I arrived in Achallader just after midday, and decided to press on to the Altnafeidh Hotel. I felt really hungry, and I wanted to clear things up with Dougie.

Dougie's police car was outside the hotel, and Dougie was inside, at his window seat.

'Malco, my man!' he said, sternly, as I came into the restaurant. 'I was wondering when you'd turn up. I hear you've been a bad boy. Withholding facts pertaining to an enquiry? Mislaying material evidence?'

But I could tell he wasn't entirely serious.

'Och, Dougie,' I said, sitting down opposite him. 'I'm so sorry. I feel really bad about the whole thing. But I didn't want to drag either of us into something that sounded so crazy.'

'It certainly does sound crazy,' said Dougie. 'Still, your cousin's taking it seriously. I'm not sure I would have done, but, hey, there you go, eh?'

'What's Steven said?' I asked.

'Seems this Patricia Harper lass is bad news,' said Dougie. 'There's some link to the Lewis corpse. And it looks like you were the last person to see her alive. Yes, I know you told me about her. But you didn't tell me she was dead.'

'But we don't know she is dead!' I protested. 'That's the whole point!'

Dougie laughed.

'I'm really not bothered,' he said. 'It's not in Highland's jurisdiction. The Menzies Stone marks the border, and the F2 plant is just over the other side, so if anyone else wants to speak with you, it'll be Tayside. All I want to do is have my lunch.'

'Are we good?' I said, anxiously.

'Always,' said Dougie. 'Until the next time, that is. Look, here's Jeannie.'

Jeannie took my order, entirely by eye contact.

'Is Glenys at home today?' I said, when Jeannie had gone off to the kitchen.

'I think so,' said Dougie. 'But she's getting ready for some big hooley on Sunday. She's certainly been buying up lots of Prosecco.'

So what's Glenys heard?

'I hope the cat's not being a hassle,' I said.

'Not in the slightest,' said Dougie. 'After all, a witch needs a familiar. It's a shame I'm allergic to cats. Anyway, how was the wedding?'

I regaled Dougie with tales of family fractiousness, until my food arrived.

Once we'd finished eating, Dougie set off north, on patrol as he put it, in his best Lone Ranger drawl. And I returned south to the cottage.

I parked, went upstairs and unpacked my bag. I was hanging up my new suit, when I began to remember.

I'm at the stones. We're at the stones. Helen and I. But not just us. There's a cat. And an owl. And the young waitress. Her hair's wild, and her eyes are glowing green. It's like a surreal dream.

The moon is high, and nearly full. The stones are glowing silvery. The broken central stones are made whole by shining wraiths. And we're surrounded by a completed circle of silvery ghost stones.

The owl and the cat are glowing. Ghostly forms encompass them. Forms of people! Patricia Harper! McMalkin!

The young woman moves with graceful precision, and begins to intone. I can't make out the words. But I know I have to find my green stone.

Helen and I hold our green stones out towards the young woman. Green lights arc towards her from the stones. The young woman weaves the lights into curling knots, that meld together to form an eye, that spirals, and weeps a green tear, into the mud at her feet.

The pool of green tear coalesces into a new green stone. The owl swoops down, clutches the new stone in its talons, and drops it into the young woman's outstretched palm.

And then I was back in my bedroom.

What the fuck was that? What the fuck just happened?

I felt badly shaken. I went back down stairs. There was no sign of the cat. Maybe it was round at Dougie and Glenys's. Maybe Glenys would know what just happened?

Glenys was by the side of the house, stooped over the vegetable plot lifting tatties. The cat was sitting on a pile of sacks, watching her intently.

'Hello Malcom!' said Glenys, standing up and stretching. 'Gosh, that feels better.'

Glenys looked me up and down.

'Are you all right?' she said. 'You look like you've seen a ghost. Would you like a cup of tea?'

I followed Glenys into the kitchen, and sagged onto a chair.

'How was the wedding?' said Gleny, filling the kettle.

'It was more hard work than fun,' I said. 'I'm so glad it's over. Still, Alison's happy, and that's all that matters, really.'

'Did you get to Nether Largie?' said Glenys.

'Yes,' I said. 'I went this morning.'

'Not last night, then?' said Glenys, looking me straight in the eye. 'Are you quite sure?'

I broke her gaze and fumbled in my pocket. The stone pulsed green between my fingers.

'Why would you think I was there last night?' I asked.

'It was an educated guess,' said Glenys, filling the kettle. 'I told you Kilmartin was a seat of power. We'd heard something big had happened there last night. You were nearby. You have a stone of power. You're tied by blood to Margaret MacAskill. It all adds up. Do you want to tell me about it?'

'I'm not sure I can,' I said. 'What I can remember's mad. Like a bad trip.'

'Mushrooms can do that,' said Glenys. 'Did you eat any?'

'Certainly not!' I said. 'That was a figure of speech!'

But where did those weird memories come from? Was it the nightcap the young waitress had given me? At least it hadn't been deadly. Was it a false memory, or an hallucination? It can't have actually happened.

The kettle boiled. Glenys made tea.

'I just wish this would all go away,' I said, as she handed me a cup.

'It will,' said Glenys. 'Soon. Too soon.'

What did Glenys mean? I'd not told her anything. And how had she heard that something had happened at Nether Largie? Why didn't anyone at the hotel mention it? Could I trust her?

Of course I could trust Glenys. If I couldn't trust her, I couldn't trust anyone. Maybe what I'd just recalled really had happened. But that's crazy.

Who exactly was the young woman, with green eyes and wild hair, posing as a waitress? Then I remembered the extraordinary woman, who'd spirited away Patricia Harper's bicycle. Were they somehow connected?

Glenys and I sat quietly together. The cat came into the kitchen, and weaved its way round my legs. I bent over and picked it up. The cat felt reassuringly solid. This was no ghost. I finished my tea, and stood up to leave.

'Are you sure you'll be all right?' said Glenys.

'I think so,' I said, 'but there's so much to take in.'

'You'll have lots of questions,' said Glenys, 'but you'll get better answers from Megan. She's been trying to contact you.'

'I know,' I said. 'She texted me.'

'I gave her your number,' said Glenys. 'I thought you wouldn't mind. She's found out more about Margaret MacAskill.'

'I'll get in touch with her soon,' I said

'Don't leave it too long,' said Glenys.

Glenys went back to her tatties, the cat to the pile of sacks, and I to my cottage.

I needed to talk with Helen. Urgently. She'd been in my vision, if that was what it was. Although it seemed implausible, I still wondered if she'd had a similar experience. I dialled her number, but it went to voice mail. So I sent her a text message, to contact me as soon as possible.

Next I phoned Megan. Might as well get it over with.

'Malcolm,' said Megan. 'How was the wedding?'

'Too long,' I said.

'And how was Nether Largie?' said Megan.

Some ordinary conversation would be nice right now. Not much chance of that.

'Deeply confusing,' I said. 'I'm still trying to process it.'

'Don't try,' said Megan. 'Let it process itself.'

So much psycho-babble.

'You texted me?' I said. 'And Glenys suggested that you had some new information about my infamous ancestor?'

'That's right,' said Megan. 'I was reading more of the account of Margaret MacAskill's prophecies. There's a third one that seems to connect with the two we knew already.'

'What does it say?' I said.

'*The gate that is open will be shut.*' said Megan. 'Does that mean anything to you?'

Oh, wow! That's what the woman in the shed whispered to me.

'Not a clue,' I said. 'Why do you think it's linked?'

'Well, said Megan, 'you could see the equinox as a gate between light and darkness, or darkness and light, of course. So that seems to resonate with the prophecy Glenys told you – *When the days balance the worlds balance.*'

'And the one you told me?' I said.

'*What's given to the stones remains given,*' said Megan. 'Well, you've just been at Nether Largie, haven't you. Did you leave anything there?'

'No,' I said. 'Nothing, except maybe my marbles.'

'Boom! Boom!' said Megan. 'Aye well, I'm sure they'll all fit together. We just have to find the right shape.'

'Could I have a quick word with Henry?' I asked.

'He's out right now,' said Megan. 'At a RAGE planning meeting. They're cooking something up for Sunday.'

'Dougie told me that Glenys was getting ready for a bash on Sunday,' I said. 'Are you going?'

'I certainly am,' said Megan. 'It's going to be a big one. I don't think there's any prosecco left between here and Inverness.'

She laughed and ended the call.

Then it dawned on me that, while Megan and Glenys seemed to think that something had happened at Nether Largie, they didn't actually have much clue what had happened. Still, someone must have told them something. Or maybe they were expecting something to happen. And I thought Henry was the conspiracy theorist.

I needed to talk with Helen. I tried her phone again. It still went to voice mail. I checked my email. Nothing from Helen, but there was a message from Polly:

Hope you survived the wedding. Can we meet today?

I couldn't face Polly. I replied:

I'm done in. How about tomorrow afternoon?

Polly responded almost immediately:

4pm, Tartan Trading Post?

Chapter 25

Helen – Friday 19th September

The previous week I'd woken well short of full fettle after the evening with my Stornoway cousins. The morning after the wedding put that into the shade. Not that I had a headache or was about to throw up. More a panicky feeling that something bad had happened but I couldn't remember what it was.

Had I been rude to somebody? Made an obscene joke to an elderly relation? Flattened a fellow dancer? Snogged some man in full public view? True, I couldn't remember any such wassock-like behaviour. The problem was I that couldn't remember very much at all about the evening. How many single malts must I have sunk?

I stood under the shower for a good fifteen minutes and finally turned it down to cold hoping this would shock the brain into functioning. But no joy. I thought I remembered climbing the stairs to my floor but before that was a jumbled haze and after that a complete blank until my waking.

I slunk down for breakfast hoping there wouldn't be a lot of critical glances or concealed smiles from fellow guests. It turned out I was hungry, though I limited my Full Scottish selection to the basics in case my stomach revolted later.

'Hello, Helen. Can I join you?' Oh god, Steven.

I grunted unwelcomingly but he didn't take the hint, and sat down. His appetite was certainly working well, looking at his piled plate.

'I really enjoyed last night,' he said.

Jesus wept, I hadn't snogged him had I?

'As ceilidhs go, it was a pretty good one, wasn't it?' he added, to my relief.

'Not really my thing, man' I muttered, unsure whether I had or had not joined in.

'You weren't bad,' he said, sounding rather patronising, 'though I did notice you sneaked off to chat to Alison's friends pretty quickly.'

OK, that didn't sound too terrible.

'So are you back off to Stornoway now?' I asked.

'Not a chance,' he said, cheerily. 'You and Malcolm have given us lots of new leads. I'm deputed to speak to F^2 again about all the things it appears they have failed to tell us. I'm afraid the two of you will probably have to do remote interviews with the boss to get all that on the record.'

'Again?' I groaned. 'Remember I am supposed to be climbing mountains.'

But I knew full well that if that's what they wanted, then that's what the two of us would have to do.

After breakfast, I got my packing done in mechanical fashion, checked out, and went out to the car. No sign of Malcolm, nor of Bernie and Thierry.

And no sign either of Mog. I called him and waited. Called him again.

Nothing.

Something stirred in my brain. Mog on someone's shoulder. His owner reclaiming him? Surely not, that would be someone in Troon, not in a random Highland hotel. Had there been a fellow wedding guest from Troon? No, not that either. But that strong feeling he'd been reclaimed. Someone with green eyes? No, Mog had green eyes. Well, how many times had I told myself he wasn't my cat?

But I felt sad as I popped back into Reception to leave my number in case he turned up. Against a definite feeling that he wouldn't.

Then I drove back along the road to Crianlarich. To my surprise I'd had a brief reply from Martha Gellman confirming my meeting suggestion for midday at The Leaping Fish. I was going to arrive too early but my laptop showed a couple of nice little walks in the countryside round the town and I planned to do one of those. I felt a bit nervous about the meeting.

So as I drove, I tried to focus on what I wanted to say to Martha the Prof. But I kept sliding off into trying to remember the evening before. It was infuriating, like a word at the tip of my tongue. I felt I could almost remember, but nothing came. Feet sliding in the mud in the middle of a dark field – no, that had been in the morning. But in the dark? Had I stumbled out, totally pallatic, for some night air? Thinking back to my zombie-like packing, I realised my brogues had been muddy. So I must have been outside. Doing what for Christ's sake?

I'd got no further when I reached Crianlarich and parked as before at The Leaping Fish. My walk was only a couple of kilometres up through some woods so I didn't bother with my boots. It was grey and inclined to drizzle but no problem if you had the right kit. True to its name – the Mountain Lookout Trail – there were great views once out of the woods, though threads of low cloud snaked across Ben More.

Woods, a view of lots of silvery stones, my memory suggested. Instead of dismissing the image as a confusion with yesterday morning, I focused on it. Feet sliding, someone in front of me – maybe Malcolm? That couldn't be right. It all went again.

I got back to the The Leaping Fish just before midday. I could see there was a black BMW in the car park next to my Nissan. Looked like Martha the Prof was prompt.

The next bit all happened rather fast.

As I got to my car, ready to put my rucksack back into my load space, two men shot out of the BMW. Before I had a chance to say a word they grabbed my arms and forced me into the back of their car, minus my rucksack. I managed to elbow one of them in the face along the way but ended up wedged between the second guy and a third man on the other end of the back seat. About to give the fuckers a verbal what-for, this third man took the words from my mouth by pointing gun at me. I froze.

'Can I suggest keeping your cool at this time, Ma'am,' he said in an American accent. 'We will escort you to your meeting with Professor Gellman.'

'Fuck you, man,' I said bitterly, but didn't try to move.

Yes, that email was certainly not one of my better ideas.

The four of them, including the driver, were all standard issue thirties-something goons with short haircuts and dark suits. As my heart rate dropped to something more normal I realised that they were hardly going to let off guns in the back of a car. Maybe Martha the Prof was just softening me up with this ridiculous display of force. Or maybe her friend Ethan the cultural attaché had more to do with it.

As we turned east on the A85, the man on my left took out one of those sleep masks people wear over their eyes on planes.

'Excuse me, Ma'am,' he said politely. 'Could I ask you to put on this mask. Professor Gellman is kind of fussy about her privacy.'

'Fuck you too,' I said. But put it on. Better to save the aggro for when it might be useful.

After a while we took what felt like a left fork onto a slower road, and then after that another left onto a very slow road uphill. There was no chat, and to take my mind off the situation, I had another go at remembering the previous night. I told myself to just watch whatever images came rather than trying to process them.

A dark night, a young woman, somehow familiar, her face illuminated by a light cupped in her hand. Weird. No, just watch. A cat on her shoulder. Mog! No, no, just watch.

By dint of supressing my reactions, I entered a strange dream-like narrative. I was standing next to Malcolm in the stone circle, our own stones in our hands. Joined in a green beam that flowed forwards into the hands of a young woman. She spoke:

'*Gather worlds, meld worlds*
Bind threads, spread pattern
Gather power, birth power
Under the moon, outside Time
Weave powers, birth stone.'

Then there was something like a jump in the image. Now she had one hand extended, and a green stone just like ours lay glowing in her palm. She pointed at the ground with her other hand and steam rose from it. A large bird – oh, an owl! – lifted the stone from her hand in its talons and dropped it into the hole at her feet. She brought her hands together and the hole vanished. Then…

'Ma'am, Ma'am.' Someone was shaking my left arm. 'Wake up, Ma'am.' My mask was removed.

I opened my eyes with a sigh. My dream, vision, whatever, was a lot more fun than my current situation. The car had stopped outside a long, low white building. One of those Scottish cabins. In the middle of nowhere. Well, in a green, treeless landscape, probably of hills. Low cloud cut off whatever the view was.

Maybe I should make a run for it when they let me out of the car? I could disappear into the mist quite quickly. But even if I got away and the goons didn't take pot shots at me, bolting in some random direction away from the road would probably get me lost. My phone and emergency snap were in my missing rucksack and I didn't have my boots. No, not a good option. Better to see what Martha the Prof thought she was up to.

I was ushered into a shabby sitting room, with a dingy floral sofa and two almost-matching armchairs. It smelt of damp but also unmistakably of cannabis. Martha and Dean might not be into single malts for relaxation. They got up to welcome me as if it was a routine social call.

'What the fuck is this charade,' I demanded. 'Have you all been watching too many box set thrillers?'

Martha looked taken aback. Before she could say anything, a phone started ringing, then stopped as it went to voice-mail. My phone, by the sound of the ringtone. I saw the driver had my rucksack. Well that was something at least.

'Say honey, I'm real sorry if these guys were heavy handed. I asked them to invite you up here so we could talk more privately. After all, sometimes you can get overheard.' She smiled meaningfully. 'Let's all sit down and have a chat, OK? These guys can make themselves useful by rustling us up some subs. And some coffee too, guys.'

She gestured at the goons. Two of them headed out of the room. Presumably to the kitchen. And we all sat down.

Time to seize the initiative.

'Aye, man, you're right. I did listen in that lunchtime. Sorry for being so rude. But I'd heard you talking about the F^2 Transilience Gate up Ben Lomond. I know whose body that was you found. And that she was connected to McMalkin, the body we fished out of the Minch. I asked to meet up because if I tell you stuff I think you want to know, you can tell me some stuff I want to know.'

I imagined myself lobbing hand grenades. A satisfying silence followed. Martha and Dean looked at each other.

'OK, honey,' Martha said eventually. 'So howsabout you give us the gen on McMalkin and the body?'

'Sorry, man. After all the hassle your goons just gave me, I get to ask my questions first. Or no deal.'

Risky, I knew, given the goons probably had harsher methods than mere questions, but I was terminally pissed off with them all.

Martha shrugged. 'OK, go for it.'

'Up Ben Lomond you said a Translience Gate might collect gravitons from parallel worlds. Great for us, but what happens to the parallel worlds when they lose gravitons like that?'

Their faces were a picture. Could be I didn't look like their idea of someone with a physics question.

'The math says there should be a statistical distribution of gravitons over parallel worlds,' Dean said at last.

'So shifting gravitons between worlds would change that,' said Martha. 'Change the energy balance between them and the probability distributions too. But you have a point: in theory removing gravitons could alter the ability of a world to produce others, cut off its branching ability. But that is only in theory.'

'Not any more if F^2 have actually created a gate,' I said. 'Someone I know went on a recent tour round the plant and saw something that could be an actual gate. But I wanted to ask a second question. Say you were in a world that was having its gravitons removed and you didn't like it. What if you could go through the gate and stop it?'

Dean laughed. 'No, no, no. That's a ridiculous idea. There is no theoretical account supporting that.'

I let off my nuclear device.

'I talked to someone who was on duty in the plant in June. He said that three people came through the F^2 gate. I think one of them was McMalkin.'

The food and coffee arrived at this point, but Martha and Dean hardly noticed. I got a barrage of questions as they tried to pick holes in a story they obviously did not want to believe. I did give them the downside, that my source might not be reliable, though I kept Thierry out of it and said it was Riddle who'd set up the meeting. But I also gave them the upside, that it explained why F^2 were so keen to find McMalkin and why the police had drawn a blank on him.

Which brought us round to Patricia Harper and her link to McMalkin. I told them about the arrowheads. Then I told them about the pic on my phone. They got it out of the rucksack.

'Seems someone called Malcolm is trying to get in touch,' Martha said.

'My cousin. I've just been at his daughter's wedding.'

I offered to show them the pic of McMalkin and Harper on Orkney.

'If you don't mind, sugar, we'll hold onto this for now. So it's this one you are talking about?'

Martha had fished the shot out of my phone gallery in no time flat. Showed it to Dean.

'And you think this Patricia Harper was taken inside the plant?'

I told them about the gate in the fence.

'This gate?' Martha asked, showing me another of my shots.

Oh, shit. That was the one with the dead robot dog in it.

'The robot was like that when I got there,' I said. Which didn't sound convincing even to me. Especially as there was smoke still rising from the heather.

'Sure it was,' Martha said. 'Was there a reason you were out there last Sunday, honey?'

The silence that followed was broken by the sound of a car pulling up outside. The doors slammed, I heard the cabin's front door open, and the sitting room door followed. A man entered.

'Hi Martha, Dean. Jeez, it stinks of god-damn weed in here.' A voice familiar from that overheard meal.

'Hi, Ethan,' Martha said. 'You've arrived at an interesting moment.'

Chapter 26

Helen – Friday 19th – Saturday 20th September

While Ethan's arrival got me off an awkward hook, I had a feeling it wasn't going to help me later.

Dismissed from what looked like an urgent meeting, two of the goons shunted me down the corridor to a bedroom, bringing a couple of subs and coffee.

'Please wait here, Ma'am, until you are required,' one of them said. 'If you need anything we will be right outside.' Both a promise and a threat.

The bedroom was on the side of the cabin away from the road. It had a desk and chair under the window, which looked out to the hills across a small backyard with an outhouse. And propped against the outhouse were two mountain bikes. Martha and Dean were still including tourism in their programme. The double-glazed window opened inwards. I tried it, but it was locked. No sign of a key.

Opening a door on the left, I found a tiny shower-room with loo. But its window was much too small for someone my size to get through. There was a new toothbrush still in its plastic packaging on the sink with an unopened tube of toothpaste. Also, the bed was made up. These weren't good signs. If they didn't intend taking me back to Crianlarich any time soon, then forcing the window and taking a bike seemed worth a try. But later.

I picked at the subs and drank some coffee. I guessed Martha and Dean were giving Ethan a run-down and deciding what to do next. Nothing drastic I hoped. I tried to imagine how someone working for the US Government, a professional paranoid, would react to the idea of people from parallel worlds invading ours. Then I tried to remember what else was on my phone. A pity it wasn't password-protected. There again, given the goons, that didn't matter.

I took a deep breath. No point in upping the anxiety like this. More useful, and probably more fun, to go back to what had happened – if it had happened – the previous night.

I closed my eyes. The image of the young woman dropping the green stone into a hole and closing it up. Then throwing both her arms out, she declaimed:

'*Stone to the stones*

When the days balance the worlds balance

The gate that is open will be closed.'

And the silvery light is dimming, the stones are shrinking, the young woman seems somehow smaller. Back into the darkness of the field, a glow ahead, feet sliding in the mud. Cold, tired, drained. Back into the hotel and the bedroom. Clothes off, into pyjamas, falling into a dead sleep.

I opened my eyes. Stared out of the window, thinking.

The young woman with green eyes. She had been in the hotel. Had arrived with the 'on the house' whisky, which surely must have been spiked in some way. Had the rest of it really happened or was it hallucination? Well, Malcolm was in the thing too, so checking with him would help. Not that I could in the current situation.

Hmm, muddy feet, no Mog. Both pieces of real evidence. The young woman in my images had intoned the same stuff as the old woman at the Callanish stones. She also had an arrowhead round her neck. Like McMalkin. So far I'd assumed F^2 were the main driving force of whatever was going on. What if I was wrong? What if there was also a group from the Gate, and F^2 were as far behind the loop with them as the rest of us? What if all the mumbo-jumbo Wicca stuff was just a convenient cover for people who were sort of aliens, at least to our world? And my pebble was just alien tech? Didn't some SF author I'd read say that any sufficiently advanced tech looked the same as magic?

That was as far as I had got when there was a knock at the door and one of the goons opened it.

'Ma'am, the Professors would like you back in please.'

The next couple of hours weren't the most fun I've ever had. Ethan was very much in charge, though he referred to Martha and Dean for technical backup. It was obvious questioning people was his thing. Cultural attaché, my arse.

He decided he wanted my day-by-day account from when McMalkin was fished out. Trying to keep the story consistent without telling him stuff I didn't want to tell him was exhausting. Especially as I didn't want it to be obvious that I wasn't telling him stuff. The whole thing was recorded so he could go over it later with a fine toothcomb.

The wedding was a godsend. I had to let on I'd visited Malcolm and Bernie, and had met up with Thierry. About the wedding, naturally. I blessed the caution of Thierry's text, easily found on my phone.

At some point Martha and Dean realised that Malcolm was the same Ranger they'd told about the body. So a round of questions about what Malcolm had told me. And apparently Malcolm had rung me twice since I arrived and messaged me to ring him back. What was that about, Ethan wanted to know? I shrugged. Then pointed out that Malcolm was going to worry about me if he couldn't get in touch soon. I hoped that might make them anxious to get this whole thing done and let me go.

But then Ethan was onto Bernie's F^2 role like a terrier, and wanted to know if we'd talked about the Transilience Gate. Of course I had to go over all the police stuff, though my guess was Ethan knew about that anyway since he didn't seem all that interested in it.

And as a grand finale, another run over why I thought there was a gate that people might come through. Ethan was not especially deferential to Martha and Dean's expertise. He wanted them to say it was impossible, when all they would say was that it was outside of current theory.

'We need answers, not theories,' he said. 'If we can't rule it out then I want an option for dealing with it.' Martha and Dean did not look happy.

'OK, guys 'n'gals,' Ethan said at last. 'Done for today. We can reconvene in the morning when I've gone over the tapes.'

That settled it. I definitely wasn't up for another session like this one. I was escorted back to my room, already thinking about when to make a break for it.

I had nothing to read, and after one of the goons brought me in a microwave meal for my tea, the evening stretched ahead. So, back to last night.

The two women, one at the Callanish, the other at Kilmartin. Those rather similar pronouncements – what did they mean?

Well, 'stones to the stones': I'd thought something had been buried at the Callanish stones. If last night was real, I'd seen it happening at the Kilmartin stones. Was it a fair guess that was why McMalkin and Harper had been at the Ring of Brodgar too? As to for what purpose, that was a complete mystery.

'*When the days balance the worlds balance*' sounded like a reference to the equinox. Hmm, that was in the next few days. And the balancing worlds might tie in with Martha's comment about stealing gravitons changing the balance between parallel worlds. While shutting the gate must surely refer to the F^2 gate?

But the real question was: why tell me about it? Or Malcolm. Why was any of this our business?

Oh. Other than maybe because we had the stones? Which were not buried in a stone circle but sitting quietly in our pockets. I felt myself shiver.

Then pushed that aside. The current problem was to break out. It was getting dark outside. The low cloud had dissipated during Ethan's long session. The moon would be up later, so if I could get out the window I'd have some light to bike by. Breaking the window lock with no tools and without a lot of noise was the main problem.

An idea occurred to me. I fished the stone out of my pocket and held it to the lock. Turn, damn you. There was a slight click. When I tried the window handle, it had freed. Hooray! All set for later on.

I'm used to waking in the middle of the night for mid-watches. So sleeping for a few hours and waking at around two was easy. The cabin felt quiet. I did that pillow thing where you try to make it look as if there is someone in the bed. Getting up onto the desk and out of the window was easy too. I did my best to pull the window shut behind me. The bikes were still there and not locked up – who would steal them out here? The nearly-full moon was bright enough to cast shadows.

Without my phone or a map the obvious choice was to go back the way I'd come. But when they noticed I was gone, that was the first route they'd check. My memory of looking up how to get to Malcolm's suggested that the area was all ridges roughly east-west with routes along the valleys on either side. So if I carried on I should hit a route back west on the other side of these hills. Also it was downhill and a quicker way to put some distance between us. Worth the risk.

So off I went. In the silver landscape the ride was almost as dreamlike as my memories of Kilmartin. I soon reached the next valley, with a bridge over a noisy stream. There was a hamlet with a sign 'Bridge of Balgie'. I turned west along the stream.

After nearly two hours the road was becoming more like a track. I began to worry it had wandered north or worse still, was going to peter out altogether. But to my relief it finally hit a proper north-south road. I stopped for a breather. There was a water bottle attached to the bike frame. It was almost a third full and I felt better after draining it. Another twenty minutes on I realised I was arriving at Tyndrum. This was the A82, the same road I'd used to and from Malcolm's. And after another half an hour I was back in Crianlarich. It was just before five and there was a faint hint of dawn in the easterly sky.

This was a dangerous moment since ambushing me back at my car was an obvious tactic. I dismounted and walked down the other side of the road from The Leaping Fish. Then stood and listened.

Nothing. Maybe they hadn't noticed I was gone yet.

Ten minutes later, grateful that my car keys had been in my pocket and not my rucksack, I had the bike loaded into the back seat and I was ready to go. I needed to see Malcolm, but I planned to go up there in the afternoon. Ethan and co might ring him or even turn up following his yesterday's calls. Easier all round if he had no idea where I was. For now, I was driving south, looking for some roadside inn where I could sleep and then brunch.

It was soon after midday when I started northwards again. My back was a bit sore because the bike had been set up for a shorter person than I was, but otherwise I felt OK. I'd caught up some sleep in the car park round the back of a rather pleasant droving inn, with my passenger seat tipped back. Then I'd relaxed with my swords and sorcery latest over a substantial full Scottish and some slow coffees. I'd have rung Malcolm from the inn to say I was coming, but his number was on my phone. Still, while I was getting the e-reader out of my luggage I came across his arrowhead gift and put it on. I hoped that would please him.

But when I got to Malcolm's cottage I saw his creaky old Land Rover was missing. Damn, he was out.

There was another cottage a bit further along the road, so I decided to try there and see if anyone knew when Malcolm would be back.

I banged on the front door, but jumped slightly as a voice came from my left. A capable-looking woman in a home-knit jumper had come round from the back and was standing there holding a bucket full of freshly dug spuds.

'Can I help you?' She was looking at me rather intently, her eyes flicking over my arrowhead pendant.

'Hi. I'm the cousin of Malcolm Nicholson, in the next cottage. He was trying to get in touch so I called by. But he's out. I wondered if you knew when he might be back?'

'You're the cousin that went up on the moor with him last Sunday?'

'Yes. Helen McIver.'

'I'm Glenys. I think Malcolm may be out until later afternoon. But we hold a key for him. I'm sure he wouldn't mind you waiting in the cottage. Come inside and I'll fetch it. Cup of tea?'

'Thanks, that would be great.' I was a little unnerved by her briskness.

Though the cottage looked the same as Malcolm's from the outside, it was very different inside. There was a long through room of lounge and kitchen, with French windows at the end framing a mountain view. The lounge had a fire burning and there was a big knitting frame to one side of it.

'Sit yourself down.'

I sat on the sofa. As I did, the ginger cat curled up at its other end opened its eyes. I held out my hand for it to sniff, thinking about Mog again. It decided I smelled of good intentions and nuzzled my fingers.

'Milk, sugar?' Glenys called from the kitchen.

'Milk and two sugars please.'

She came through with the mugs and handed one to me. Then sat in the chair by the knitting frame.

'Did Malcolm give you that pendant?' She gestured at the arrowhead.

'Yes, at the family wedding we were both just at. Someone told me it was the sign of Wicca.' Not sure why I said that.

Without a word she pulled an identical pendant from under her jumper.

'And is it?' I asked.

'Of course,' she said.

'I don't know anything about Wicca myself, but one of my ancestors was said to be a sorcerer.'

'Margaret MacAskill? Malcolm told me she was a relation only the other day. Yes, she was one of the earliest documented wise women and a prophet. We know her well.'

I noted the use of 'we'. I wondered what else Malcolm had told her.

'What did she prophecy?'

'*When the days balance, the worlds balance* is her best known one.'

'What?' I said sharply. Glenys looked at me quizzically. But I wasn't going to tell someone I'd only just met about the two women at the stone circles. Though if they'd been quoting my own ancestor at me, that made it all the more personal.

'So the equinox is important to Wicca?' I asked instead.

'Naturally. The balance of dark and light. We meet to celebrate it.'

'So you are meeting tomorrow?'

'Yes. At the Creag Na Caillich quarry. Where the arrowheads come from.'

That sounded horribly significant somehow. But the coincidences were making me feel queasy and I wanted some time on my own. I drained my mug.

'Well, thanks for the tea. I've taken enough of your time. If I can borrow the key I'll go and wait for Malcolm.'

She smiled gently and fished some keys out of her pocket.

'Here you go. And thanks to you for an interesting chat.'

Chapter 27

Malcolm – Saturday 20th September

I'd slept badly, despite being in my own bed. The more I ran my apparent memories of Nether Largie across my brain, the more detailed they became. And the more plausible. The restless cat didn't help.

When the phone rang, the list of possibilities had grown markedly compared with a week ago. Work? Most unlikely. Bernie? Unlikely. Polly? Not impossible. Henry? More likely. Helen? Very likely, but only assuming we'd both actually been at Nether Largie, and she'd remembered.

The phone display suggested it was Helen. But the voice wasn't Helen's.

'Is that Malcolm Nicholson?' said an American woman, in what sounded like an educated accent. 'I'm Martha. A friend of Helen's. Is she with you, please?'

'Yes, this is Malcolm,' I said. 'Why are you using Helen's phone? Has something happened to her?'

'She's been visiting with us,' said Martha, 'and she left her phone behind. I saw that you'd been trying to call her. So I thought you might know where she was.'

'She's not here,' I said. 'And, besides, if she doesn't have her phone, I've no way to contact her.'

'If she turns up,' said Martha, 'could you ask her to call, please?'

'All right,' I said.

'Thank you,' said Martha. 'Have a nice day.'

'You too,' I said.

And hung up.

So who was that? Helen hadn't mentioned visiting anyone. Maybe it was one of the Americans Helen had talked about; the same ones that claimed they saw Patricia Harper. But they're hardly Helen's friends.

It dawned on me how little I knew about Helen.

More loose ends? Well, I'd told the truth. But how was I to get in touch with Helen? I rather hoped she would turn up.

I showered and dressed, and fed the increasingly impatient cat. Then I checked the fridge, in search of breakfast. The milk had gone off and the bread was mouldy. I made myself a cup of tea, and set off to shop in Fort William.

As I crossed the Moor, the sky was clear, with high, scudding clouds in the gathering wind. The sun had lost its summer warmth, and the air smelt fresh, with a cold edge on the nostrils.

I made good time to Fort William, and drove across town to the supermarket on the northern fringe. I filled two bags with fresh produce, and a third with cat food and stores. Then I walked back into town, to Hernando's Hideaway, where I'd met Polly, what felt like an age ago. I'd a vague hope of seeing her again, but of course she wasn't there.

It struck me how little I knew about Polly: where she lived or what she liked to do with herself. I wondered if she was based in F²'s Glasgow offices. But neither she nor Bernie had mentioned each other, so maybe she was attached to the plant at Tigh Na Cruach. Still, there was time for that yet.

I ordered the full Mexican breakfast – fried eggs over spicy fried potatoes, with a side of salsa and sour cream, and fresh tortillas. That certainly made a nice change from hotel cuisine, no matter how haute. I was washing it all down with a cup of tea, when the phone rang. Henry Craig. Urgent business. Could I come round? No, we couldn't talk on the phone. I could stay for lunch.

With some misgivings, I accepted this kind offer. I'd little energy for Henry's puppy dog enthusiasms, and the prospect of more of Megan's cooking wasn't appealing. Still, seeing Megan was. And I wanted to make sure that RAGE weren't going to try anything totally stupid on Sunday.

I walked back to the supermarket, drove the Land Rover round to the pumps, and filled it up with diesel. An electric car would be hopeless in this part of the world, with potential charging locations few and far between. Maybe I could get an exemption, when they brought in the new climate control regulations.

As I drove down Lock Linnhe to Port Appin, I wondered what Helen was up to. She'd said she was on a climbing holiday. But surely she'd have missed her phone.

This time, I found the Craig's home without getting lost. Henry ushered me into his office. On the table was a plan of the F² facility, blown up from the back of the brochure, taped together from four A4 sheets of paper.

'Could you check this, please?' said Henry. 'And tell me about anything that's missing.'

I pored over the plan.

'It's a pretty good overview,' I said. 'I'll mark up the offices I know about, inside the main building. You'll especially need to look out for security.'

'Here you go,' said Henry, passing me a pencil.

Soon, the plan was covered in circles and arrows, and spidery scribbles.

'I think that's just about right,' I said. 'There's also that gate I mentioned, on the west side of the enclosure, near the Menzies Stone. I'd better mark that as well, in case you need to make a quick getaway.'

'Thanks,' said Henry. 'If there's a gate, maybe there's a way in underground.'

'Like the other end of an emergency exit?' I said, as I amended the plan. 'I've not noticed anything, but the heather's high, and I've never been through the fence.'

'Is there anything else I should know about?' said Henry.

I told Henry about the railway station checkpoint, and the robot dogs.

'That's all I know,' I said, handing Henry back his pencil. 'How many of you are going in?'

Henry looked abashed.

'So far, just three of us,' he said.

'Just three?' I said. 'How come? RAGE meetings are always well attended.'

'People are full of talk,' said Henry, 'but no one wants to actually do anything.'

'I'm surprised you're so keen,' I said. 'You kept a low profile at that meeting.'

'I was keeping my powder dry,' said Henry. 'This is the big one.'

'Well,' I said, 'good luck with it.'

'Actually,' said Henry, 'I was rather hoping you might join me.'

'Me?' I said. 'No way!'

'Aye well,' said Henry. 'Megan thought you'd say that. She's far better at reading people than I am. Thanks for all your help, though. Shall we have some lunch? It's the kids' turn to cook.'

Glad I'd had a big breakfast, I followed Henry into the living room. But I was pleasantly surprised. Megan and Henry beamed as the children took charge. Their cooking was at least equal to their mother's. Lunch was a hearty soup with fresh bread, followed by thick slices of a substantial omelette.

Replete, we retired to the sitting area, while the children tidied up and served hot drinks. As much curious as polite, I asked Henry and Megan about the next novel. Henry said it involved slave runners, who had been blown off course by a storm on a North Atlantic passage. As the ship floundered, the captive Africans overpowered the crew, and beached it on the small Inner Hebridean island, where the Preacher Man was due to conduct a wedding. After much derring do, and not a little romance, the slavers were taken into custody by the Redcoats, and the Africans sailed off for southern shores.

I thought it sounded contrived, though I could hardly say so. It certainly caught the moment.

Still, the Craigs were certainly good company, and we talked for far longer than I'd intended. By the time an afternoon snack was suggested, I feared I'd left it rather late to meet Polly.

As before, Megan saw me out.

'It's all happening tomorrow,' said Megan. 'I gather you're not going with Henry, so maybe you'd like to join us?'

'I thought it was women only?' I said.

'Wicca knows no gender,' said Megan. 'You'll be most welcome. And, besides, there'll be prosecco.'

'Thank you,' I said, 'but I've had enough excitement for one weekend. And enough to drink.'

'As you like,' said Megan, 'But if Margaret MacAskill's prophecies bear fruit, this is going to be the big one.'

'What do you mean?' I said. '*The big one*?'

'There have been reports,' said Megan. 'Strange signs and portents. From Callanish and Brogdar, as well as Nether Largie. The prophecies seem to point at the equinox as the pinnacle. And Creag Na Caillich is the fourth seat of power.'

'Well,' I said, 'my plans are to put my feet up. I've had enough chasing around.'

'I know you're sceptical, said Megan, 'but be that as it may, be sure to wear your arrowhead tomorrow.

'I'll do that,' I said, climbing into the Land Rover. 'Thanks for your hospitality. Please do thank the children.'

'See you the morn',' said Megan, with strange conviction.

I made my way back to the main road, and hammered south and east to Crianlarich. Polly was waiting at a table in the Tartan Trading Post cafe.

'Sorry I'm late,' I said, as I sat down opposite her.

'You are late, aren't you,' said Polly.

'I got held up,' I said. 'I was talking with RAGE about tomorrow.'

'What exactly are they planning?' said Polly.

'I'm not entirely sure,' I said.

'You can trust me, you know,' said Polly.

'I wouldn't be here if I didn't think I could,' I said, 'but I genuinely don't know. Henry had mentioned doing something at the main entrance, to get maximum publicity.'

'I'm not sure that'll do him much good,' said Polly. 'It'll be heavily guarded, and, besides, it's all happening after dark.'

'What exactly is happening?' I said.

'Now it's my turn to not know,' said Polly. 'I've only just been briefed. It seems they've not just been conducting passive experiments.'

They? Not we?

'What else have they been up to?' I said.

'They've built something they call a Transilience Gate,' said Polly.

Helen mentioned that.

'A gate?' I said, as I rootled around in my long forgotten secondary school physics. 'Like a transistor? To control the flow of gravitons?'

'Well, no,' said Polly. 'They're actually talking about a literal gate. I'd heard mutterings, but I thought it was all a metaphor for lay people.'

'Is that what I saw?' I said. 'On the screen? The big dodecahedron?'

'So you did see it,' said Polly. 'Good. I'd hoped you might. Yes, that's it. The physics sounds just about plausible. But they've yet to see if they can actually get more energy out of it than they have to put in. Just like fusion power.'

'If it's a gate,' I said, 'where does it go to?'

'I'm not entirely sure about that,' said Polly. 'And I don't think they are either. Actually, I feel a bit miffed that I've been kept in the dark for so long. I do have a PhD. And I am supposed to be their science communicator. Bloody patriarchs.'

I made sympathetic noises, and suggested that we order some tea.

'Have you any more details about what's happening tomorrow?' I asked, as we waited for our number to be called.

'It's all kicking off quite late,' said Polly. 'They're firing things up after 6pm. But I don't think anything's happening until around eight. I'm supposed to be there, to prepare a press release. If it all works.'

'That is late,' I said. 'I'd better let RAGE know. You're right, though. They'll not get much publicity unless they pull something spectacular.'

'Anything is better than nothing, I suppose,' said Polly. 'Will you be there?'

I sighed.

'No,' I said. 'I don't think so.'

'Why on earth not?' said Polly. 'I thought you felt strongly about this. That's why I approached you in the first place.'

'I do,' I said, 'but it's complicated.'

Polly laughed.

'You said that before,' she said.

'It's my job,' I said. 'I've been warned off doing anything that could be misconstrued as involving Rural Resource. Protesting about developments on the Moor seems to come into that category.'

'I can see that,' said Polly. 'That's a shame, though. I'd have felt better if I'd known you were going to be there.'

Goodness me!

Our number came up, and I collected a tray from the counter.

'I'm got a bad feeling about tomorrow,' I said, as I poured the tea. 'This is going to seem silly, but I'd like you to have this, as a sort of good luck charm.'

I handed Polly the arrowhead that Bernie had declined.

'A Neolithic arrowhead!' said Polly. 'Thank you! How lovely! It's not calc-silicate hornfels, is it?'

'Blimey!' I said, astonished. 'You and all! Yes, it certainly is. How did you know that?'

'When I was an undergrad,' said Polly, 'in my first year, I did an outside option on Scottish Archaeology. In some ways, I wish I'd stuck with it. I prefer known unknowns to unknown unknowns. What's your interest?'

'According to my wife, well, ex wife,' I said, 'I can bore for Britain on geology. I've never studied it formally, but it's always fascinated me. Our world is so old. And it was built up, layer by layer, fracture by fracture, over the millennia. What we see now hides so much past. Every stone tells a story, if we know how to read it.'

'Gosh!' said Polly. 'You really are serious about it.'

'And working on the Moor,' I went on, 'I need to know about the local formations, which is a great opportunity to find out more.'

'So where's the arrowhead from?' asked Polly, looping the cord over her head and round her neck.

'The quarry you followed me to,' I said. 'Creag Na Caillich.'

'That was a strange day,' said Polly. 'The way the mist just rose up like that. Maybe you could take me back there some time?'

'For sure!' I said, too eagerly.

'Well,' said Polly, looking at her watch, 'I'd best be on my way.'

'Where do you stay?' I said.

‘Perth,’ said Polly. ‘It’s handy for Glasgow. And it’s not too hard to get to the plant.’

‘Och, you should have said,’ I said. ‘I’m sorry you’ve had to come all this way. We could have met somewhere nearer.’

‘It’s fine,’ said Polly. ‘I wanted to see you. And it’s a nice day for a drive.’

Go on, then.

‘Have you family?’ I said.

‘Fishing, are we?’ said Polly. ‘No, it’s just me. Anyway, how was the wedding?’

‘Pretty strange,’ I said. ‘I’m glad I went, but I’m so glad it’s over. I’ll tell you another time.’

‘Maybe when we go to visit your quarry,’ said Polly.

‘Maybe we’ll have better things to talk about,’ I said.

We parted far more amicably that I could ever have hoped for. As I drove the short distance back to Achalladar, I mused on how the last week hadn’t been a total disaster.

The week wasn’t over. Outside the cottage was a familiar car. Helen’s car. And inside the cottage, conked out on the sofa, was Helen.

Chapter 28

Malcolm and Helen – Saturday 20th September

Malcolm lent over the sofa, and gently shook Helen by the right shoulder.

'Helen!' said Malcolm. 'Wake up! What are you doing here?'

Helen sat up suddenly and pushed him away, looking startled. Then relaxed.

'Oh, sorry man, I wasn't sure who you were for a moment. It's been a difficult couple of days.'

'Sorry if I surprised you. I've been trying to contact you, but you're the last person I expected to see. Is everything all right?'

'As you weren't who I thought you might be, it's all cool for now. Yes, I know you were trying to get in touch but I dinnit have my phone any more, so not a lot I could do about getting back to you. And I needed somewhere to go. Do you think I could stop over tonight?'

'Of course you can stay. There's so much we need to go over. Especially what happened after the wedding. But I knew you didn't have your phone. Some American woman called Martha's been using it to look for you.'

'Fuck. That was why I didn't come round a lot earlier. I thought they might try and trace me. What did you say to them?'

Malcolm briefly recounted the phone call.

'Good. So they won't know I'm here.'

'Are you hungry? You can tell me all about it while I cook.'

‘I had a late great brunch back in Crianlarich, but yes, some scran would be good.’ Helen sighed. ‘Mind me to be more careful about my so-called canny ideas. For sure this one was not so canny.’

They both went through to the kitchen. While Malcolm prepared dinner, Helen told him all about her dealings with the Americans, including Ethan’s interrogation and her night-time escape.

‘That’s so heavy!’ said Malcolm. ‘And these are the same Americans I saw a week ago? They seemed pretty harmless then. Just goes to show.’

‘Well, I think Martha and Dean have been supping with the devil using a short spoon. Ethan is the heavy one. Martha and Dean are really into their physics. They were looking pretty uncomfortable when I last saw them.’

‘I’m glad you’re here now, Helen. I’ve been having really weird flashbacks about what happened the evening after the wedding. At the Nether Largie stones. They don’t make much sense. Have you experienced anything like that? Sorry if that sounds crazy.’

‘No man, it doesn’t sound at all crazy. I’ve been getting – not flashbacks exactly – more images, from a strange sequence of events at the stones. But I think maybe they do make sense even if I dinnit have the complete story. How’s about you tell me about your flashbacks? Maybe my images fit in.’

Malcolm told Helen about the apparent sequence of events leading up to the birthing of the new green stone.

‘You mean Mog is actually McMalkin?’ Helen asked, sounding really upset. ‘But that’s crazy. Well, not just crazy, really scary. Given Mog was sleeping on the other side of my bed. And then the owl is actually Patricia Harper? Maybe they are sort of ghosts if they are both dead. Yerk.’

‘I think it’s maybe the other way round. McMalkin is actually your cat, and Patricia Harper’s the owl. It’s like the people are emanations of the animals. So you’ve been having the same sort of experiences?’

‘My images fit to your flashbacks like jigsaw pieces.’

Helen took up the story from the new stone and its burial, to when they got back to the hotel.

‘So the young woman repeated the same things I heard from the old woman at the Callanish stones,’ said Helen. ‘And your Wicca neighbour says they come from our ancestor Margaret MacAskill. That's even scarier,' she finished.

'Glenys? I suppose she let you in. I'm now not so sure about her. They're good people, her and Dougie, but some of her ideas seem pretty whacky.'

'You think so, man? She seemed pretty focused to me. Not as if weird things haven't been going on. The old woman was Wicca, the young woman must have been, and what about the woman you saw as well?'

'I suppose that makes some sort of strange sense. The striking woman did say one of the prophecies.'

'Which one? Sounds like three witches and three prophecies, if I was reading one of my swords and sorceries.'

'She said something like *'The gate that is open will be shut.'* If it's three witches, is that like Macbeth? We're in the right part of the world, but that seems even more ludicrous.'

'No idea man, didn't do that one at school. The big take-home is they want the F^2 gate shut. And why would they quote all our ancestor's stuff at us if we weren't involved in doing it?' asked Helen.

Malcolm sighed, put the casserole in the oven, and sat down heavily at the table opposite Helen.

'The gate shutting's precisely what isn't going to happen,' said Malcolm 'F^2 are planning on opening the gate on Sunday.'

Malcolm recounted his meeting with Polly Sharp.

'What! You're telling me that F^2 are going to power up the gate after what apparently happened in June? Are they crazy, man? Does your contact not know about all that?' Helen asked.

'Polly didn't mention anything happening in June.'

'I never got to tell you about Thierry's patient did I? He was there in June and it crashed his brain. And if you believe his story, man, three people came through the gate then. God only knows what will happen if they open it again.'

'That's mental! People came through the gate! So what happened to them? Did they survive?'

'They might have been McMalkin and Patricia Harper. Why else would F^2 be after them? Or maybe it was the three women. Which would make them sort-of aliens in my book. Either way, yes, on the loose I'd say.'

'Aliens? Witches? This is all spinning out of control. I'm most worried about what might happen tomorrow if F^2 succeed. But I can't see how they can be stopped.'

Malcolm told Helen about Henry Craig's plans.

'Henry really wants me to join them tomorrow,' said Malcolm, 'but I can't see what good that'll do. Anyway, I'm really not keen. My job could be on the line.'

'Hah! Well if it all goes pear-shaped your job might be the least of our worries,' said Helen.

'How is making a protest at the plant going to change anything? They need to be stopped from firing up the gate.'

Malcolm opened the oven and prodded the casserole.

'Should be ready soon,' said Malcolm. 'You know, I still don't get how this all links to the three women.'

'Look, it's clear what they're up to,' Helen said vehemently. 'They want us to go in there and use our stones, don't they man?'

'Why on earth do you think that? We've not actually talked with any of them. Well, you did at Callanish, but that all sounded pretty obscure.'

'OK. Here's how I think it goes. They dragged us off to Kilmartin to see a new stone being made using our stones to do it. They know we have the stones that belonged to Mog and the owl, or McMalkin and your Patricia Harper. They are quoting prophecies right at us from our own ancestor with a big stress on closing the gate. And obscure seems to be how they do things.'

'Well, that's a theory. And what Megan was saying seems to back it up. To be honest, I don't have an alternative. So are you actually saying we should go into the plant with the RAGE folk?'

'Maybe. I get the idea your RAGE guys dinnit have a clue what they are doing or how dangerous it might be. And I think the stones would get us in through that back gate we spotted. RAGE might be a handy diversion. But there again, having more people with us might help.'

'Och, Helen, that's such a big ask. And we'd have to get from the back gate to the plant. It must be a mile at least. And those bloody dogs'll spot us before we've even started.'

'Well man, let's sleep on it. But if it goes the way I think, those women might not give us the option.'

'I wonder if there's some way we could contact them. Maybe Glenys would know?'

'That's a plan. Ask her tomorrow, man. Now, how's about the scran?'

Chapter 29

Malcolm and Helen – Sunday 21st September

Helen woke with her back feeling sore again, after a night on Malcolm's fold down sofa. She got up and went to the bathroom.

Malcolm's phone rang. Malcolm appeared, looking bleary.

'Helen!' called Malcolm.

Helen emerged rubbing her eyes.

'It's for you,' he said. 'From your phone. Must be that Martha woman. My turn.'

Malcolm handed Helen the phone and disappeared into the bathroom.

Helen held Malcolm's phone for a moment, looking confused and then indecisive. She wondered whether to speak to Martha, then wondered whether it was really Martha and not Ethan. Finally she shrugged, realising Malcolm had as good as said she was there.

'Hi. Good of you to ring, man. I really would like my phone back.'

'Hi honey'. Yes, it was Martha, but at rather less than her usual volume. 'Gotta to keep my voice down, Ethan doesn't know I'm making this call.'

Oh.

'OK,' said Helen, sceptically.

'I wanted to apologise for all that stuff, honey. Believe me, it wasn't what Dean and I wanted. Ethan kinda gets carried away sometimes.'

No shit Sherlock, thought Helen.

'Yes, so I noticed. Well, thanks I suppose,' she said.

'But that wasn't the only thing. Dean and I have been thinking about your physics question. And about people coming through the gate.' Martha paused. 'There are some assumptions in the math that nobody has questioned yet. They might just support that. But the key item is what happens if you siphon gravitons off from a parallel world. That decays its probability level.'

Helen felt it was a bit early in the day for a physicist in full cry. Still, it sounded like Martha was trying to be helpful.

'Martha, you know I'm not a physicist myself. What does that mean?'

'It means that excess graviton transfer could actually kill off a parallel world. Make it so improbable it ceased to exist. If you lived in one and worked that out, you sure might be unhappy.'

'Wow, serious stuff man. Hey – did you know they were going to run the gate again today, Martha?'

Silence on the other end of the phone.

'Well yes, honey, we did,' Martha said at last. 'I'm afraid we are going to be there when they try to do that. Ethan is a tad worried about it and decided we have to intervene.'

'What? You are going to be in the plant?'

'Yeah, we're a Health and Safety team for the purpose. Emergency inspection. That young police officer is going to front for us. Your cousin I think?'

'Steven? Has he agreed?'

'I don't think he has the option, sugar. Ethan is in with his high-level bosses.'

Poor Steven, thought Helen. He probably doesn't know how dangerous this could be. But without her phone she didn't have his number. There was nothing at all she could do to warn him.

'Thanks for letting me know. Well man, good luck.'

'You too honey. And sorry again.'

Martha ended the call. Damn, Helen thought, she hadn't asked Martha how she'd get her phone back. Neither had she mentioned Malcolm's RAGE friends and their plans. But she was certain that if Ethan was involved it was much better to stay out of the whole thing. In any case Malcolm might not be anyone's first choice for something like storming a plant.

'Malcolm!' Helen shouted. 'Change of plan.' Malcolm emerged from the bathroom looking pink. Helen told him what Martha had just said, and how it explained why people from parallel worlds might want the gate shut for good.

'But I think that bollixes us going into the plant,' Helen concluded. 'No way am I meeting Ethan again.'

'That's a relief,' said Malcolm. 'I thought Henry's whole scheme was mad. So where does that leave us?'

'We've still got those three women to worry about,' said Helen. 'And I really do want to get shut of this stone. So let's go to the Wicca thing at the quarry and see what happens. It is the equinox and there was all that stuff about balancing worlds then.'

'That sounds even madder than Henry's plan,' said Malcolm, 'but, hey, what the hell. At worst we'll get wet feet and a glass of prosecco.'

'Prosecco? Now you're talking, man. This Wicca crowd can't be all bad,' said Helen.

'Sorry Helen,' said Malcolm, 'but I think that's a running joke. It's what their men think they're doing. We could take a hip flask, though. Anyway, I'll need to contact Henry. And then I better see Glenys to find out what they plan.'

'OK, sounds good. But can we have breakfast first? Maybe I'll go for toast this time if you have some bread?' said Helen.

'I did a big shop yesterday,' said Malcolm. 'Oh bugger, it's still in the Land Rover!'

'Let me get my keks on and then I'll give you a hand unloading.'

They both finished dressing. Then they brought in the shopping, and Malcolm made breakfast. After eating, Helen tidied up and Malcolm phoned Henry.

'Malcolm!' said Henry. 'I was hoping you'd get in touch. We're all set to go. But we don't know the timing. Have you learnt anything?'

Malcolm explained that things were supposed to get going by eight. Then told Henry he wasn't going with them.

'I'm sorry Henry,' Malcolm said, 'but there's bigger stuff happening.'

'What do you mean?' said Henry. 'That sounds like a weak excuse. Or is there something you're not telling me?'

'I've heard that there's going to be a big police presence,' Malcolm said, desperately making it up as he went along.

'A big police presence is just what we want!' said Henry.

'But they'll round you up in no time at all,' Malcolm said 'and then it'll turn into one of those '*Defend The Rannoch Three*' things, and everyone'll lose sight of what F^2 are up to.'

'We'll just have to make sure we don't get caught then,' said Henry.

'If you need someone on the outside to bail you out, you can always contact me,' Malcolm said, 'but I'm really not going in.'

'Aye well,' said Henry. 'Megan said you wouldn't come. You'll regret it when you see us on TV.'

'She's a wise woman, Megan,' Malcolm said. 'Be careful.'

'Surely will,' said Henry. And rang off.

'Am I wrong, or is that man a bit of a wassock?' asked Helen.

Malcolm laughed.

'Well,' said Malcolm, 'at least that's settled. I suppose we'd better go and see Glenys, and find out what they're up to this evening.'

'OK. I bet it involves stumbling around in the dark again, going on Kilmartin,' said Helen.

The cousins left the cottage and went up the track to Glenys and Dougie's house. Malcolm knocked on the front door. Dougie answered it, in full police uniform.

'Malco, my man!' said Dougie. 'Is this your cousin Helen?'

'That's right,' said Malcolm. 'Helen, this is Dougie, Glenys' husband. Is Glenys around, Dougie?'

'Another cousin!' said Dougie. 'Nice to meet you. Glenys said you'd turned up out of the blue. Do come in. I'm just off. There's been a robbery in Tyndrum, and I've been called out.'

'Hope it's easier to sort than my break in,' said Malcolm.

As Dougie drove off in his police car, Malcolm and Helen went through to the living area.

'Hey Malcolm!' said Glenys, getting up from her knitting frame. 'Hello Helen. I hope you've had a good night's sleep. You certainly looked like you needed one. Cup of tea?'

'Thanks,' said Malcolm. 'But we've just had breakfast.'

'So how can I help?' said Glenys.

'When I was here yesterday,' Helen began 'you said you had a do this evening. In the quarry the arrowheads come from.'

'It's not a do,' said Glenys, patiently. 'It's the Autumn Equinox ceremony. It's one of the cardinal events of the seasons. And this year is particularly important. You both know the prophecies.'

'Sorry to get that wrong,' Helen said. 'I didn't mean to be disrespectful. I was wondering whether we might be able to come along. We have been told the prophecies several times in the last week or so by different people. It sounded like we might have some role to play.'

'Your stones combined would be sources of great strength,' said Glenys.

'Stone? How do you know about that?' Helen demanded.

'It told me,' said Glenys. 'Besides, you've been fiddling with it the whole time. We knew you'd join us.'

'That's a big assumption!' said Malcolm. 'We need to know what's likely to happen, before we agree to anything.'

'Anything can happen,' said Glenys. 'When the moon rises, and lights up the cliffs surrounding the quarry, great forces are unleashed. And it's a full moon tonight. That's particularly auspicious on the Equinox. They only coincide every twenty years or so. And we have two stone bearers.'

'This is all just vague supposition,' said Malcolm. 'You don't buy this, do you, Helen?'

'Normally no, man,' said Helen. 'I dinnit believe in boggles nor brags. But what about Kilmartin? Either it was the two of us in one hallucination or it happened. So let's give this the benefit of doubt, but.'

'You were at Nether Largie as well!' said Glenys. 'You didn't tell me that, Malcolm. Of course you must both come! The moon must rise above Tarmachan to illuminate the quarry. So you'll need to be there just before sunset. We'll be there around seven.'

Chapter 30

Malcolm and Helen – Sunday 21st September

The sun was low in the sky when Malcolm and Helen pulled up on the verge below the path to the quarry.

'Here we are,' said Malcolm. 'I still think this is crazy.'

'Go with the flow, man!' said Helen. 'Dinnit be such a wet blanket. So now where? The sun's setting and it'll be easier to find our way if we get gannin.'

'I'm not sure what we should do. Do we wait here for someone else to turn up, or just head up the hill? Glenys didn't say.'

'If you're sure you know the way, let's go for it,' said Helen.

'The path starts just across the road, and then we follow the stream.'

They put their boots on and set off up the hill. At the old shielings, Helen paused to look back.

'Cool sunset! If I had my phone it would make a good pic.'

'We're about halfway,' said Malcolm, 'so I reckon we need to keep moving.'

Beyond the shielings, they followed the second branch of the burn, up towards the quarry. As they approached the plateau, they could see the flicker of a fire across the mountain flank.

'Looks like we're going to be on time,' said Malcolm. 'I wonder if I'll know anyone besides Glenys.'

They came off the rise into the quarry. People dressed in white were illuminated by the flames from the fire in the centre. Glenys came across and joined them.

'Helen! Malcolm!' said Glenys. 'Welcome. Here! Put these on.'

Glenys handed them each a white robe.

'Do we have to get undressed?' said Malcolm.

'No we dinnit,' said Helen very quickly. 'This is Scotland, for Christ's sake.'

'You can if you really want to,' said Glenys, 'but we're all wearing thermals.'

Helen and Malcolm pulled on the robes over their coats.

'This way,' said Glenys, walking across to the fire. 'We're just about to start. Could you stand here please.'

She led them behind the fire to a large flat rock, at the entrance to the defile that led through the mountains.

'I don't remember this rock being here,' muttered Malcolm, as they climbed up onto it.

A drum sounded a single solemn beat, and Glenys rejoined the people gathered round the fire. The drum sounded again, and a young woman stepped forward, took up a twig broom and swept her way around it.

Malcolm nudged Helen.

'That's Mary,' he said, sotto voce. 'Henry and Megan's eldest.'

When she had completed her circuit, Mary put down her broom and rejoined the circle.

The drum began to sound a low beat, and two older women stepped out of the circle towards the fire.

'*With salt I bless you,*' said one woman, scattering sparkling crystals from a clay bowl.

'*With water I bless you,*' said the other, shaking shining drops from a clay beaker.

'Bloody hell!' said Malcolm. 'That's Jess and Jeannie!'

'Is this your friendly neighbourhood Wicca club then?' asked Helen. 'Very Scottish. We have the Women's Institute in Sunderland.'

The circle reformed.

Glenys raised her arms: '*Come powers of earth, of soil, of growth, come join.*'

The woman opposite Glenys in the circle raised her arms: '*Come powers of the air, of change and season, come join.*'

Megan raised her arms: '*Come powers of fire, of vigour, of light, come join.*'

Finally a fourth woman raised her arms: '*Come powers of water, of moon and tide, come join.*'

As they began to dance and chant in unison – '*Come powers of fate, of time and space...*' – the moon rose through the pass, bathing the quarry in silver.

The air above the fire began to quiver and expand in a silver blur. The circle halted and all the women stared upwards.

Three figures formed in the disturbed air, larger than life. They resolved into the shapes of three women.

'That's the old woman from the Callanish!' said Helen.

'And that's the woman who hypnotised me!' said Malcolm.

'And the young woman...' Helen began, '... from Nether Largie!' Malcolm finished.

Most of the circle huddled backwards, away from the fire, astonished. Only Glenys and Megan stood their ground.

'Hail spirits,' said Megan resolutely. 'What are your wishes?'

'*What's given to the stones remains given,*' said the young woman.

'*When the days balance, the worlds balance,*' said the old woman.

'*The gate that is open will be shut,*' said the hypnotic woman.

Then they gestured at the assembled Wiccans, and Malcolm and Helen saw them become rigid and unseeing.

'What the fuck have you done to them?' said Malcolm angrily, getting down from the rock and approaching the three women.

The women stepped casually from the air above the fire onto the ground, and shrank to a more human size.

'Don't you worry child,' said the old woman. 'This is a private conversation. They are out of the temporal lattice for now.'

'Who the hell are you?' said Helen, joining Malcolm. 'Did you come through the F_2 gate? Are you from a parallel world?'

'Not at all,' said the striking woman. 'The Wiccans called on the Powers of Fate, Time and Space, didn't they? We are the guardians of all the worlds.'

'Come on!' said Malcolm. 'Guardians of all the worlds! We weren't born yesterday.'

'But you were born yesterday,' said the old woman.

‘And your ancestor Margaret MacAskill just the day before,’ said the young woman.

‘But let’s cut the cackle,’ said the woman with shimmering skin. ‘Yes, we came through the gate, and we have come here to call on you to help close it.’

‘So why do you need us,’ said Malcolm, ‘if you really are Powers of Time and Space?’

‘Oh!’ said Helen. ‘It’s the green stones, isn’t it?’

‘Well-spoken, child,’ said the old woman. ‘You carry the stones of our familiars, Greymalkin and Harpier, which are now bound to you. Their purpose is to focus the web of energy we will weave from the stones we planted in places of power. Without them, we cannot close the gate.’

‘We’re very keen to stop the gate functioning,’ said Malcolm. ‘We think tapping graviton energy is a huge danger to the environment. But why do you want to close it?’

‘We are the guardians of space and time,’ said the woman with agate eyes, ‘The gate threatens all of this part of space and time. See!’

She gestured upwards, and the air thickened into a silvery shimmering fabric above their heads.

‘This is a fold of the web of worlds,’ said the young woman. ‘Your thread is there.’

At her gesture a thin green thread shone out of the fabric, connected to a glowing green point.

‘And this is what will happen if the gate continues,’ said the old woman.

Around the glowing green point, the fabric withered and dimmed, leaving only the single shining green thread.

‘All that is left is your world,’ said the old woman.

‘We cannot allow this to happen,’ the three women said in unison.

‘But what happens if you take all that energy to close the gate?’ Helen asked. ‘Someone told me that removing gravitons lowers the probability of a parallel world – what happens to our thread then?’

‘You are right, child,’ the old woman said gently. ‘Your thread must decay into the web to save it.’

The green line faded from the fabric.

'But all of you exist everywhere in the fold around this world. So you continue in the web even when this thread dies.'

'But we are what we remember,' said Malcolm. 'Will we still be us?'

'Those who witness and bear the arrowhead will remember,' said the young woman. Helen touched the arrowhead at her throat, and Malcolm felt for his in his pocket.

Then all three women said in unison, 'Time is running out. You must decide!'

'What time is it?' Helen asked Malcolm.

Malcolm checked his phone.

'Bloody hell!' said Malcolm. 'It's nearly eight o'clock.'

'Let's do it,' said Helen. 'If we still can.'

'All right,' said Malcolm, reluctantly. 'All right.'

The three women raised their arms, and began an incantation in some unfamiliar language. Malcolm and Helen found they were reaching for their stones.

The stones flared green tongues of light, gathered up into a beam by the women's hands. Then the air around them filled with new rays of light, coming from beyond the mountains all around them. The women glowed so brightly, Malcolm and Helen wanted to look away.

'Follow the shining path,' the three women said, pointing behind Malcolm and Helen.

They turned. 'Oh wow!' said Helen.

A broad path built of silver moonlight floated across the landscape, as far as they could see.

Malcolm groaned.

'Are you OK with this?' Helen asked him.

'Have we any choice?' said Malcolm.

They linked hands, stepped onto the path and began to walk. The land flowed under their feet, as each step covered kilometres.

'Canny path,' said Helen. 'Seems like we can get there in time.'

'We're over the Moor already,' said Malcolm, now more entranced than scared. 'And the path goes straight down into the F_2 plant.'

As they came to the roof of the plant, it dissolved around them. Then the path dived downwards through the main building, through the floor and into the cavern housing the Transilience Gate.

The brightly lit chamber was thronged with people. Red warning lights flashed on the control pedestal. The dodecahedron throbbed purple.

Polly, wringing her hands, stood with a film unit to one side of the dodecahedron. Next to the pedestal, a group of F_2 staff in white lab coats milled around. In front of them, Dr Sam Crawford remonstrated with Ethan. Two muscular young men in suits, waving automatic pistols, backed Ethan up. Martha and Dean stood nearby with Steven, looking on, aghast.

'What's going on?' demanded Crawford. 'Who are these lunatics with guns? You claimed you were Health and Safety!'

'You don't know what the hell you are doing here,' shouted Ethan. 'You have to stop the experiment! Now!'

As Malcolm and Helen appeared, everyone swivelled and froze. The silver path faded as they stepped onto the concrete floor.

'Helen!' cried Steven. 'What in god's name are you doing here? Get out right now! This is really dangerous!'

'Malcolm!' exclaimed Polly, moving towards him. 'Thank goodness you're here! I need your help! This is really crazy!'

As the dodecahedron vibrated more rapidly, the chamber lights dimmed.

'Ethan,' Martha yelled. 'Look out, there's another power drain. Something is tapping the energy supply.'

In a burst of silver, the path reappeared. Ethan's henchmen leapt forward, brandishing their weapons. A large tabby cat stepped off the path. As its paws touched the concrete, it transformed into McMalkin. An owl alighted behind McMalkin, and changed into Patricia Harper. The embodied familiars pointed at the gunmen, whose weapons glowed red hot and dropped from their hands.

Helen went white. 'Jesus Christ, Malcolm! McMalkin was dead. And now he isn't!'

'It's all right, Helen,' said Malcolm. 'He's just an aspect of the cat, like we thought.'

Before anyone else could speak, the three women arrived in a huge burst of green energy. Without pausing, they advanced inexorably on the dodecahedron.

'My god!' screamed Crawford. 'Those women! They're the ones that came through the gate when we first fired it up! This is a nightmare!'

Ethan flung himself in front of them.

'This is unauthorised! I demand you halt!' he shouted.

The old woman gestured at him. Ethan stopped in mid-step, as if paralysed, and toppled over.

'*When the days balance, the worlds balance. The gate that is open will be shut,*' intoned the three women.

Again spellbound, Malcolm and Helen held their stones high. A wave of green light broke over the gate as the three women glided through it and vanished.

Behind the gate, the emergency exit burst open, and Henry Craig rushed out of the tunnel into the chamber, waving a banner: '*Grouse Not Gravitons!*'

Smoke rose from the control pedestal and, as the white-coated F_2 employees scattered, burst into flames. Crawford grabbed an extinguisher. As he rushed towards the fire, the dodecahedron flared with rainbow colours, and slowly folded in on itself.

'Everybody out!' shouted Helen. 'Now!'

She grabbed a dazed-looking Steven by the arm, and dragged him towards the tunnel. Two large ceiling panels fell with a crash into the chamber, as the walls began to buckle.

'Come on!' said Malcolm to Polly, taking her hand. They pursued Helen and Steven into the doorway, Martha and Dean close behind.

'Look!' exclaimed a transfixed Henry, blocking their way, gesturing at the vanishing dodecahedron. 'Look!'

'Come on!' yelled Malcolm, brushing past Henry. 'The whole place is coming down!'

'Follow me, everybody,' said Steven, with regained authority, shining a torch down the pitch black tunnel. 'Please keep calm. But let's be quick.'

The group fled into the tunnel, followed by a rush of F_2 staff. Ominous sounds came from behind them.

The tunnel smelt damp and was only just head height, but the floor was paved, and they made rapid progress. Martha and Dean deployed their phones as extra flashlights.

'How long is this god-damn thing?' muttered Dean at last, checking the time on his phone. 'We've been down here a good fifteen minutes.'

'Not much further,' said Henry, illuminating the metal-runged ladder at the tunnel end with his own flashlight.

Henry ascended the ladder and opened the hatch. One after another, they clambered up the ladder, and tumbled out onto the moonlit heather, the mountains silhouetted against the silvery sky.

'That sure was a lucky escape,' said Dean, dusting himself down.

'Is everyone out?' asked Steven. 'Maybe we should check the tunnel.'

But over to the east, the sky lit red, and there was an earth-shaking explosion. Then the world began to dissolve.

Chapter 31

Helen – Tuesday 9th September

How can you describe what you cannot describe? I was standing in a moonlit evening watching the F^2 plant explode and feeling the ground shudder. Then something. And the next moment after that, I was watching what was clearly a Kongsberg dynamic position controller in broad daylight on what had to be the Alba na Cuan, at sea.

I've thought about it a lot since, tried to focus on it the way I did with the Kilmartin images. Maybe I saw that same silvery fabric that the three women had showed us in the quarry? But much closer, with only a few visible threads? And slid from one thread to another? And a feeling of doubleness, like after one too many single malts? But there again, maybe I'm just making it all up. Sometimes I wonder if any of it really happened at all.

Anyway, I didn't have much time to think about things just then. Bodger Jones stuck his head through the door.

'Hey, Hulkie, Skipper wants you, main deck aft, pronto. Bring your med kit, he says.'

'What's up man?' I croaked, my voice compressed by the terror that I was in some sort of *Groundhog Day*, and the whole thing was going to happen again.

'Don't panic, nobody died. Riddle's cut his hand on the winch gear. That boyo is a walking disaster on a ship.'

'Aye, aye Sir' – the only possible response. I grabbed the First Aid Box and a box of latex gloves.

When I got aft, there was a huddle round the trawl net, only just winched in and still streaming water. Tangled in it was the lost signal buoy we'd been looking for. Bullseye from the sonar. I felt a terrific surge of happiness. No *Groundhog Day*. Just a bit of time travel. Wow, I'd read about it in countless stories, and here I was actually doing it!

Riddle was off to one side holding his right wrist and looking pale.

'Cheer up laddie,' I said, probably sounding far too happy. 'Worse things happen at sea. Let's get you fixed up.'

It was a nasty gash in his palm, and so I took him below to clean it up properly. I used steri-strips to hold it together, and added a light bandage on top.

'Well Riddle, just as well we're nearly done. You need to take care of that for a day or two. Avoid any pressure on it and keep it dry.'

Then, as I was filling in the incident book, and quite without thinking, I asked: 'How's that brother of yours now?'

'Jackie?' Riddle asked in an astonished voice. 'How do you know about him?'

Not only should I not have known about him, I shouldn't have asked about him either. Crews don't welcome nosiness about their shore life, so I'd broken protocol.

'Apologies Riddle, must be confusing you with someone else.'

'No problem, Hulkie,' Riddle said. 'Jackie's just found another job. He was working over at Rannoch Moor, but they let him go back in the spring. He's just been taken on by Elizabeth Yule. As a driver,' he added when I looked puzzled. 'They run the buses, such as they are round our way.'

'Good for him,' I said.

Luckily the PA started up at that point, relieving my embarrassment.

'Captain from the bridge, all hands. We have a Shipping Forecast for a NNE gale force 10 moving to storm force 11 in Minch from 02.00 hours tomorrow. I have therefore taken the decision to abort our final task and return to port. Starting in about thirty minutes when the new schedule is plotted.'

So this really was a different world. Even the weather was different. And my slip with Riddle showed that it was different for other people too. That was more than a bit scary. The F^2 plant had sacked Riddle's brother back in the spring when I remembered him working there in June. How could I know that what I remembered from before this contract was still OK?

What about my family? Was Wilf still my on-off boyfriend? I felt in my pocket. I did have my phone, or the Hulkie of this world had. What had the Hulkie that was now me been up to that I didn't know about? My head spun. There was now one Hulkie where there had been two. What happened to the other one? Had I kind of killed myself?

I was dragged out of the rabbit hole by Bodger reappearing.

'Hulkie, are you done with Riddle? We need to get started.'

On the checks we carried out before starting the main engines, he meant. It was about fourteen hours to Troon, though luckily the coming storm was behind us and would speed us up a bit. But it wouldn't be a good time for an engine problem.

While I was in the engine room I felt in my pockets again. There had been something else there when I looked for my phone. I pulled out the green stone. And nearly had a heart attack. The whole point had been to get rid of it.

Hang on though, it did feel different. No glow, no vibration.

'Hey, Bodger. Any idea where this pretty pebble I picked up comes from?'

I handed it to him. I felt nothing, no panic. Not even a twinge.

Bodger turned it round.

'Same colour as the pendant I got my wife back in Tobermory. Iona green marble that was, boyo. Though I'm no geologist. You should get it polished.'

'Maybe I will,' I said, taking it back.

Phew, it was just a stone in this world. Thank Christ for that.

There was something very comforting about shipboard routine. We were busy until it was time to eat, and because we were underway, it was one on and one off. I was first for Gammon Findlay's specialty chicken leg.

When I relieved Bodger, I got my phone out, feeling weird about it. Partly because I was on duty and mobiles on duty were banned, and partly because it wasn't really my phone.

But it looked just like my real phone. The one the Americans had confiscated. It had the annoying scratch on the top left of the screen where I had dropped it, pretty soon after I got it – which was when? Beginning of last year. So did that mean the two Hulkies were still one at that point? I really hoped so. That was after I'd dumped Jed and just as I was beginning to get matey with Wilf in the hill-walking club. Or at least, he was beginning to get matey with me, I corrected myself.

Yes, I did still have Wilf's number.

But there were no phone numbers from later than today. No Steven. No Malcolm either. Duh. Of course not. But I did remember Malcolm's email. Though from a lookup several days from now. Hmm.

I hesitated. Malcolm was the only other person in the whole world I could talk to about what had happened. On the other hand, could I be sure he had reappeared in the same world as me? Or that he was a Rannoch Ranger in this world, come to that? An email could make me look like a raving idiot. But I didn't have long to work it out. Bodger would be back soon and later we might not have any signal. So I went for it. I suggested if he fancied a chat he should let me have his number.

I also sent a short email to Dad. He's not what you'd call a digital junkie but he does use email. Reassuringly, the few recent emails of his I remembered were on the phone. I told him the voyage was finishing a day early because of the weather and I'd be in touch the next day. He often used the computer in the evening because he was into classic cars (don't ask – there's an ancient sports car in pieces in his garage) and chatted with others similarly obsessed. So he should read it today.

When Bodger came back, we set up the Scrabble as we had most evenings on the voyage. We went through two hard-fought games. My biggest triumph was when Bodger put down 'Elect' and I added 'rolytes' for a double word, the 'y' on a double, and using all my letters too. But Bodger won both in the end.

We arrived at Troon about 6.30 as the sun rose, though only in theory, as it was windy and wet. But Troon is sheltered from storms, so the wind wasn't as fierce as out in the Minch. We docked and then had breakfast before finishing.

I walked to the car with that sense of déjà vu all over again. As I loaded my kitbag in, I found myself looking round for a cat. Duh again.

Anyway, Mog hadn't been a cat in the usual sense. 'Hadn't been'? Wouldn't be? Not that either. If a tree falls and there is nobody to hear it...

It was underwater driving on the A77 with lorries throwing up fountains of spray. I stopped at the Kilmarnock services for another coffee. I was in no hurry and it was a good place to make calls.

First I rang home.

'Oh hello, Pet. Your father said you'd be ringing.' Mam went off into one of her spiels from which I extracted now familiar items. A letter had just arrived for Dad's hernia op, they'd miss Alison's wedding, would I go. Fate seemed determined to rub my face in this wedding. Though I was even less keen than my first time round, I had to agree. Especially when Dad came on the line.

'Sorry to have landed you with standing in, Topsy, but very happy you are doing it. Say something nice to them all from us. Your Mam has sent off a present. Maybes you could let Bernie know, we're off to get me admitted to the hospital next.'

So far so good then. The world didn't seem to have changed very much at all. Maybe that was the point? Assuming the three women had some control over where to dump me?

I rang Bernie. Now this felt very odd, since she'd not seen me for years but I'd seen her only a few days before. Or so my memory claimed. I told her about coming to the wedding in place of my parents and struggled hard not to mention anything I'd learned from chatting to people at my version of the wedding. She gave me the earful about Malcolm that sounded just like the one I remembered.

'So how's work?' I asked her.

'Oh Helen,' she said. 'Such a difficult time. You know I work for F^2? Well, it all went wrong last year. There was some crucial experiment over at the Rannoch plant that didn't work, and the venture capitalists who'd been supporting us backed off. We'd all have been down the road if one of the partners in our EU project hadn't rescued us.'

I made sympathetic noises.

'So wasn't the rescue a good thing?' I asked.

'Well yes,' she said. 'But they're French. They've mothballed the plant and moved some of the scientists to Paris. I'm on gardening leave now

– they are a huge company and they don't need an HR person in Glasgow.'

'Can't you move to Paris too?'

'Well, I have got a French Higher, and they have offered, though it would be a demotion. But it's such a big change Helen, I dinnae ken what to do.'

'I can see it's a big decision,' I said slowly. 'But maybes it's a good moment for a change? That'll be your youngest child married, and you know I think it's long since time you and Malcolm called it a day. You never know, you might meet some nice French guy.'

'Aye well,' she said, 'Pigs might fly.'

'No, really. Go for it I'd say. Hey – I just left a ship at Troon and I'm coming through Glasgow today. I plan to climb some Scottish mountains. Can we meet up for a coffee and a better chat?'

'Why didn't you say! Come and stop over, it would be great to have a really good blether.'

So that was me sorted for the night. The F^2 stuff might be a problem for Bernie, but it was a big relief for me. No *Groundhog Day* again. And no Thierry either. At least not yet.

My last call was the trickiest. Wilf.

Come on, Hulkie, I told myself. Maybes you dinnit feel as independent as you think. He's no Jed. You'll not get a bigger adventure than the one you were in. Take your own advice – time for a change?

'Hi, Wilf,' I said.

'Hulkie! I was really hoping you'd ring. Canny trip?'

'Aye, it had its moments. Listen – do you fancy coming to a family wedding with me, Thursday next week?'

Chapter 32

Malcolm – Tuesday 9th September

The world scintillated and reformed. I felt as if I had momentarily blacked out. Dazed, I looked around.

I was alone. I was standing by the Menzies Stone, on the other side of the fence. There were no lights on the horizons. The sun had set, the quarter moon was rising, and the stars were beginning to appear.

Thank god I'd escaped from that tunnel. I thought I was going to die down there. The longer there was no sign of a way out, the more the sides seemed to press in on me, the more I felt I was going to suffocate. I'd tried to get past it, but it all came back to me: when the jerry built school started to collapse, when I went back in to look for the missing child, when the wall crumbled on top of me...

But now I was safe.

The Land Rover was parked nearby. Above the Land Rover, an owl sat on the fence, watching me.

Automatically, I reached in my pocket for the green stone, and held it up to the owl. The owl just sat there. I inspected the green stone. The stone was dull, just like any old stone. I put the stone back in my pocket.

What had happened? Had we closed the gate? Had the worlds rebalanced? Had the probabilities summed to one? I knew where I was, but I didn't know when I was.

I took out my mobile phone, and turned it on. The home screen showed the date: Tuesday, the 9th of September. Twelve days earlier.

The day everything changed. Maybe we had closed the gate. Maybe the worlds had rebalanced. But, then, what was this world like?

That Tuesday – today – I was here – I had been here – looking for Patricia Harper. If this world was different, then maybe she'd never been here.

I went over to the Land Rover and took out the torch. Then I inspected the heather around the Menzies Stone. There was no sign of a bicycle. Next, I scrutinised the ground alongside the fence. There was no sign of the green stone. Of course not. It was still in my pocket.

Grouse rose from the heather as I started the Land Rover. I drove back to the hut, my brain buzzing. Where had the stone in my pocket come from? It couldn't have come from Patricia Harper if she'd never here.

So why could I remember her?

Inside the hut, the visitor's book was still on the reception desk. Today's only entry was for two Americans. Martin and Deanna. From North Carolina. Wishing me a nice day, in the comments column. So, no Patricia Harper. And no Martha and Dean. What else had changed? If anything had changed.

I went round to the back of the hut, and inspected the lock on the store room door. There was no sign of an attempted entry. I undid the lock and checked the store room. The store room was empty. So, was the bicycle missing, or had it never been there in the first place. Without Patricia Harper, maybe there had never actually been a bicycle. So maybe there was never a woman who took it.

But why could I remember them?

I returned to the Land Rover, and drove south back to the cottage, my brain overflowing. No Patricia Harper and no green stone. No bicycle and no striking woman. So, no Transilience Gate. No quarry. No Nether Largie. And no wedding. Well, not yet. What about Alison and the boys? And Bernie. And Helen.

Polly?

As I was parking the Land Rover, Glenys came past my cottage. Without stopping.

She smiled broadly, and fingered the arrowhead on the thong round her neck.

Was she smiling because she usually smiled? Or was she smiling because she thought she knew something I knew.

Glenys and Megan had insisted on the efficacy of arrowheads. Maybe I remembered because I had an arrowhead. So, maybe Glenys's arrowhead protected her. And I gave arrowheads to Helen and Polly. So, if they're still in this world, maybe they remember as well.

Outside the front door, the cat paced impatiently. Behind the front door, was a pile of letters on the mat. I couldn't face them right then, so I added them to the stack on the hall table.

I felt unaccountably hungry. I fed the cat, banked up the stove with peat, and made myself an omelette. As I ate, I watched the local news bulletin on TV. The main story was the impending sale of the lease on the mothballed F^2 plant at Tigh na Cruach.

Wow! So, in this world, whatever F^2 had been up to on Rannoch Moor must have been a failure. I wondered if Bernie and Polly still had jobs, if there were still Bernie and Polly to have jobs.

As I finished eating, the phone rang. Bernie. Why didn't I respond to my post? Did I even open it? Was I even going to the wedding? Was I bringing anyone? She wasn't.

Strangely relieved, I ended the call, and began to tidy up.

The phone rang. Henry. Had I heard about the sell off of the F^2 leases? Maybe the facility could be used for the good of the local community. Maybe RAGE could morph into REAP – the Rannoch Environmental Action Plan. Would I like to help?

Strangely annoyed, I ended the call, and scrolled through my contacts. Nothing for Helen. Nothing for Polly. So maybe they no longer existed. Or, if they did, they hadn't yet told me how to contact them. Yet?

I could always get in touch with Helen through her parents. That was what I'd done before, in a future that might not now happen.

But I'd no way to contact Polly. I should have asked Bernie. But Bernie would never give out a colleague's private details. And how would Polly react to a random message from some strange man? I supposed I could surf for Polly, to contact her in a vaguely official capacity, about the knock on effects of the plant closure.

I fired up my laptop. There were two unread email messages. The first read:

```
This is your cousin Helen. I'm on holiday
in your area. I thought it would be nice
to chat about this and that, the state of
the world, shared memories and all that.
I don't have your phone number though, so
if that seems good, maybe email it to me.
```

The message from Polly was much shorter:

```
If you're still here, so am I.
```

I wonder if Polly would like to go to a wedding.

Acknowledgements

We would like to thank our first readers Alistair, George, Ian, Malky, Nancy, Sue, and Rob, for their most supportive engagement.

Other novels, novellas and short story collections available from Stairwell Books. Sci-fi, fantasy and Climate Change-themed books are highlighted.

Eboracvm: Carved in Stone	Graham Clews
Down to Earth	**Andrew Crowther**
The Iron Brooch	**Yvonne Hendrie**
Pandemonium of Parrots	**Dawn Treacher**
The Electric	Tim Murgatroyd
The Pirate Queen	Charlie Hill
Djoser and the Gods	**Michael J. Lowis**
The Tally Man	Rita Jerram
Needleham	Terry Simpson
The Keepers	**Pauline Kirk**
A Business of Ferrets	Alwyn Bathan
Shadow Cat Summer	Rebecca Smith
Shadows of Fathers	Simon Cullerton
Blackbird's Song	Katy Turton
Eboracvm the Fortress	Graham Clews
The Warder	**Susie Williamson**
The Great Billy Butlin Race	Robin Richards
Mistress	Lorraine White
Life Lessons by Libby	Libby and Laura Engel-Sahr
Waters of Time	Pauline Kirk
The Tao of Revolution	**Chris Taylor**
The Water Bailiff's Daughter	Yvonne Hendrie
O Man of Clay	**Eliza Mood**
Eboracvm: the Village	Graham Clews
Sammy Blue Eyes	Frank Beill
Serpent Child	Pat Riley
Rocket Boy	John Wheatcroft
Virginia	Alan Smith
Looking for Githa	Patricia Riley
Poetic Justice	P J Quinn
Return of the Mantra	**Susie Williamson**
The Go-To Guy	Neal Hardin
Abernathy	Claire Patel-Campbell
Tyrants Rex	**Clint Wastling**
A Shadow in My Life	Rita Jerram
Thinking of You Always	Lewis Hill
How to be a Man	Alan Smith
Tales from a Prairie Journal	Rita Jerram

For further information please contact rose@stairwellbooks.com

www.stairwellbooks.co.uk
@stairwellbooks

Milton Keynes UK
Ingram Content Group UK Ltd.
UKHW010041290923
429540UK00001B/9